"You are a sp

He smiled that warming smile.

"I feel very special tonight," she said. "It's a lovely meal and the wine is delicious." Suddenly she felt tongue-tied. To make conversation she asked, "You've seen a lot of the world, haven't you?"

"Guess so, but I never saw anything I like better than what I'm looking at right now."

"That's very extravagant, Mitch." She tried to put a bit of reproof into her voice, but still her words came out in a breathless rush. He was too close to her.

"I meant that, Lucia," he said, leaning still closer. "There's something between us, something that happens when we're together. I feel like I have a life after all, and I'm not a used-up old-timer yet. Do you feel it, too?"

"I . . . well . . . I . . ." she fumbled. He was sitting so close. Why couldn't he have asked that question from across the room?

He smiled.

She whispered, "Yes, it's happening."

He leaned over her and she bent her head back to look at him. His mouth came down and touched hers, a butterfly touch. Their lips barely brushed, but she felt the kiss, powerfully, through her old body.

A KISS TO REMEMBER

HELEN PLAYFAIR

ZEBRA BOOKS
KENSINGTON PUBLISHING CORP.

ZEBRA BOOKS

are published by

Kensington Publishing Corp.
475 Park Avenue South
New York, NY 10016

First Printing: April, 1993

Printed in the United States of America

Chapter One

"All right, open the door! I know you're in there!"

Lucia opened sleepy blue eyes and blinked into the darkness of her bedroom. A glance at the faintly lit dial of the clock confirmed her suspicions. Yes, it was two in the morning and yes, somebody was banging on her front door. Somebody very loud and angry.

Picking up a lace-bordered pillow, Lucia pressed it over her eyes. Maybe if she ignored the racket long enough, it would go away, or maybe one of her sons would deal with it. Probably one of their friends anyway, making unfunny jokes in the middle of the night. Unfunny jokes strongly indicated a friend of Georgie's.

No, not Georgie's. Georgie had gone away. Lucia pressed the pillow more firmly to her face. The fact that her older son had left for a good job among his beloved computers in a beautiful northern California valley may have mitigated her loss, but nothing could change her feeling that she was bereft, impoverished. Her house was half empty; she had a shortage of sons.

Only Tommy left. Tommy still lived at home, and since he did, let him deal with their nocturnal visitor. Why didn't he? The banging and shouting continued. Oh, yes, now she remembered. Tommy had gone on a date with that nice girl from his physics class.

Two in the morning? Lucia snatched the pillow from her head and sat up, wide awake, snapped to attention by her trouble sensors, those mysterious maternal mechanisms that are somehow implanted in every mother upon the birth of her first child. She felt the familiar parental dread of the call in the night, the highway patrol at the door . . .

She grabbed the robe that was lying on the foot of her bed and put it on. It was more peignoir than robe, a confection made chiefly of ruffled lace, but she had no time to search for something less frivolous. She didn't try to find slippers. Lace fluttered around her bare ankles as she raced down the uncarpeted stairs.

She called, "I'm coming, I'm coming!" and her voice echoed in the big hallway.

The lights were still on, the front door only latched against Tommy's return. She threw open the door and peered out.

The elaborate old fixture on the front porch held eight bulbs, but it was hard to reach and nobody

6

had replaced one for years. The two dusty bulbs that still worked cast a dim light on her visitor. Not a policeman, thank the Lord. Who then? Some friend of Georgie's who did not know he was gone? Georgie's friends were likely to be large, muscular, and noisy. Tommy's, on the other hand, tended to carry around stacks of books and talk in such long sentences that they had no breath for shouting.

This one had lots of breath for shouting. About all she could see of him was that he was tall, and so deep in the chest and wide in the shoulders as to look a bit top-heavy. Large and angry.

He demanded, "Who the hell are you?"

Fresh, too. Lucia answered as coldly as she could manage in the rush of her relief, "I could ask you the same question. Why are you banging on my door at two in the morning?"

He asked, surprised, "Isn't this a fraternity house?"

"Are you drunk? You are several blocks off Fraternity Row, and this is my home."

He ducked his head and mumbled, "I'm trying to find my daughter. She went out with some student; I figured this was his fraternity house."

"You must be drunk. You're not making sense."

"I am too!" His voice rose again, and he waved a long arm toward the street. "That's her car right there. She must be here; it's parked right in front of this house!"

Lucia squinted at the white blur that was an automobile sitting at the curb in the darkness, and then she looked up again at the shadowed face of her visitor, and she understood. "Oh, you must be Debbie's daddy!"

"So! She is here!"

Lucia stepped back, pulling the door wide open. "Why don't you come in?" When he hesitated she added, "Parenting has this in common with nuclear physics; you can't practice either one very effectively on the front porch."

He came inside, and in the brighter light of the entry hall she could see that this was no adolescent fullback but only another worried parent. His face was angular, truculent, and his dark brown eyes were hooded by his brows. He wore jeans and a casual shirt of a cotton fabric so fine it clung to his muscular chest like silk. His jaw was wide and the stubborn mouth bracketed by deeply carved lines. He was staring at her, obviously taken aback by her white gown.

Well, why shouldn't she wear it if she felt like it? She had the slim figure for it, and just because she was the mother of two almost-grown boys didn't mean she couldn't look pretty once in a while in the privacy of her own home.

It covered her; she knew for a fact that every ruffle had been perfectly placed for modesty and even a certain dignity, but under his searching look she had to restrain a schoolgirl impulse to wrap her arms across her breasts. She stood stubbornly straight, throwing back the dark hair that hung in waves just above her shoulders. What was there for

8

him to stare at so astonished? The gown? Her oval, high-cheekboned face? Or the startling contrast between her bright blue eyes and the brown-black hair?

She held out her hand and smiled. "I'm Lucia Morgan. You'd be Mr. . . ."

"Colton, Mitchell Colton. Where's Debbie?" He took her hand with a brief, warm shake.

"I can't tell you exactly. She went out with my son Tommy, and they aren't back yet. I believe they said they were going to a movie."

"That's what she told me," he growled, flexing those heavy shoulders, "and it's two in the morning. A movie takes an hour and a half. What time did they leave?"

"Six-thirty, seven. They didn't eat here. They said they were going to get something . . . uh . . . somewhere. I'm afraid I wasn't paying much attention."

"How long has her car been there?"

"She brought it here right after her last class. They went to the movies in Tommy's car, but she didn't want to leave hers on campus all evening, so she put it there. Mr. Colton . . ." She looked at that stubborn, unconvinced face and knew there was no hope of getting him to go away and let her get a night's sleep. "Mr. Colton, would you like a cup of coffee?"

"I could do with one," he admitted, rubbing a hand over his somewhat bristly chin. "Are you sure they're not here? If you were asleep, they might have come back and you wouldn't have heard them. . . ."

"If she were here, she would have heard you. They must have heard you on the next block. I hope you won't mind sitting in the kitchen while I make the coffee."

He followed her down the long hallway to the kitchen, where she snapped on the lights to the usual dazzle. It was a big room and there was lots of white tile. Little hexagonal "chickenwire" tile covered the floor, the countertops, the wall behind the range. The range itself stood tall on white legs and was surmounted by two large white warming ovens.

"Sit down, won't you?" Lucia indicated one of the mismatched chairs grouped around the table. She didn't want him just to stand there; for some reason it made her nervous. Somehow, just because he was there, he made her aware of her bare feet, of her outfit that had been deliberately designed to be provocative. Well, she could hardly rush upstairs now and slip into a pair of coveralls. He would just have to bear it.

She went to the cupboard and hauled out her favorite coffeepot, battered and well broken in to make good coffee. She carried it to the sink and filled it, her movements deft and economical. "This will take only a minute," she promised.

He sat down but leaned forward tensely, watching her. In fact, he was squirming. She observed him from the corner of her eye as she measured cof-

10

fee. First one shoulder came forward, then after only a moment the other. He opened his mouth and closed it, cleared his throat. When it came out at last, it was an apology.

"I'm sorry if I made too much noise," he said. "I'm pretty upset. Did I wake Mr. Morgan, too?"

Her mouth tightened, but she answered easily, "Not very likely. I'm a widow."

"Oh, I'm sorry."

She snapped the lid onto the pot and took it to the stove. "It's nice of you to say that, but you don't need to. He's been gone for ten years, and I'm quite accustomed to it."

He stood up abruptly. "Are you saying you're alone in the house?"

"Of course."

"And you opened the door in the middle of the night? To a complete stranger? While you're dressed in that . . . that *thing?*" Looking more upset than ever, he waved a big, hard hand at her clothes.

"It's a robe. Please sit down, Mr. Colton. It may be decorative, but it's also quite practical. I ought to know; I designed and made it myself."

He sat down slowly. "Is that what you do? Design clothes?"

Lucia shot him a glance. Was he going to settle down and make conversation? He looked as if he might. He was obediently sitting in the chair and, as nearly as she could figure out, the expression on his strongly-modeled face was intended to be meek. It was a pretty poor imitation.

11

She explained. "What I do for a living is work in the office of a freight company, but on my own time I design and make gowns and robes. And specialty items sometimes, like pillows and spreads. It's more a hobby than anything else, but a friend sells my stuff in her boutique and I pick up a few extra dollars. I'm sure you know how important that is when you are raising children."

"Sounds like you're holding down two jobs at once. Are you a workaholic?"

She sat down opposite him and put her elbows on the table, her chin in her hand. "No, I'm just broke and trying to keep things going. And I don't have two jobs, I have three. Raising kids is at least a full-time job. I like things that way; it's being idle that drives me up the wall. Does that make me a workaholic?"

"Maybe. Maybe we all are. I'm not very good at just sitting around, either. Do all the gowns look like that one?" His eyes were a warm brown and his hair was cut too short. It looked as if it would be curly, dark brown, and iced with gray if he didn't keep it cut to a thick stubble.

"This gown is special," she said. "It was a custom order for a bride, but she canceled the wedding and the order. I liked the outfit and it fit me, so I just kept it for myself."

"Why did you open the door?"

"I thought you were a kid, clowning around. Anyhow, why not? I've been a single parent for years. There isn't much left that can scare me."

"It was a foolish thing to do." But he was smiling and he had a warm smile that pulled his lips back tight against his teeth and warmed up his whole craggy face. She found herself thinking that Debbie's mother was a very lucky woman.

She jumped up and took a pair of mugs down from the cupboard, thick crockery mugs with the strength to survive family life. "How do you take your coffee?"

"Black."

"Me, too." Now, why did she feel the need to tell him how she took her coffee? There was a mood of intimacy growing between them, as if they knew and understood each other, as if they were friends. And something inside her kept pushing her to encourage it. Dumb. A really useless thing to do, when probably she would never see him again after tonight. After the kids got home. Unless, of course, his Debbie and her Tommy were to fall in love, and one day marry, and then they would all be family. She poured the coffee and put the pot back on the stove over the pilot light, where it would keep warm.

He was sitting back in his chair now, watching her move about the kitchen. A slight smile softened the angles of his face. He asked, "Do you mind if I call you Lucia?"

"Not at all. What do they call you? Mitch?"

"Naturally. Have I got your name right? LU-see-ya?"

"Yes, that's right. The family is Italian and I

should have been a Lu-CHI-ya, but somehow I've always been just Lucia."

"Pretty name." He actually seemed to be loosening up, but even as she thought so he asked, "Where did the kids go, really?"

What an annoying man! He never gave up. She replied as evenly as she could manage, "They said they were going to a movie. They didn't say which one."

"Even if they saw two movies, every place in town is closed by now."

She sat down opposite him with her coffee and hooked a bare foot over the battered rung of her chair. "I can think of at least a hundred reasons why they might be late, and only a couple of them are bad. Why don't you just try to relax and see what happens?

"Are you always this calm? It's your son, too."

"I try. I really try hard to keep cool. It takes nerves of steel to be a parent, and yours seem to be giving you some trouble tonight."

"My nerves? They sure are." He smiled again apologetically, and she was charmed by the way the crinkles next to his eyes curved down. He would be her age, of course, maybe a little older. Well into his forties, but the years had treated him kindly. The lines of his face were strong and cheerful and his athletic body looked more powerful and resilient than that of a man half his age. It was only that his shoulders, broadened by the heavy muscles of his upper arms, seemed too wide.

14

He explained, "I tried to stay home and wait for her, but it got so I just couldn't stand it anymore, just sitting there. So I got in my car and started looking for her. About all I had to go on was the name of this street. She had said it was near the USC campus and the guy was a student. I thought this would be his fraternity house. Aren't most of these places?"

"Fraternity houses? The big houses along this street? Some of them are places for groups to live in, but all of them were homes first. The Victorians built big. I'm astonished that you were able to find the right place."

"It's not hard to find a car if you don't have too much area to cover. You know the color, you know the plates, you can move pretty fast and not miss it. But it took me a long while, and by the time I got here, I was ready to break somebody in half. I didn't mean anything personal, not to you. You can understand that, can't you?" He leaned forward, his hands gripping the edge of the table. Big, capable hands with hard knuckles.

She said, "Of course I know what you were going through. Only a parent can understand what it's like to wait like that, wondering, where is my child now? What is he doing? Is he in trouble? Does he need me? Why doesn't he call? Why doesn't he come home?"

Mitch nodded slightly and hunched over his coffee. She was reaching him. She continued. "You can wrestle with those demons for hours and then your kid comes home and he was playing arcade games or something and he's sorry, Mom. You're a rag and he's sorry."

"That's just what it's like," he agreed. "I thought it was bad with the boys, but Debbie's a girl, and it's worse."

"It's hard to do, but you have to distance yourself from them. It isn't that you don't love them anymore, but when they get to this age, you have to start letting go. I find it a valuable technique not to ask when they will be home. That way, you can't tell if they're late."

He lifted his head, almost a little angry. "And do you believe they are charmed? Protected by angels, maybe? Nothing can ever go wrong?"

"There's a million things that can go wrong. I try not to worry about them until they do. I have a theory about bad news. You could go to the most remote place you ever heard of, Siberia or Montana or someplace, and hide in the bottom of a mine and if there was bad news for you, they'd find you. Good news can wait, but bad news will always find you."

"I wish I had your steady nerves." His eyes were sad; he was worrying again, but he forced a smile and asked, "How old are your children, Lucia?"

"Tommy's the one you'd be interested in; he's the one who's out with your daughter. He's eighteen and a freshman. He has a chemistry scholarship. He's really rather shy and doesn't date a lot. He obviously thinks your Debbie is special. My older boy is Georgie. He graduated last June and has gone up north to do something with computers. I never have understood exactly what his job is, but it sounds rather as if he feeds the computers, burps them, and changes their diapers."

He laughed, and she tried not to observe what a good laugh it was, comfortable and unashamed, and how attractive his face was when he smiled. A man with a smile like that was dangerous.

He said, "Some machinery has to be treated about like that. I have two boys. Debbie's my youngest; she's the only girl."

"She's charming and must be very bright. Isn't she majoring in physics?"

He blinked, surprised. "I guess she is bright. I never thought about it that way. She always gets good grades in school. She even skipped a grade back in elementary school. But she never acts smart."

Lucia laughed in her turn. "Wouldn't she be obnoxious if she did?" she asked, and was rewarded with another of Mitch's big laughs. She took a sip of her coffee. "Tell me about your boys."

He shifted forward and began eagerly. "The older one is Jared. He's studying to be an accountant. He lives with his mother. Darryl is the other one, and he's at UCLA and lives in a dorm there."

"Don't you and your wife live in town?"

"I've got a condo in the Hollywood Hills. My ex-wife lives in Oxnard with her husband. Debbie's usually with her, but she came to live with me last month when she started at USC. She decided all by herself that she was going to USC and live with me. She could have gotten into UCLA, she had the grades, but she didn't want anybody to think she was following her brother. You know how kids are. Ten thousand people on that campus, and because Darryl's one of them, she has to go someplace else. Her mother didn't want her to live alone. . . . She's still only seventeen. . . . And of course she couldn't commute from Oxnard. It's nearly fifty miles."

Ex-wife. Ex. Why did that information fill her with a secret delight? Lucia's eyelashes fluttered, then covered her downcast eyes. She murmured, "Oh, I'm sorry."

"For what?"

She looked up and smiled faintly. "I don't know exactly. Sorry you had to divorce . . . It must have been very painful. Sorry all your children aren't with you. Sorry you have two in college at once. I'm close to bankruptcy and I have only one there!"

"The divorce was entirely my fault," he said flatly.

"What an astonishing thing to say!" she exclaimed. "I've never heard anybody say that before. It's always the other guy's fault."

"Ione was not to blame. That's her name, Ione. It was my profession that broke us up, I guess you might say, but I'm the one that chose that profession. I'm a tool pusher."

Lucia tried not to look confused. "Oh, yes."

He explained. "That's what they call the boss on an oil rig. I have to go where the rig goes and stay

18

with it until the job's done. The rigs go all over the world, and I expected Ione to follow me wherever I had to go. She complained some; she complained a lot, but I guess I never realized how hard it was for her, with the kids and all."

"A lot of moving and three little children? Yes, that would be very hard."

"Some people like to travel, but Ione always kept talking about going back to her hometown and getting a house and settling down. She's from Oxnard. I kept saying okay, okay, right after the next contract. Then one day, we were living in Lagos at the time, she just picked up everything, the kids and the furniture and everything, and left. Went to Oxnard and put the kids in school and got a house."

He shrugged with a sour grimace. "I don't think she even knew this guy, the one she married later, when she did all that. But he was in Oxnard, and by the time I'd finished my contract and came to the States, they were together. I just had to face the facts; it was too late and our marriage was down the tubes. I've tried to keep up with my kids the best I could, but I haven't lived with them since they were little."

"No wonder you're having so much trouble adjusting to Debbie! All the steam you're putting into it, I should have known you were a new father. An old one never would have survived this long."

He sighed heavily, lifting his shoulders. "It's a skill, being a parent, and I'm out of practice. I don't know what to do with Debbie."

"Does anybody know? I'm sure I don't."

His eyes were the rich, warm brown of very old brandy, and there was a smile in them when he looked at her. Her ruffled sleeves had fallen back, leaving her forearms naked, and she felt that brandy-warm glance on her skin. He asked, "How did you end up here, all by yourself in this big house?"

"I'm not by myself; I live with my family," Lucia insisted, but then she added almost sadly, "I guess there's not much left of the family. Only Tommy, and he'd love to go live with his friends on campus. I couldn't let him go even if I could afford it, because I need him to help me with the house. There are emergency repairs about once a week and I have to have his help. Especially when there are falling bricks or broken duct work or something like that."

"Heavy work for a woman."

She got up and went to the stove. "A little more coffee?"

"Yes, thank you."

She poured. "I've become a pretty good carpenter, even if I do hold the hammer in both hands a lot of the time, but I never loved that kind of work. My husband did. He was very into chisel and grout and plane and plaster and paint. All that stuff. We bought this house because he wanted to restore it. He was going to make it look just like it did when it was new, around the turn of the century, and he was going to do all the work himself."

The pot was empty and she put it next to the sink. It was too hot to be taken apart, but she shifted it vaguely as she talked. "We didn't have much money, but we figured we wouldn't need a lot because we'd be living in the house and he would be doing the work a little at a time. We had just finished paying back what we borrowed for the down payment when he was killed. There was an accident . . ."

She went on quickly because there was still pain in the memory of that useless death. Just one more traffic statistic. "It's still my dream to have the house restored, or at least fixed up so it's fit to live in, but I've never had the money."

"This close to campus, seems like you could rent out rooms to students, make some money that way."

She turned and smiled at him. "We tried that once, and it was a disaster. You see, in this whole vast place there's only one bathroom. Young people these days expect something better."

"I'm not much into antiques and that stuff, but even I can see it's a beautiful old house. It can't be very comfortable, though. This kitchen looks like an airplane hangar. How can you work in here?"

"People in those days never went into their own kitchens; they had servants to do that for them. You're right, I hate this kitchen and everything in it except the stove. Love that old stove. It's made of solid steel and always cooks evenly. Heats in a flash. Weighs a ton. They must have put it in here with a derrick."

He chuckled. "You are some special lady. It sure must take a lot to get you down."

"Oh, I get down. Everybody does sometimes. Do you—did you hear a car?"

He listened. "I think so."

"It is! That's Tommy's car; I recognize the squeak in the brakes. He's parking in the driveway." Lucia leapt up and rushed to unlock the back door. "Quick, Mitch! You can go out this way."

He said, "Huh?"

"Hurry! If you slip out the back door and go around the house that way"—she pointed—"that's the side of the house away from the driveway. Maybe you can get to your car before she sees you."

He got up and ambled agreeably toward her, but then he just stood there, looming. He asked, "Why am I running away from my own kid?"

It made her breath come short, thinking about how he had to hurry. He was close to her, so near she could almost feel the warmth of his big body. She answered urgently, "She mustn't find you here! She'll know that you went looking for her; she'll know you were worrying."

"There's a law against worrying?" He sounded amused. She just wasn't communicating with him.

"She'll be angry with you, Mitch. She'll say you don't trust her."

"It's three o'clock. This time of the morning, I don't trust anybody."

"Trust me. If you want a friendly relationship with your daughter, she must never find out that you went cruising the streets, looking for her when she was on a date."

"I thought maybe she needed help . . ."

"That's not a reason, it's an alibi." She stood up to him, straight and serious in her fluttery ruffles. Barefoot, she just reached to his shoulder. "Tell me something. When you found her car, if she had been in it with a boy, what would you have done? Risen in her window like the morning sun?"

He thought about it for a minute. "I guess it's time for me to skulk quietly away."

But he didn't. He stood there, smiling and looming. Those big arms . . . He could squash a person. Somebody her size, easily. He said, "Dinner tomorrow?"

Lucia said, "Huh?"

"Will you have dinner with me tomorrow?" he repeated patiently.

"Oh, Mitch, get going! If they're out of the car, they might see you crossing the front yard."

"Lucia, pay attention. Watch my lips. You. Me. Eat. Food. Dinner. Tomorrow."

She couldn't help laughing. "Sure, sure, anything! Yes! Just go!"

At last his legs were activated and he was moving. Out the door he went, down the pair of steps to the darkness of the yard beyond. He called back, "I'll pick you up at six-thirty."

"No, wait!" she cried, but when he paused and turned she quickly amended, "No, don't wait. Okay, okay! Just go!"

He waved and disappeared around the corner of the house. He didn't show much talent for skulking, but the night was dark and he was probably going to get away with it.

Lucia locked the back door and, moving swiftly as was her habit, picked up the coffee mugs and washed them. As she pulled apart the coffeepot, she wondered why she had done that. Why had she accepted an invitation to dinner? She didn't date. Well, hardly ever. She didn't have time, for starters. Between her children and her job and the big house to care for, she had enough complications; she didn't need any new relationships.

Also, she sincerely felt that one of the advantages of maturity was the chance to opt out of the dating scene. She didn't need competition and scorekeeping. She wasn't crazy about dancing, and she did not feel like coping with the demands of men to whom a date was synonymous with a one-night stand.

So why had she made an exception for Mitch, and after only an hour's acquaintance? He was attractive, but certainly he wasn't the first attractive man she had ever met. Those little shivers of awareness that ran along her nerve endings when he looked at her . . . Exciting, but scarcely unique. One can feel that kind of response with almost any man. At the moment she couldn't remember when it had last happened to her, but . . .

She had accepted his offer of dinner to get rid of him. That was it. It was the only thing she could do to speed him on his way, and the slightest delay might have been disastrous.

A friend indeed was Lucia. She was so quick to help that she could assist a friend even when he did not see the need as clearly as she did.

Lucia put the cleaned cups and the pot into cupboards, methodically destroying every evidence of her visitor and even as she worked she knew her excuse was a cop-out. As necessary as it had been to get Mitch out of the house, she had agreed to have dinner with him simply because she wanted to see him again.

She turned off the kitchen light and started through the hall, muttering to herself, "Sure, Lucia. Santa Claus and the Easter bunny will be along in their season, too."

It was then that she heard a car engine start in front of the house, where Debbie's car was parked. Almost immediately Tommy's key turned in the lock of the front door. She considered slipping quietly upstairs to her room, but he would have seen the lights and he would know she was not asleep. She waited.

Her son was tall and slender, his hair a dark blond and somewhat shaggy. There was a small frown of puzzlement on his face as he opened the door. He saw her there at the foot of the stairs and said, "Hi, Mom. What are you doing up?"

"I thought I heard water dripping." It was a good lie; plumbing problems in the old house kept them all constantly on the alert, but she wondered how it was that she was lying, when she had always prided herself on being truthful with her children. It made her testy and she added more abruptly than she had intended, "It's very late. Why did you stay out so late when tomorrow is a school day?"

He twitched his shoulders impatiently. "Mom, I work weekends, every Friday and Saturday night. If I don't go out on Thursday, I don't go out. I didn't mean to be this late; we got to talking. You know how it is."

But there was a hint of sarcasm when he said this last, for how would a person's mother know what it was like to be so engrossed in conversation with an attractive member of the opposite sex as to lose track of the time?

Chapter Two

In the gray light of morning Lucia faced the problem of clothes. There were several things she would have asked Mitch had there been time for questions. She needed to know how to dress, and she would have arranged to meet a little later. Six-thirty was the time she usually arrived home, and traffic delays could make her later. There would be no time to change her clothes; what she wore to work would have to do for the dinner.

One of the advantages of working for the freight company was that she needed no fancy clothes. Her office was in the back and she talked to customers only on the phone. Cotton trousers and a casual shirt were almost a uniform for the people who worked in her section. If she were to appear at her desk wearing a dressy outfit and high heels, everybody would know she had a date and there would be questions and friendly teasing. She would have to tell lies, or admit she was going to dinner with a man she had met only that morning, who worked at a job she had never heard of. If she wore her usual clothes, Mitch might take her to some nice place where she would look like a hick in her chinos and T-shirt.

But was he likely to take her to the kind of place where the fashion plates dine? He had called himself a "tool pusher," and had explained only vaguely what that was. It sounded like somebody whose idea of entertainment would be an evening of bowling. Would she be getting all dressed up for a dinner of hot dogs and beer at a place where her shirt with the freight company's logo on it would be more appropriate?

Well, she could hardly call him up at six in the morning and ask him what she should wear to work. She settled on a neutral outfit, a cotton dress of classic cut in a subdued plaid. There was a bright burgundy blazer she could throw over it if she felt the need for a bit of dash, and she tucked a pair of espadrilles into the hall closet in case she needed to dress down.

At least her ploy was successful at the office, where nobody noticed her at all. One person remarked that she "looked nice," but it was an off-hand comment, almost lost in the rush of the day.

She got home on time, even a trifle early. It was as if the traffic on the freeway had opened up on purpose to let her through. She would be able to brush her hair and touch up her lipstick.

Pleased, she was starting up the stairs when Tommy's voice began calling her. "Mom, is that you?"

"Yes, dear."

"I have to go to work tonight!" was his frantic reply.

"Yes, dear, I know. Where are you?"

Dressed only in brown trousers, Tommy burst out of his room on the floor above. "I don't have a white shirt!" he cried accusingly.

Tommy's job at the fast-food outlet demanded that he look crisp in a white shirt and brown pants. She said kindly, "You can probably find a clean shirt in the dryer. There were a couple in the load I washed yesterday."

"Oh, fine. I've got to leave in ten minutes and I get a shirt that's all wrinkled in the dryer."

She made her voice severe. "We do have an agreement, Tommy, that you look after your clothes and I look after mine. You are tall enough to do your own ironing now."

"Aw, Mom!"

"I'll check for you and see if the shirt is there," she offered, and he went back into his room, the door closing with a peevish slap.

It had been a struggle to get modern laundry equipment installed in the antique house when they had first moved in, but Lucia had always been glad she'd insisted. The old washer that had scrubbed so many pairs of tiny jeans and grimy

29

little-boy socks was still washing away. The dryer had been replaced with a more efficient model that was still referred to as the new dryer, although it was five years old.

She pulled Tommy's shirt from the new dryer and observed that it needed pressing to meet the standards of his employment. The ironing board was nearby and she laid the shirt on it and plugged in the iron.

She was almost finished with the shirt when the doorbell rang. She hurried down the hall to the entry and opened the door—to confront an entirely new Mitch.

While it would have been impossible not to recognize somebody his size, his appearance had changed enough for a double-take. Besides being combed and closely shaved, Mitch wore a suit. Not an ordinary suit, not at all. Her eye trained to the nuances of sewing, Lucia instantly observed the skillful roll of the lapels, the hand-set-in sleeves. Custom tailoring, probably English. The conservative lines and careful fit made Mitch's big body look more in proportion, while still flattering the width of his shoulders. The color was dark gray and his tie was gray-blue silk, with tiny figures marching across it like a stripe.

It was disconcerting. She was already struggling against a feeling that last night had been only a vivid dream or fantasy, and there was no Mitch, or perhaps this solid body actually did exist, but the warmth and appeal she had felt from him were not really there.

And then he smiled that smile that pulled his lips tight against his teeth and somehow made her tinglingly aware of his mouth and he said, "I'm sorry I'm late, Lucia. Are you ready?"

"Please come in," she replied. "I have one tiny thing to finish and then we can go. Come with me if you'd like."

He followed her down the hall, through the kitchen to the service porch, where she picked up the iron again. Mitch eyed the appliance with a touch of exasperation.

"I hoped you would be ready and we could leave right away," he said. "If we're late, we could lose our reservation."

Lucia skillfully smoothed the front of the shirt. "Nearly finished. You look very elegant, Mitch. Am I dressed all right?"

He regarded her dress without admiration. "Yeah, it's all right. You haven't got time to change anyhow."

Lucia gave him a level look. The evening did not seem to be starting out on a positive note. Maybe there was some deeply-buried childhood trauma that made him get surly anytime he saw an ironing board.

Sill half naked, Tommy padded through the kitchen, calling, "Mom, have you got my shirt?" He stopped, staring with surprise, to see Mitch standing there. Perhaps he had not heard the doorbell.

Lucia handed him the finished shirt and said, "You two haven't met, have you? This is my son, Tommy. This is Mr. Colton, Tommy."

Mitch put out his hand. "Oh, yes. I understand you are acquainted with my daughter, Debbie."

"Uh . . . Debbie." Tommy presented a flaccid hand and allowed it to be shaken. He was clearly getting what the children would describe as "a lot of input with no readout." For the time being, Lucia thought it just as well.

She said, "You had better hurry, Tommy, or you'll be late. We have to leave right now. Don't forget to lock up."

Tommy said, "Sure, Mom. Nice to meet you, Mr. . . . Colton." He rushed off, perhaps glad to escape.

On her way out Lucia picked up her purse and slipped on the blazer. It was a good one, the nicest she owned. It made her feel a little less intimidated by Mitch's suit.

Intimidation returned in force, however, when she saw his car. A silver-gray Porsche gleamed at the curb. Mitch held open the door, and she slipped into the seat, which somehow combined an incredibly soft leather covering with the Spartan firmness demanded in their seating by sports-car customers.

Mitch started the engine, a deep, thrilling

rumble, and they were away. He didn't say anything, but concentrated on darting through the rush-hour traffic.

At last she asked, "Do you get good gas mileage?"

"Not terrific," he admitted, then glanced at her and smiled. "It doesn't matter, because I use this car only for special occasions, like taking a beautiful lady to dinner."

"Now, how am I supposed to take that?" Lucia questioned. "That you drive it all the time, or that it's hardly ever out of the garage?"

"What do you think?" he countered.

"I think it's in remarkably good shape for all the use it must get. Where are we going?"

"Papa Choux's. Do you like it?"

A sudden vision of herself sauntering into a classy restaurant like Papa Choux's in her cotton plaid dress made Lucia answer almost sharply, "How should I know?"

She recovered herself quickly. After all, there was her good wool blazer. She could button it up and look nonchalant. "I mean, I've never been there to eat. When I drive by the place, there are all those guys in red coats, parking cars, and I have this rule of thumb. If a place has valet parking, I can't afford it."

He actually laughed. "I'm not crazy about valet parking, either."

She agreed. "Besides all the money you have to

pay some guy to park the same car you park yourself a dozen times a day, there's the embarrassment. Have you ever tried to explain to a valet that if the car doesn't start, you have to slam the door a couple times?" She looked at the elegantly uncluttered dashboard before her. "No, I guess you haven't."

"Sure I have."

"I doubt that. What did you say your job is? A tool pusher? I got this picture of somebody checking things out in a toolroom."

"I push only one tool. The drill."

"Huh?" It occurred to Lucia she was saying that a lot lately.

It was getting dark, and his profile was almost a silhouette against the graying sky outside the car window. Heavy brows, jutting chin, and a high-bridged nose. "I'm in the oil business, and I'm the guy who makes the drill go. If you're going to be formal about it, they call me a vice president now, but I used to be a tool pusher and essentially that's what I still do, only now I have a lot of rigs to push instead of just one."

"Push," said Lucia thoughtfully. "I guess that's one way to describe what the boss does."

"The way I see it, the tool pusher has the most important job in the industry," he went on. "There's all those other departments, accounting and pipeline and marketing and acquisitions and even management, but none of it means anything unless the drill is doing what it was designed to do. I'm proud of being the guy who brings up the oil."

"Do you still follow the rig around the world, like you used to?"

"About every chance I get, but I don't get to a lot now. They like to keep me here in L.A., making like an executive." As he spoke, Mitch put the car into a turn and slipped into a parking lot that was little more than a wide space in front of the restaurant. A valet appeared immediately. Mitch joshed with him and slipped him a tip in advance to ensure tender care of the car.

As they climbed the steps to the elaborate front door, he said with a grin, "In some ways, life was simpler when I had to slam the door to start my car."

Papa Choux's presented a dazzling impression of crystal and mirrors, of chandeliers, red carpet by the acre, and large numbers of aquaria for fish. To look at, or to eat? She didn't have time to guess at the species in the tanks. She had to see what everybody was wearing.

It was a relief to find that Southern California style, there was no consistency. A few of the ladies were expensively gowned, but most wore casual clothes. One young girl sported a tank top and an old man had on his baseball cap from Disneyland. It made her feel better.

Mitch murmured his name to the headwaiter, and they were ushered to a booth. Mitch asked her, "A booth is okay, isn't it? I asked for one when I booked because I figured it would be quieter and we could talk."

"It's delightful," Lucia answered. "The whole place is perfectly grand. You were going to tell me about your old car."

He pretended to lean back and think, but he was looking at her; she felt his eyes like a touch. Something in his little smile made her feel that she was desirable, beautiful, charming, and even intelligent.

"What car?" he asked. "I've had dozens over the years. My favorite of them all was an old bathtub Porsche, though. It was ugly and the body rusted and you had to fiddle with the timing every couple of hundred miles, but I loved that thing. It was just fun to drive."

"But you turned it in for the new Porsche?"

"Not on purpose. One of my sons totaled it."

"Totaled! Oh, dear! Was he hurt?"

"My son? Not even a bruise, but the car was done for. He didn't get hit all that hard, you see, he just put himself where he'd get knocked around by a big, solid old Cadillac. Everything on my car was sort of lifted up and set down someplace else. Couldn't have been fixed in a hundred years." He was leaning forward, eyes bright and laughing, but she sensed that he had

36

not always been this amused by the destruction of his car.

She said, "I guess I'm lucky. They say every kid totals a car before he learns to drive, but all my boys have ever done is bend a few fenders."

Mitch's smile turned rueful. "I'm afraid I wasn't very nice about losing that Porsche. I yelled at Jared so much, he went home to his mother. He's been there ever since. It's two years since I've seen him."

"Was he living with you when all this happened?"

"It was summer. Usually I have the kids most of the summer. Winter, they're in school and I wouldn't want to take them out. So I arrange to be in the country and we do something together. We all like camping, especially at Yosemite. Back when Jared was talking to me, I took them all to Europe one year. It gives Ione a break and a chance to go someplace with what's-his-name."

"It sounds like you have managed to be with your kids a lot in spite of everything."

"I've tried. A kid needs a father, especially a boy. A boy raised only by women is likely to be a wimp."

"A girl raised entirely by men would be a slob," Lucia countered. "It's called the balance of family life."

A waiter came with menus and chatted about

the specialties. Mitch observed, "The lobster is good here. Do you like lobster, Lucia?"

"Love it," she replied. "However, I'm not going to eat anything I have to look in the eye before it's cooked."

"I'll make the selection for you personally," the waiter promised.

"Some white wine would go well," said Mitch. "Is there a special kind you'd like?"

"Tell you how it is with me and wine," said Lucia. "I can tell white from red. But only with the lights on, of course. Please, order what you'd like."

He must have already picked something, because he ordered immediately and the waiter disappeared. They were alone, and they looked at each other and smiled. His smile warmed her; she could feel the heat rising through her body, rising to meet the heat she saw in his eyes. And it was silly, because they weren't alone at all. The room was full of people, but it was like being alone because they were in a place where only the two of them could go, a place where they understood each other perfectly.

Lucia wondered what they needed wine for. She was already light-headed. She decided to return to the subject at hand, whatever that had been. Oh, yes.

She said, "Surely you're not worrying that Jared will be a wimp just because he's with his mother. She doesn't live in a vacuum, after all. And there's always what's-his-name."

"What's-his-name?" Mitch raised an eyebrow and chuckled. "Did I say that? I guess it's pretty obvious he isn't one of my favorite people. The kids don't give him very high marks, either."

"As highly intelligent children, I'm sure they have figured out that saying nice things about their stepfather is not the way to put you in a good mood."

"Probably," he admitted. "It's just that I'm having trouble seeing any son of mine turn into an accountant. I've always had this theory that someday there's going to be a company that doesn't have any accountants in it, and when there is, I'm going to go to work for them right away. Seems like everybody would be happier there, and have more time to do their jobs, too."

Lucia laughed. "What an enchanting idea! Nobody to tell you the company can't afford it!"

"None of those long forms to fill out."

"Of course they wouldn't pay any taxes!"

"No wonder they can afford anything anybody wants!"

They were still laughing when the waiter brought their lobsters. He tied amusing bibs around their necks and gave them nutcrackers and little sharp forks.

Mitch picked one up and eyed it disapprovingly. "They sure make this look like a chore. I've got enough tools here to assemble a carburetor."

"Well, please don't. It would probably spoil the tablecloth." It wasn't very clever, but it made him laugh, and that was what she wanted. To hear him laugh, just to sit next to him and watch the way he moved. The way his hand closed around the fork; she watched him roll a bite of lobster in melted butter and lift it to his mouth. She did the same, swirling the yellow butter and letting it drip back into the dish, tasting the sweetness of the lobster countered by the mild bite and saltiness of the butter.

Their eyes met and they were sitting there with forks in their hands, just looking, lifted to that plane where they communicated without words. He took up the end of her bib and gently touched the corner of her mouth with it, wiping away a speck of butter. His hand was not entirely steady, and she understood that. His nearness made her quiver, made her fumble.

She needed a topic of conversation. She began, "I think . . . I think it would be easier to understand your children if you had a perfect memory."

"Who me?"

"Anybody. Can you remember what it was like, I mean, exactly what it was like, to be sixteen? For instance, what were you doing then?"

"When I was sixteen? I was roughnecking in the oil fields. I was big as a grown man and then some. I've always been a little oversized."

"A little oversized . . ." she murmured, and lost her train of thought completely, because of course he was not just a little. Not just a little of anything. He had managed to fit himself behind the table, but his width of shoulder and depth of chest kept him from looking like other people did there. His size gave him authority. No, just being Mitch gave him authority.

She asked, "Do you find that people think you will fight their battles for them just because you are bigger?"

He looked up from his lobster, surprised. "Yeah, it's a real hazard. How would a little thing like you know that?"

"I'm very observant."

"People do try to manipulate me sometimes, people who are practically strangers. Try to make me lose my temper for their own purposes. They don't realize that the bigger you are, the better control you have to have over your temper, and I'm pretty big."

She took a sip of her wine. She liked it a lot, so much that she was taking a second glass, although she feared it was making her talk at random. Maybe nobody would notice. She remembered what she wanted to ask him. "How did you manage, when you were only sixteen, to go to school and work in the oil fields at the same time?"

"I didn't. I dropped out of school until I realized that without an education I was never going to be anything but a roughneck. That's when I went back to school. I never liked it a lot. All I wanted out of it was the knowledge I needed to get back to the oil fields. That's where I like to be. To me, the rig floor is the most exciting place in the world."

"I can tell you love your work, so you must be good at it."

"I'm good at talking about myself all evening, too," he admitted with a wince. "Do you like your job?"

"Not for the kind of reasons you like yours. It's easy and the hours are regular and I like the people I work with. It doesn't pay all that well, but it leaves me time and energy for my family and even for my hobby, and I've always been grateful for having it."

"Have you ever thought about making your life easier by getting married?"

She smiled, somehow touched that he would think of that, and answered, "Never seriously. Oh, sometimes the idea has sounded good in the abstract, but you don't get married in the abstract. You need somebody pretty special if it's going to be a real marriage."

"Your husband must have been special."

"He was, of course." Lucia toyed with a fork and looked up, a glance swift and almost shy. "I'm not used to talking about my marriage; most people don't want to hear. We were happy. He's gone and I've adjusted to that. I haven't forgotten, you understand, I've adjusted. You don't forget people just because they are gone."

"Maybe you should," Mitch said quietly.

"Well, you can't, and I don't believe you should. Haven't you lost friends that you will miss forever? I have. Even one old aunt."

"Sometimes you sound, forgive me, just a little flip about it."

"Do I? Well, I'm not, but ten years is a long time. These days when one of the boys says or does something that's exactly like his father used to say or do, it delights me. I don't feel sad, I just remember, and what I remember is that I loved him."

"You must have had some hard times."

"I've been through grieving, being bitter and frightened and desperate. When you finish all that, it's like sunrise. You're a new person and it's a new day and you can be happier than you ever knew how before. I'm happy with my life. I have my boys. I wouldn't change anything even if I could."

He smiled that warming smile. "A lot of people would complain about how hard things are. You are a special lady."

She smiled back. "I feel very special tonight. It's a lovely meal and the wine is delicious."

"Would you like some more?"

"No, thank you. I've had enough." Or maybe it was something else that was making her flutter. Just to prove she could still make conversation, she asked, "You've seen a lot of the world, haven't you?"

"Guess so, but I never saw anything I like better than what I'm looking at right now. When you're smiling at me, that's the prettiest sight I ever saw."

"That's very extravagant, Mitch." She tried to put a bit of reproof into her voice, but she couldn't sound more sensible than she felt and it came out in a breathless rush. He was too close to her. It made her feel foolish and reckless, like somebody who could listen to fulsome compliments all night.

He leaned slightly toward her, and his expression was serious. "I meant that, Lucia. There's something between us, something that happens when we're together. I started feeling it the first minute I saw you, in your nightgown."

"Oh, my stars, you'll make me blush! It wasn't a nightgown, it was—"

"Whatever it was, you looked mighty pretty in it. I'm happy when I'm with you. I feel like I have a life after all, and I'm not a used-up old-timer yet. Do you feel it, too?"

"I . . . well . . . I . . ." She fumbled. He was sitting so close. Why couldn't he have asked his question from across the room? She couldn't think straight when he was so near, and if he smiled, she was really going to do something foolish.

He smiled.

She whispered, "Yes, it's happening."

He leaned over her, and she bent her head back to look at him. His mouth came down and touched hers, a butterfly touch. Their lips barely brushed, but she felt the contact powerfully through her whole body. She pulled back quickly and darted a glance around the room to see if anybody had noticed them. Nobody had, of course. They all were too busy with their food, their conversations, to bother with anybody else.

He whispered, "Do you want dessert?"

"No."

"Coffee?"

"We should."

They drank coffee, impatient for it to cool so they could finish it and be on their way. She floated out of Papa Choux's. It must have been the wine. She felt so light, it was ridiculous that her feet were still churning along, quite as if she needed them to propel her.

He ransomed his car from the attendant and they got in. He drove to a nearby side street and parked the car under a large, dark tree. The seats of the car were separated by a bulky map compartment, but somehow they managed to connect across it and share a long kiss — tender, searching, almost testing. His lips moved slowly, warmly over hers, not even needing to deepen the kiss, for it was complete in itself, a message, a greeting, a recognition. Their bodies were communicating with kissing. She could feel his need almost as strongly as she felt her own, burning through her. She was aware of heat low in her body, surprising her with its suddenness and its blatant sexuality.

After a long time his hand came around to cradle her shoulder. He didn't touch her anywhere else; again, there was no need. They both knew. There was a faint taste of lobster and wine on his lips, and she could have continued exactly where she was forever.

When he let her go she was embarrassed to realize that there were tears in her eyes. She wanted to weep because it was so right, so perfect, and because he had moved a few inches away from her on the other side of the map compartment.

He smiled, and, as always, it warmed her, even as she was trying to blink away her inappropriate tears. He put a big warm hand under her chin and tried to turn her face toward the light, but there wasn't much there in the shadow of the tree. He said, "You're not crying, are you?"

"Of course not."

"That's good." He brushed her lips again with his and kissed her eyes. He must have known she had lied, but he didn't mention it.

Instead, he said, "Lucia, you're wonderful. We'll go to my place."

She asked, "Isn't your daughter there?"

"She won't bother us."

"Not bother . . . Well, I should think she wouldn't!" Lucia's mind was suddenly crowded with images of Debbie not bothering them. Confined to her room, perhaps? Sent out in search of a left-handed monkey wrench? Sitting alone by the dead kitchen fire with her feet in the cinders?

She protested. "Last night you followed her all over town for fear she would . . . And tonight you want to . . . This isn't going to work, Mitch!"

"Maybe she won't be home," he suggested hopefully.

What was she doing, Lucia wondered suddenly, sitting under this sinister tree with a man she scarcely knew? How many of his dates had he grabbed across that map compartment? She said, "Please, we'll go to my house. I'll make a pot of coffee."

"Isn't your son home?"

"Of course, and even if he should not be, coffee is all you're going to get." Sensible Lucia turned firmly to face the windshield.

"What's gotten into you all of the sudden? Did I say something?"

"Nothing, nothing at all. I'm just having a small attack of common sense, belated though it may be."

Lucia's hands clenched quietly in her lap. "Do you have a lot of success with this line? The booth, the lobster, the wine? All that masculinity and those hound-dog eyes of yours? How many women have you charmed with that routine? Just lately, I mean. You don't have to strain your memory."

Reproachfully he began, "Lucia, I thought we had something going. . . ."

"Yes, I'll bet you did, and probably we would have if the fact that you aren't living alone right now hadn't brought me to my senses. I never used to be this gullible. I wonder if it's senility?"

"What do you mean?"

She decided to tell him. He had asked, hadn't he? "I was ready to fall right into your arms. A real California romance. One torrid evening and then . . . and then nothing. Somehow, nothing else ever happens and you never see the guy again. Try to call him and he's out of town."

"Is that how you've been treated?"

"Not me," she replied stoutly. "I'm too cautious, normally. But I do have friends, and as I told you, I'm very observant."

"It's not like that with us, and you know it."

"Sure I do. I'm just like every other human being. Every one of us thinks he's different from everybody else. The laws of nature are suspended just for him."

"Lucia, this is you and me!" He had his brows

drawn down, almost hiding his eyes. "We've got nothing to do with the laws of nature or the way other people do things. We're us, and what we have is real, and it's just starting."

"It is? Then why don't we have any plans? Not even one date lined up, and the whole weekend ahead of us? It seems like you might have committed yourself to something tomorrow, at least, since it's Saturday."

He sat sullenly staring at the windshield for so long that she prompted him, "Well?"

He muttered, "I'm going to be out of town tomorrow."

"Yes, naturally. A business trip, of course. Everybody starts them on Saturday."

"I knew you'd take that attitude!" he stormed. "I'm in the oil business, and trouble on the rig is no respecter of weekends. I've got to go, and I don't know for sure when I'll be back. It might take a week."

"Do call me when you get back," she said in her ice-cream voice, cold and sweet.

"You could give me your phone number," he grumbled.

"Yes, of course I will." And he would call. Surely he would call, and when he did she would feel even more foolish than she felt now. She felt foolish and sad, sad because he probably wouldn't call, not now, not after her tirade and suspicions. How could one person get this confused?

She wanted Mitch; she had as much as admitted it, and then balked like a frightened schoolgirl. She couldn't think of anything relevant to say, and asked only, "If you're going to be gone all week, will Debbie be alone?"

"She belongs to a sorority and she's going to stay at their house on campus."

"Tell her to call me if she needs anything . . . or anything." It was the thought of poor little Debbie needing something, and her mother in far-off Oxnard, that was stinging Lucia's eyes with tears. Sure it was.

She said miserably, "I've blown it, haven't I? I've blown it with you. I just never learned to be tactful."

"Let's not say blown. You're making me pretty uncomfortable, but we've got too much to let it blow."

He cupped her chin in his strong, warm hand and turned her head toward him. "Look at me, Lucia. I don't care what happened to your friend, or whatever; I'm not the kind to hit and run. You believe that, don't you?"

His touch held her. He wasn't forcing her, but she couldn't look away. And since she couldn't, she had to tell the truth. "Yes, I believe you. God knows why, but I do."

"You'd understand if you'd pay attention to your own feelings instead of to your observations about other people. You and me, we're just starting out, and that isn't the best part but it can be one of the best parts if you'll just stop fighting me and let it happen."

Relaxing as if hypnotized, she leaned across the map compartment toward him.

"One of the best parts," he repeated, "and one of the . . . most . . . exciting . . ." His fingers slipped under her hair at the back of her neck. She trembled at the touch but held back when he kissed her, deliberately keeping it light, pulling back from the hunger she could feel in his mouth, his hands.

"Time, Mitch, I need time," she whispered as he let her go. "I'm not a kid who can close her eyes and leap. My life isn't that simple. Please take me home now."

He said, "Okay," and put the car in gear. His weary sigh was almost inaudible.

Chapter Three

Lucia always got up early Saturday morning and used the first fresh hours of the day to do her yard work. She mowed the lawn and watered and pulled weeds around the shrubs under the breakfast room windows. Low maintenance was her goal in gardening, but in just this one spot she encouraged bushes of flowering jasmine. The breakfast room, with its pretty bowed windows looking into the backyard, was the most used room in the house. It was there the family gathered for homework, to watch TV, play games, and eat most of their meals. The green bushes flecked with fragrant white blossoms looked lovely outside the windows.

She was grubbing around the roots of a plant when the phone rang. It was on the window seat next to the window that had a broken screen, so Lucia opened the pane and picked up the phone. She had left it there deliberately, knowing Terrilee was going to call. It wasn't extrasensory perception; Terrilee tended to get frantic around opening time on a Saturday morning.

Terrilee owned the boutique where Lucia brought her gowns and robes to be sold. A clever, inventive, and hardworking woman, she seemed to attract misfortune. Her background included an unfinished education, a failed marriage, and a thriving business that had been stolen from her by a man she had loved and trusted. Her problems with her weight kept Lucia counting calories. Her troubles with the men she dated were the basis of Lucia's caution. They had been friends since school days, and Lucia loved her almost as much for her reckless boneheadedness and occasional lapses of good taste as for her earthy humor and the devotion to hard work with which she was building her new business.

Terrilee opened the conversation by booming, "Hello, Lucia! How's your love life?"

Even with a friend as dear as Terrilee, Lucia couldn't begin by saying, for instance, "I think I'm falling in love with a man who's such a smooth operator, we've had one date and he's already out of town."

So she said instead, "I'm fine, Terrilee. How are you?"

"This is me you're talking to, remember? I'm so healthy I can eat anything, and the trouble is, I usually do. I could do with a little ill health to make me pale, interesting, and best of all, thin. What I asked about was your love life."

"Oh, just like usual. I have to beat them off with a stick," Lucia evaded. "How's yours?"

"The usual here, too. Some guy asked me to dinner at the Queen Mary and I thought it sounded like fun, going onto the boat and everything, but it turned out he didn't mean the boat, it was some dive in the Valley with male strippers."

"That's terrible!"

"As a matter of fact, the show was good, and funny, and I had a good time. Lucia, do you have any gowns for me?"

"A couple. Two that are finished, one that's almost."

"What color are they?"

"Off-white. One has ecru lace."

"What I need is some color. Can you give me some color? The racks are full but the place looks dead. Everything's white."

"Well, I could make something . . ." Lucia said.

"You know what I'd like? Some of those floaty things you made last spring. With spaghetti straps. You know the design I mean?

"Yeah, sure."

"It's a great design. Always fits the customer, no matter how fat she is. I need about six of them, all in colors. No white."

"Sure, I'll do that," Lucia promised, although the idea of six identical gowns was already boring her. Then she had an idea. "How about rainbows?"

"Great! What do you mean?"

"Each gown in rainbow colors. It will be easy. The things are gored anyway; I'll just cut them all at once and alternate the gores."

"I don't know what you're talking about, but a rainbow is just what I need in here. Do it for me, will you?"

"Sure, and can I send along the ones I've already finished, too? I could use the extra money. Tommy's scholarship doesn't cover books."

"Sure, send them. Are you sure you're all right? You don't sound a hundred percent."

"Everything's fine," Lucia lied.

"Do you know what I admire about you? It's your ability to survive all kinds of disasters without losing your figure."

"I hope I'm not about to survive another disaster," said Lucia.

* * *

She didn't finish gardening, for gardening is never finished, but she stopped in time to run the errands and get back with the groceries to cook lunch for herself and Tommy. He worked the evening shift on Fridays and Saturdays and he would get a meal at the fast-food outlet, but he was so tired of the hamburger that was their only offering, he seldom ate much. Lucia liked to be sure he got a hot, nourishing lunch.

After she had cleaned the dishes and the kitchen, she made a quick run through the downstairs rooms, straightening and picking up. As quickly as she could, closing her eyes to a dozen things that should have been cleaned, repaired, or at least dusted, she worked her way up the stairs and into her sewing room. At last, it was her time to sew! A whole afternoon was ahead to do what she wanted, like a reward for finishing all the rest.

She was aware that the labor she put into the gowns brought her a relatively small return, but she liked working with the pretty fabrics and creating something new. It was lovely to do work that stayed done and did not, as her usual work at home and in the office did, have to be done all over again the next day. She felt relaxed and happy in her workroom, her favorite room in the house.

It was on the second floor in the front, with

another of the big bow windows looking right into an old laurel tree that grew on the street. The wainscot and doors of this room were all of oak, and in good condition. The closet was as big as another bedroom, for it was a Victorian dressing room.

She had recently been to the wholesaler for a supply of the delicate silks she liked to work with. They were lined up on their special shelf, each bolt covered with protective paper, but she knew what the colors were. Rose, lavender, azure, teal. Green, chartreuse, yellow, and tangerine, a color for each of the eight gores of the gown. She must have been thinking rainbows when she made the purchases. Everything fitted in perfectly except the peacock blue.

Now, why had she bought that bright peacock blue? It was not even the same type of fabric as the rest. It had a hard finish that give it sheen, and the color was too bright for the pastel rainbows she was planning. She opened the bolt and spilled the vibrant blue onto her worktable. There was a sensuous feel to the fabric. She would make something lovely from it, something that would sell at once.

But what it was making her think of was a dress. Simply cut and loosely fitted, this dress, to make the most of the subtle shadings in the fabric. It would have long sleeves, a tailored neckline, and a narrow belt to flatter her waist-line. A dress, in short, to wear out to dinner with Mitch.

And what if he never asked her out again? What if, as she had angrily predicted last night, he never showed up again? She shouldn't be sewing for herself in any event. She should be using these precious hours to fulfill her promise to Terrilee and to earn the money for Tommy's books.

But it would be a lovely dress. It would catch the color of her eyes and set off her dark hair. Really, she needed a pretty dress. There would be lots of places she could wear it. The boutique could wait. Lucia selected her pattern and began to pin.

By the time the light was fading she had the dress assembled and ready for hand finishing. She could easily do that under artificial light in the long evening that stretched ahead, what with Tommy working most of the night. He would probably not come home even at the late hour he finished work. He and his friends complained that working around food all night made them hungry, but not for the dishes they were handling. They would get in the car and drive someplace to sample another chain's food.

She hung the dress on a padded hanger and stood back to look at it. It was particularly successful. The elegant lines and glowing color went together. She would look good in it, dressed up enough for the places Mitch liked to go and for the suits he wore. Would he like how she looked in it? Would he ever see her in it? Was he ever going to call?

She snapped off the light over her sewing machine and brushed a few trimmings into the wastebasket. "You're a fool, Lucia Morgan," she said aloud.

She would fix herself a snack and then she would watch television, or maybe she would read, or telephone her friends. What did people do in the evening . . . people who weren't workaholics?

Around midnight, as she was sewing on the last few buttons, he called. She wasn't surprised to hear the phone ring at such an hour, nor to hear his voice on the other end. She had known all along that the world is a good place and he was going to call.

"I've been thinking about you," he said.

"That's nice."

"Have you been thinking about me?"

Lucia smoothed the silk of her new dress where it lay across her lap. "I guess you might say that. Where are you?"

"Outside Bakersfield about thirty miles. It isn't even a place, just a motel. I hope you don't mind that I phoned so late. I just got in off the rig a little while ago."

"I don't mind."

"There wasn't much going on, so I thought I'd drive to the motel. Get a shower and a night's sleep where it's quiet."

"Do you usually sleep on the rig?"

"There's a bunch of trailers out there. You can stay for a month at a time if you want. Trailers to sleep in, one to cook and eat in . . ."

"Why isn't there anything going on? I thought you had this big dramatic problem."

"We've still got the problem, but the equipment we need is in Ecuador. There isn't much we can do right now."

She couldn't help laughing. "Ecuador? How did it get there?"

"That's where they used it last. It's okay; they'll get it here in a couple of days, and if they don't, I'll probably think of something. I always do. Anyway, I have to, so I can be back in town by Saturday. I'm giving a party."

"Saturday?"

"It's no big deal. Just some friends coming over for barbecue. Will you come, Lucia? Bring Tommy if you want. The rest of them are bringing their kids."

"I'd be happy to come, but Tommy can't. He works Saturday evenings."

"Okay, that's settled, then. Remind me to give you the directions to get to my house. Dress casual. Now, what have you been doing all day?"

"Oh, the Saturday usual. Errands, yard work."

"Yard work? You shouldn't have to do that. You have two big boys to do it for you."

"Well, Georgie's away, and Tommy's so busy. I don't mind the work. It's my one chance all week to get outdoors. Just think what a gym would charge me for the same amount of exercise! It's a good workout and it's free."

They talked for most of an hour, not about anything in particular, just talking. She made him hang up when she found out he was at an outdoor pay phone, standing up and swatting mosquitoes in the hot desert darkness.

Tommy was home all day Sunday and some of his friends came over to study. One of them brought his motorcycle along and he tuned it up for hours, running it, gunning it, stopping and starting the engine in a noisy symphony under Lucia's window.

She was hurrying to catch up with the neglected rainbow gowns and the racket got on her nerves. She kept herself closed in her workroom, away from the boys, afraid she might snap at them. But by the time the afternoon was over and the motorcyclist had roared away, she was making good progress and felt more positive. She went to the breakfast room where the boys were studying and invited them all to dinner.

She concealed her astonishment when they said they wanted to eat hamburgers from the fast-food chain. They pooled their money and sent somebody to fetch the food. Lucia ate hers, although she was not fond of it. She thought if you closed your eyes you would not be able to tell if you were eating the hamburger or the paper container it came in.

There was the advantage of a clean kitchen afterward, and no dishes to wash. She was so charmed, she made a cake. It was a simple recipe; you did not frost the hot cake, but made a topping of butter, brown sugar, and coconut and ran it briefly under the broiler. It was intended to be eaten warm, and Lucia knew very well that five boys could easily eat the whole thing. They did.

Late Wednesday night she finished the rainbow gowns, and Thursday after work she hung them on the rack that was mounted in the back of her station wagon and took them to Terrilee's home. She lived in a couple of rooms behind the shop, so she had only to unlock the connecting door and hang the new merchandise in the showroom.

As they put the gowns on the store racks,

Terrilee protested, "You didn't have to bring them over, Lucia. I could have sent someone for them."

"I wanted to talk to a real live human being," Lucia admitted. "It seems like I've spent this whole week with telephones instead of people."

Terrilee wore jeans and a sweatshirt, not at all an attractive outfit on her, for the jeans were tighter than the skin on a sausage. Lucia thought the only way they could possibly fit like that was if Terrilee had gained five pounds since she pulled up the zipper.

She was thrilled with the gowns. Throwing out her arms with characteristic enthusiasm, she cried, "Lucia, they're wonderful! I want one for myself; that's how I can tell when something's really good. These are good. I love it that each one's slightly different from the others." She riffled the gowns as they hung on the rack. "Look, the colors rotate! I know just how I'm going to display them."

They moved back into Terrilee's living room and she locked the shop door. Lucia was pleased with the praise for the gowns, but she said worriedly, "You've fallen off your diet again. You were doing so well, too!"

"Was. Past tense," Terrilee agreed, shoving back a strand of her unruly red hair. "That was before I met the guy with the line about—Oh, well, never mind. We all know there aren't any good ones left."

Lucia couldn't help the smile that bubbled up in her. "There might be one," she said.

Terrilee's nose flared with astonishment. "Lucia! You? Can it be true? You do look absolutely glowing. Are you in love?"

"Oh, no . . . Yes . . . I think so! Oh, Terri, I think I'm in love! I've known him only a week, but he's so sweet and so nice and he has such nice eyes!"

Terrilee's expressive nose turned sharp with suspicion. "He sounds like a cocker spaniel. Where did you meet this paragon?"

"His kids and mine. They know each other."

"Hey, wait a minute. He's got kids?"

"Practically everybody our age does. He's divorced."

Terrilee's nose went even sharper. "Let's go a little slow here. How do you know he's divorced?"

"He said so. And he must be, his ex-wife is remarried."

"One of them. How do you know how many ex-wives he has? You've got to learn to be a little careful, Lucia. You don't know the ropes like some of us scarred veterans. Never get involved with a guy until you know what his marital status really is, and then if you're smart, you'll run a credit check. I'll do it for you. I've got TRW. Give me his social security number."

Lucia drew herself up, somewhat offended. "Where would I get that? And I wouldn't run a credit check on him if I had it. I know without doing anything like that that he's good and honest and kind."

"Oh, boy!" Terrilee combed her fingers dramatically through her russet curls. "This sounds more every minute like a man to look out for! Don't fall for a man you don't know anything about, Lucia! You're going to get yourself hurt!"

"You're the one who's always telling me I ought to have more fun," Lucia protested.

"Fun! Yeah, fun! You weren't listening! I said have fun. I didn't tell you to fall in love!"

"I don't know what you mean."

"Let him chase you, take you places, give you presents; let him fall in love, but don't you fall. That's when the fun stops."

"It hardly seems equitable that way," Lucia objected mildly.

"If you fall for him, do you think he's going to worry if it's equitable?" Terrilee returned.

"I could get hurt," said Lucia thoughtfully. "You're right about that."

"You're probably going to," was Terrilee's heartless reply. "Nobody wins the decathlon the first time out. But you'll have a chance to come out of it alive if you just don't fall in love!"

"Living's living," Lucia said firmly. "It's the chance we all take. It's like crossing Wilshire Boulevard. Everybody knows it isn't safe, but you have to do it sometime. You can't spend your whole life on one side of Wilshire."

"Oh, Lucia, I wish you'd be careful!"

"I will, Terrilee." Lucia smiled at her friend. "I promise you I will."

She had scarcely arrived home when the phone started to ring. Of course, it was Mitch. Lucia sank down on the window seat with the phone in her hand. She was grinning all by herself, but she remembered that she was supposed to be suspicious and asked, "What do you want, Mitch?"

"Is everything all right? I've been trying to get you for an hour."

"I was out making a delivery. You sure make a lot of phone calls. Where do you get all those quarters?"

"Don't need 'em. I've got a piece of plastic. How are you, Lucia?" His voice already sounded familiar, deep and masculine with just a little roughness in it, a little rasp.

"I'm fine. How are you, Mitch?" She loved listening to that voice, even if it was only on the phone. She stretched out on the seat, tossing a badminton racquet onto the floor. The hell with Terrilee, too. "It's nice to hear from you."

"I've got Saturday night all set up. We won't be finished here, but I'm taking the night off anyhow and driving into L.A. You'll like the Larchmonts; they're some of my oldest friends."

"It sounds like fun."

"Did Tommy change his mind and decide to come?"

"No, he couldn't get off work, but I'll manage somehow to get through the evening without him."

"We'll be finished out here probably early next week and then I'll be back in town. How about Saturday a week from now? Would you like to go to a show?"

"Of course."

"Do you like what's at the Shubert? If you do, I'll order some tickets."

"Well, of course I'd like that, but you don't have to go to a lot of trouble. We could just take in a movie."

"Nothing's too much trouble," he said with a small chuckle that was almost a purr. "Not for Lucia."

She nestled into the cushions of the window seat, comfortable as a cat on the radiator vent. "You'll spoil me," she murmured.

That chuckle again. "I'm trying not to rush

you. Just a quiet evening with friends, that's all. For something as important as this, I can be patient."

He paused, and there was a long silence broken only by the crackling in the wires between them. Then he whispered, "It's important to you, too, isn't it, Lucia?"

A dozen coy answers presented themselves, a hundred ways to follow Terrilee's advice and string him along while staying aloof. And just one answer that was mature and honest. She said firmly, "You are important to me, Mitch, and I am looking forward to being with you again."

There, she had said it. Probably Terrilee was right and he was handing her a line. She was rushing out to get her heart broken, but what of it? If she was to have only a taste, a tiny taste, of living and loving again, she would have it. It was better than pushing it away, better than starving forever.

Mitch said slowly, "I didn't think this could happen. I didn't know a person ever got a second chance, but it's happening to us, isn't it?"

"Yes, I think it is."

"I know it is. Lucia, we have a future. We have a future together."

"I can hardly wait to see you."

"Is that so?" The chuckle entered his voice

again. "You talk a great game on the telephone."

"I may surprise you," she warned. "You're talking to the new Lucia. The one that has crossed Wilshire."

He said, "Huh?" but she refused to explain.

Chapter Four

Finding Mitch's condo was not easy. The road ran all over a mountain and all the street signs hid in dense brush. With perseverance and the wonderful maps in her Thomas Guide, Lucia found it at last, perched high above a spectacular view of the Valley.

The number was painted on a cluster of mailboxes at the roadside, and behind them, an arched gateway led to a flight of stairs. Several condos, loosely linked together, rambled up the cliff, some of them out of sight in the primeval forest they favored up in these hills.

Next to the arch was the garage entrance, guarded by serious black gates. Visitors parked outside, of course, taking their chances on the steep, narrow road.

She mounted the staircase and found Mitch's door. He opened it at once when she rang, almost as if he had been standing behind it, waiting for her to arrive. He wore jeans and a colorful shirt, very much at home. Why was it, relaxed in his own place, he looked bigger and more formidable than ever?

But his smile beamed and he said, "Lucia, I'm glad you could make it. Did you have any trouble finding the place? You look beautiful."

There were shadows around his eyes; Lucia thought he looked tired, but she knew he had been working long hours out in the field. But he was the same Mitch, with that same smile she remembered so well. He stood there smiling, approving the way she looked.

She had chosen her outfit carefully, a patio dress in a colorful print. It had a full skirt and the neckline was cut just a bit low and bordered with a ruffle. He must have liked it; he stood blocking the doorway, and there was a flame deep in the brown depths of his eyes as he ran his gaze admiringly over the warm hollow between her breasts. He carefully observed the tight waist of the dress and traced the curve of her leg down to her high-heeled sandals before he murmured at last, "You look beautiful."

"You said that already," she reminded him. "I'm glad you approve, but since you do, may I come in?"

"Oh . . . uh . . . sure." He seemed to jerk himself back to reality. He stood aside, but not very far aside, and she brushed lightly against him as she entered. The slight contact crackled with power. Somehow that touch, just her shoulder against his chest, made an imprint on her mind as if she felt his whole body against hers.

She found herself in a spacious living room that seemed even larger than it was because there was little furniture. A pair of large white couches had a low table positioned between them. The stereo and TV were together in a big cabinet, a table held the telephone, and scarcely anything else dented the expanse of pearl-gray carpeting. The fireplace was part of a wall of fieldstone; the opposite wall was entirely of glass, for full advantage of the view.

Debbie sat on one of the couches, chatting with a pretty, dark-haired girl of her own age. They both waved but otherwise paid no attention to Lucia.

She said, "What a lovely room, Mitch. I see you go for the elegantly underfurnished look in interior decoration."

"Well, I've been meaning to get some furniture and stuff, but I haven't gotten around to it yet," he explained.

"You haven't lived here long, then?"

"Not long. Three years, I guess. You didn't bring Tommy?"

"I told you, Mitch. He has to work on Saturday nights."

"I thought he might change his mind. Come and meet my friends."

He introduced Jim Larchmont, who rose from a couch like an animal coming out of its lair. He was almost as big as Mitch and very bald. He had a dark tan and a ready smile and he took Lucia's hand with obvious delight.

"So you're Mitch's little lady!" he boomed. "He is one lucky guy! You're sure beautiful!"

Not quite sure how to deal with the effusiveness, Lucia stammered, "Well . . . uh . . . thank you."

"Come on, I'll fix you a drink. How does a frozen daiquiri sound?"

"Sounds lovely," said Lucia, and she followed him, Mitch trailing along behind them both.

He led the way to the kitchen, where a short, shapely woman was washing lettuce at the sink. She cried, "Oh, thank God you're here!"

On high-heeled clogs she clattered toward Lucia and offered a wet hand to be shaken. "I'm Nancy Larchmont. Now we can get the food going before the guys get any more cocktails."

Her face was round and charming and she had a warm, honest smile. Her eyes were black, her hair black and curly. She wore jeans and an apron, making Lucia wonder if she had overdressed.

She asked, "Are we doing a pot luck? You didn't tell me, Mitch. I would have brought something."

"No, no, it isn't that," Nancy answered for him. "I always cook when we're at Mitch's. It's the only safe thing to do. He could ruin shelled peanuts."

"I do it on purpose," Mitch chuckled. "Gets all the ladies looking after me."

"Can I help?" Lucia asked Nancy.

"Get your drink and relax," Nancy replied. "I'll have the salad ready in a minute, and the potatoes are on, and Mitch is just about to go out and get the barbecue fire going."

Mitch caught her meaningful look and said agreeably, "Okay, I'm going. Come with me, Lucia, and see the view from my patio."

"I'll be out as soon as I get my drink," Lucia promised.

Jim had taken a container from the freezer and attached it to the blender. The slush in the bottom of the container turned to froth, and he poured some into a glass for Lucia.

She tasted it and realized at once that it was

dangerously cold. With the tongue frozen, a person could not tell how strong it was, and she suspected it was very. She smiled at Jim and said it was delicious.

Jim accepted her praise placidly. "It's my own special recipe," he said. "I'll go see if Mitch wants some more." He went through the door to the patio, carrying the container.

Lucia asked again, "Are you sure I can't help you?"

Nancy was shredding lettuce into a bowl, and she grinned, eyes sparkling. She said, "He never did this before."

"What?"

"Mitch never asked us to meet a girlfriend of his before. I think you must be pretty special."

"Me?" But Lucia smiled because she was beginning to feel very special indeed.

"You've got him so nervous, he's scarfing up those lime daiquiris like he was expecting an outbreak of scurvy."

"Oh, come on, Nancy . . ."

Tossing lettuce, Nancy spoke portentously. "Something going on here! We shall see events! Why don't you get out there on the patio and see if you can calm him down? Go on!"

Lucia went out the kitchen door. They called it a patio but it was actually a terrace, probably on top of the bedrooms of the condo, which had several levels. The floor was of redwood planks and brushy plants in large wooden containers were scattered around it. The air was fresh and cool and the Valley was spread below as flat as a lake of lights, surrounded by the dark bosky shoulders of mountains.

Mitch seemed calm as one could reasonably expect, working away at firing up the charcoal briquettes. Jim had disappeared, leaving behind him on the wide wooden railing a stemmed glass of pale green froth.

She moved to the rail and put her glass down next to Mitch's. "What a splendid view! You can see the whole Valley!"

He came over to stand beside her. "Yeah, on clear nights like this I feel like I own it and they turn on all those lights just for me, because it looks so pretty from up here."

She felt a shiver. The night air was already turning cool and he was standing so close to her. She whispered, "Yes."

"I've missed seeing you all week." He smiled but made no move to touch her.

"I've been looking forward to tonight." She leaned just a little toward him, her eyes wide as she looked up, her lips slightly parted.

He didn't do anything. He just stood there.

At length he said, "Yeah. Jim and Nancy are a couple of my best friends."

"They're very charming," she replied, but suddenly everything was awkward. The easy camaraderie they had on the telephone was missing. She wished he would put his arms around her, touch her some way, but why did they need that for communication when they could talk so easily on the phone?

She found herself wondering if she was reading too much into his attentions, his phone calls. Was it possible that all he wanted was a telephone buddy, somebody who didn't mind being called in the middle of the night or whenever things shut down on the rig?

He said, "Let's go see if Jim made any more of these drinks."

She was surprised how fast his glass had emptied. Maybe Nancy was right. She ventured, "Are you thirsty?"

"Well, tonight's special."

She smiled up at him again. "Is it?"

"Well, I hardly ever get to see my friends."

They returned to the kitchen, where Nancy handed Lucia a tray of chips. "Put that in the living room," she directed. "We're all going to sit down and talk until dinner's ready."

As Lucia took the tray, Nancy startled her by leaning into the doorway and bellowing into the next room, "Debbie! Where the hell's the pepper?"

Then she looked at Lucia and grinned a bit sheepishly. "Well, she's the only one who knows where anything is around here."

"I'll carry that for you," Mitch offered, and took the tray from Lucia's hands.

"It's not heavy," she protested, laughing.

"You've got a free hand, take this," commanded Nancy, and gave her a bowl of dip.

They trooped into the living room and arranged the snacks on the table between the white couches. Nancy introduced her daughter, Jean. She had her mother's luxuriant black hair and seemed rather quiet.

Nancy flopped down on a couch and took up her drink. "That sure is a pretty dress, Lucia."

"How nice of you to say that," Lucia replied. "It's my own design."

Nancy blinked with surprise. "You mean you just think of something and then you make it? Just like that? From scratch?"

Lucia smiled. "It's not as hard as it sounds. I make most of my clothes."

"She makes stuff to sell, too," Mitch put in. "Nighties and stuff."

Lucia gave him a glance. "It so happens that the outlet I have for my work is a boutique that specializes in loungewear, so that's what I make the most."

"You design it and make it both," Nancy repeated. "I wish I could do that. Then I'd know what to do with the silk I brought back from Hong Kong."

"You went to Hong Kong? How exciting! Were you on a cruise?"

Nancy waved her drink carelessly. "No, just on our way back from Sydney."

Lucia pretended to select a potato chip while she thought that one over. Sydney was in Australia, so what did it have to do with Hong Kong, which was near China?

Mitch's hand hovered over the tray, and he picked up the chip adjacent to hers. Their fingers didn't touch, but it was as if the chips were conductors, completing her electrical connection with Mitch. She lifted her eyes to find he was smiling at her, and she couldn't remember what it was she had been about to say. She smiled in return.

Mitch explained. "When you're halfway around the world, it doesn't matter if you go east or west to get home; the distance is the same and the airlines don't care."

Lucia said, "Oh."

Jim decided to join the conversation. "Did you have any trouble getting here, Lucia?

That road's an obstacle course. I don't know why anybody lives up here. I'll bet I bottomed out my car three times."

"It would help if you didn't drive a Cadillac that's as big as a truck and a lot less practical," Mitch teased.

"Big car like that is the only way to be comfortable if you're going to drive any distance," Jim insisted. "A person gets all hunched up sitting in something like that Volkswagen of yours."

"It's not a Volkswagen," Lucia protested. "It's a Porsche."

"That's sort of a joke," Mitch explained. "Both cars had the same designer." He rose. "Fire ought to be about ready. I'm going to put on the steak."

"Yes, do that," Nancy agreed, and handed him her glass. "On your way back, bring me another daiquiri."

Mitch took the glass and left. Nancy asked, "Do you have kids, Lucia?"

They began comparing families. Nancy had a boy the same age as Lucia's Georgie and she was launching into a description of his current activities when the phone rang. Quite naturally, Nancy got up and answered it. Just as naturally, she began an animated conversation.

Well, maybe she had call forwarding. Lucia

turned to Jim and pumped him for the rest of the information about the Larchmont son, who was married and about to make grandparents of Jim and Nancy.

Nancy's phone conversation continued until Mitch came back into the room, and then she handed him the receiver and said, "For you, Mitch. It's Ione."

Mitch put down the drinks he was carrying and took up the phone. Lucia watched, astonished. Nancy's breezy way of taking over everything was hard enough to get used to, but Ione? How many Iones might there be, say, in the state of California? How many with Mitch's phone number?

There could be only one. His ex-wife.

At least nobody noticed that she had gone silent. Everybody else had, too, and they all watched Mitch. He wasn't saying much, just, "Yes, yes," occasionally. Lucia thought it interesting that he never once said no.

When he hung up, Nancy was still standing beside him. With the bluntness of an old friend she asked, "What did she want?"

He began poking through the drawer of the table that held the phone. "She hasn't heard from Darryl for a couple days and she wants me to check up on him. I'm going to have to make some calls."

Nancy asked, "Who can find a college boy on a Saturday night?"

"Oh, I've got some numbers." Mitch pulled a scrap of paper from the drawer. "This happens all the time, so I've got a list of the friends he hangs out with. I'll find him." He began dialing.

Nancy shrugged, turned away, and went into the kitchen. Lucia followed her.

A pot holder in each hand, Nancy was rolling hot baked potatoes out of the oven. Her expression was exasperated, but when she saw Lucia, all she said was "See if you can find the plates, will you? They've got to be someplace."

Lucia began opening cupboards. She asked tentatively, "You know Ione, don't you?"

"Sure. Mitch and Jim have been best friends for a donkey's years."

Lucia found the plates and took down a stack. She said, "Oh."

Nancy put both hands on her hips, wadding up the pot holders with which she had been fielding the potatoes. "You've got to understand, Ione and I were overseas together."

"That was very important," Lucia guessed.

"Where I first met Ione was at a camp," Nancy began. "Oil camps are all pretty much the same; a fence around nothing in the middle of nowhere. This one was in Venezuela.

About all that was out there was thousands of miles of grass, and that was the wet season. The rest of the time it was just thousands of miles of miles."

Nancy leaned back against a counter. "The company builds a bunch of houses so the families can come out. The house is made of metal because otherwise the termites will eat it, and all the nuts are on the inside, like living in a battleship. It's hot and humid three hundred and sixty-five days of the year and the same number of nights. Cooking's a losing game. The vegetables are canned and all the meat has been frozen for years. The lettuce comes in once a month and it always looks like last month. The fruit is local, that is, it's bananas."

Lucia listened silently. She was the alien here, she realized. All the rest had traveled such long roads, been such places as she could only imagine. Mitch had a whole life she had not shared; he lived in a world she did not know.

Lucia shrugged and folded her arms. Well, what of it? She could find out. She could learn.

Nancy was rattling on. "The rigs are right outside the fence, and one or the other is always pulling pipe, so it's always noisy. The nearest hospital is five hours away. At the camp there's a doctor who doubles as the vet, and he doesn't speak much English even when he's sober, which isn't very often. And there you are with a couple of babies to look after."

"It must take a real pioneering spirit to live like that," said Lucia.

"It does, and what the wives are to each other is a support group. Ione was in mine and I was in hers. Debbie and Jean were babies together in the same playpen, bopping each other with their toys. And Darryl outside the pen, being a terrible two."

"I can understand that you are loyal to Ione," Lucia said.

"She's my friend." Nancy's pleasant little face was buttoned into an earnest frown. "Don't get me wrong; I think she handed Mitch a raw deal, but I don't expect perfection from my friends. I figure if you do, you're not going to get perfect friends, you're going to get no friends. I can even see where she was coming from when she left Mitch. She wanted to live in a real house with regular walls and familiar food in the kitchen and a supermarket around the corner and raise her kids to be Americans."

"But they are Americans," Lucia protested. "Don't you feel that your children are Americans, even though they have lived in other countries?"

"For me it's different. I've lived in oil camps from Valdez to Djakarta and I loved it all and my kids did, too. Jean still does. She wants to be a petroleum engineer just like her dad. Then there's people like Ione. She could travel the whole world and never find anything but inconveniences and people who won't speak English and plumbing that isn't up to American standards. She couldn't make the adjustments, she hated the sacrifices, she didn't like the life; she just couldn't hack it. Maybe there's a tipping point. Maybe Ione could have handled it with two children. Or one kid. Or maybe not."

"Under those circumstances, I don't know if I could handle three children," Lucia admitted. "I was surprised that Ione called him. Does she do that often?"

"I think so. Well, you know how Mitch is. Solving problems is what he *does*. And that guy she married, whatever his name is, he's no use when things go wrong. So when there's a problem, Ione calls Mitch. The trouble is that he always takes care of things for her."

"What kind of problems?"

"Oh, anything, especially anything to do with the kids. Ione's always been the kind of mother who calls the paramedics if one of the kids looks at her cross-eyed."

Lucia said, "I think we had better do something about the barbecue before it sets the whole complex on fire."

Nancy screamed, "Gaa! The steak!" and rushed outside.

Lucia filled a big glass with water and followed. She was glad for the interruption, glad the subject was dropped, for no matter how long they kept talking about it, there could be no conclusion. The questions she wanted to ask she could not ask, and Nancy could not answer.

She wanted to say "What were they like together? Was their love so passionate they had three children before they found out they were incompatible? Is he still in love with Ione?"

When the fire was doused and the steak on a platter, they returned to the kitchen. Mitch was there.

Lucia asked him, "Did you find Darryl?"

He answered, "Yes, and I told him to call his mother. Looks like I forgot about the steak."

"We'll slice it thin and serve ketchup," Nancy decreed.

"I didn't mean to burn it . . ." he began apologetically.

Nancy told him, "The trouble with you is, you're no gourmet. That's not burned, it's flambéed. Here's a knife. Carve."

It did taste good, garnished with a lot of laughter. They sat on the couches and ate from the coffee table, since there was no dining room furniture.

Lucia encouraged them to talk about their life in Venezuela. Jim tried to escape the subject, or pretended to. "Oh, that was a long time ago," he demurred, and then went right on talking. "Jean was born out there, and you're what, Jean? Seventeen? Debbie was born there, too. I remember them together. Cute little babies, looked like twins, both walking around with their diapers drooping down."

Jean clattered her knife into her plate, but he did not seem to notice. He said to Nancy, "Remember when the cow got in?"

"Cow, hell," Nancy replied around a bite of steak. "It was a bull."

"They breed a special kind of cattle out there on the llanos," Jim related. "Got to, so they'll survive in that climate. I don't know what they really are, but they look like a mix of Brahma for size, Texas longhorn for horn, and Miura for mean. This one was black. Big and black and he stuck his head right inside the enclosed patio where those two kids were playing, and Nancy socked him square on the nose."

"He's exaggerating as usual," Nancy said. "All I did was hit that critter with everything handy and then I snatched up the kids, one under each arm, and ran into the house."

Jim chuckled. "Whatever you did, that was the most intimidated bull I ever saw."

Nancy finished the story. "It was still standing around when the guys got home for lunch, so they herded it out of camp. I noticed they never got out of their pickup truck to do it, though. Just drove along behind it, both of them snug inside the truck, waving their hats and singing, 'Ti-yi-yippee-yay!' "

"Why should we walk all the way to the front gate?" Mitch asked reasonably. "It was half a mile or more. Probably the way the bull got in, by the front gate. There was a guard there, but he was asleep half the time. The fence was sound; we checked it."

"You don't go overseas to live anymore, do you?" Lucia asked.

Jim answered, "Nah, we live in the Valley now."

Nancy explained. "Now that Jim and Mitch are executives, they still travel a lot but they live here. That's the trouble with the oil business. When the kids are little and you have to carry them everywhere with a diaper bag over your other shoulder, the company moves you constantly. Now that the kids are big enough to be on their own, and traveling would be fun, I'm all settled down in a real house. For the first time in my married life I've got junk in the garage. When I plant something, I get to see the little green things come up, even watch them flower."

"You want to go traveling?" Jim asked with some surprise. "I'll fix you something. I've got to go to Bahrain for three, four days. You can come along if you want."

Nancy screamed with laughter. "Bahrain! It takes three days just to get to Bahrain, and then we'd turn around and come back? No, thank you!"

Jim shrugged. "You said you wanted to go somewhere. Go there and come back, that's what most of my trips are like."

Lucia liked the Larchmonts. The dinner was fun and the conversation lively, although the two daughters took very little part. Debbie was almost as silent as Jean. Perhaps they were overwhelmed by the presence of two such large, cheerful fathers.

Everybody pitched in to do the dishes, even the two girls, and the job was done in record time. The last dish was being put away when

Jean began shooting meaningful glances at her mother.

Nancy at once consulted her watch and said, "Oh, dear, we're going to have to go. I promised Jean this would be an early evening. She has homework to do."

"So do I," said Debbie.

"Do you have to leave so soon?" begged Mitch. "I thought you'd stay awhile. We could have a game of bridge."

But Nancy, or rather, Jean, was adamant, and the Larchmonts were soon on their way out the door. Jean was far in the lead and stood in the hall, jingling the car keys, for she was going to drive home.

Nancy whispered, "You don't mind, do you, Lucia? I had to promise her we'd leave early; it was the only way I could get her to come at all. She can't stand Debbie, and the feeling is mutual."

Lucia whispered back, "That's too bad. Why do you suppose they feel that way?"

"Probably thsoe stories about the two of them spending their babyhood in the same playpen."

Lucia smothered a giggle. "Are you having a learning experience, Nancy?"

"Hell no. I love that story. How they feel about it is their problem. Good night, Lucia.

I'll see you again soon."

Debbie's eagerness to get to her homework seemed to have evaporated, and she flounced around the room, checking the titles in a rack of stereo cassettes. She was a tall girl, strongly built like her father, with his same clear brown eyes.

Mitch's attention was on Lucia. There was an anxious note in his voice as he said, "I'm sorry. I didn't know they'd have to leave so early. Can you stay awhile anyhow? Would you like a drink?"

"Certainly not. I didn't bring along a minor to drive me home. Have one if you like."

"No, I've had enough. Coffee?"

Lucia sat down on a white couch. "Come and talk to me, Mitch. This is the only chance we're going to get. I do have to go soon, and you'll be driving back to Bakersfield tomorrow."

He came and sat down beside her, not close, but close enough so that the interchange of electricity that always arced between them began its rapid bounce, one to the other. Lucia thought she would have known where Mitch was just by the electric feeling he gave her, even if she could not see him. She would know he was close to her even if it were dark, she wore earplugs, and couldn't feel the springs of the couch sag beneath his weight, couldn't smell the faint scent of his warmth and masculinity.

"I should be back for good sometime next week," he was saying. "We've about got the situation licked. On the rig, I mean."

"Our theater tickets are for next Saturday, aren't they?" Her words were almost at random; she kept forgetting what she had meant to say. The heat that flickered between them had more reality than their conversation. His heavy, bare arm was propped on the back of the couch near her, the hand closed into a loose fist. Broad hands, red with new sunburn, the fingers thick and blunt. A worker's hands.

"Two weeks from now, that's the only tickets I could get, but you're saving next Saturday for me, aren't you? We'll take in a movie, or just dinner."

"Of course." She raised her eyes to his face, and he smiled and the heat flickered again. It was in his eyes. She knew he was watching her, watching her eyes with the same intensity with which she was watching him, and the thought made her hands quiver in her lap.

"I'm excited about that," she murmured. "The theater tickets, I mean. I love going to the theater. It was thoughtful of you to . . . to think of taking me . . . to the theater, I

92

mean."

"Oh, I like musicals."

Debbie impatiently snapped shut the cassette rack. "Dad, is it okay if I go watch television?"

Mitch barely glanced at her. "You can watch the one in here, honey."

Lucia looked at him reprovingly. He tried to pretend he didn't notice, turning his head away. His strong brown throat arched up from the V neck of his shirt to the clean line of his jaw. Lucia willed her hands to return to their relaxed position in her lap. Surely he didn't want Debbie to stay any more than she did.

She said nothing but waited quietly for him to turn his head back toward her. When at length he did, he was trying to look as if he were thinking of something else. It was such a transparent effort that she was afraid she might laugh.

Lucia closed her mouth firmly against laughing, but laughter had already twinkled into her eyes and she saw it leap into his. They shared their silent amusement, and with it an unspoken acknowledgment of their need to be alone together. Mitch's voice was steady but just a little gruff as he told Debbie, "Go watch the one in your room if you'd rather."

"Is it okay?" she questioned eagerly. "All

right! Good night, Mrs. Morgan." Debbie scampered off with the first enthusiasm she had shown all evening.

Lucia asked, "What did you tell that poor child?"

"Just that she had to be polite to our guests."

"And she wasn't to leave the two of us alone together?"

"I didn't say that exactly. . . ."

She demanded, "What are you trying to prove?"

"I'm not proving anything," he said a little defensively. "I'm just trying to show you how respectable I am. That you don't need to be afraid of me."

"What makes you think I'm afraid of you?"

"Well, you've sure made it clear you don't trust me."

Lucia leaned just a little toward him. "Maybe I owe you an apology. My performance last week suggests a very overgrown schoolgirl." There was still a space between them, but across it she could feel the heat of his body responding to the heat in hers. Yearning for his touch and yet not quite able to close the small gap between them, she waited, for she knew he longed as she did, and she needed his response, needed to be met halfway.

He got up and moved to the other side of

the table.

She stared with astonishment at him, standing there with that awkward barrier between them. "Mitch, is there something wrong?"

He ground a fist into his own palm. "All that's wrong is I'm having a hard time proving how trustworthy I am, and you're not making it any easier."

She repeated the word, wondering. "Trustworthy?"

"I said this was just going to be an evening with friends, no funny stuff, and that's what you agreed to, and that's what it's going to be."

"Mitch, I said I was sorry. Aren't you going to let me change my mind?"

"Oh, Lucia, Lucia." His voice deepened as he said her name. He opened his hands slowly, palms toward her. "I want more than anything in the world for you to change your mind about me. Do you think you might be going to?"

"There's a distinct possibility." She patted the cushion beside her. "Why don't you come back over here and we'll discuss it?"

He sank down where he was, onto the couch opposite her. "I think it'll be easier to keep my promise from over here."

Lucia's eyes widened angrily. "Promise? Are

you still being trustworthy? I'm starting to feel like I'm on a date with a Boy Scout!"

"You could turn a Boy Scout into a satyr," he retorted.

"What a thing to say!"

"Well, you're sure doing a job on this Boy Scout."

"You know what you're doing?" she asked sharply. "You're playing games with me."

"I'm keeping my promise," he repeated stubbornly.

Lucia stood up and started looking around for her purse. "Well, I guess I could stick around and see how long it takes for you to crack, but I never have been into games. Thank you for inviting me to your party, Mitch."

He jumped up and came toward her, but not too close. "Are you mad at me?"

"Some," she admitted, picking up the purse from on top of the television set. "But I'll probably get over it. There's something to be said for a man who keeps his word, even when it's silly."

"If that was a back-handed compliment, I accept it," said Mitch. "I'll ride along with you, make sure you get home all right."

Lucia blinked at him. "That's dumb. Then you'd be at my house and I'd have to ride back here with you and make sure you got home all right."

That made him laugh. "You wouldn't worry about me, would you?"

"Why should you worry about me? I've been going home alone for years."

He moved closer to her. "Lucia . . . I'll walk down to your car with you and you call me up as soon as you get home, okay?"

"Why don't I call you if I don't get home okay?"

"Come on, don't make me worry. Promise you'll call me."

She reached up and touched his face, feeling the slight rasp of his beard. "I promise. Do you Boy Scouts ever kiss good night?"

His arms went quickly around her and his mouth came down on hers. She put her arms around his neck to pull him closer, to pull him into the warmth they shared when they were together. She responded to the pressure of his lips, parting her own at the first touch of his tongue. She knew she was behaving badly, that she would not have been so aggressive if she had not known that he had himself on a leash, that he would hold back. But she had dreamed of this kiss, dreamed of hearing him say . . . Oh, she didn't quite know what, but she did know he hadn't said it.

She let him go reluctantly, and they stood looking at each other. Their eyes spoke a promise that had nothing to do with the one she had made, about the telephone call, but was about something else entirely.

When she got home she called him and they talked for an hour. Tommy came home from work and complained that he never got to use the phone. Lucia ignored him, but it put something of a damper on the conversation, and it wasn't long before they said good night and hung up.

Chapter Five

Lucia had scarcely arrived home Monday after work when the phone started ringing. It was Terrilee. She yelled into the phone, "I told you so!"

Lucia said mildly, "Hello, Terrilee. How are you?"

"The gowns are a smash! I sold all six of them over the weekend. How soon can you get me a dozen more?"

"Really? How nice to hear it!" It wasn't just the money she would earn, although her mind was already clicking off a dozen places she might put it; the success of the gowns was a deep satisfaction. She had known they were good.

"Can you get them to me by the weekend?" Terrilee was demanding. "The design is hot; let's pour it on."

"A dozen gowns by the weekend? In five days?" Lucia protested. "You know I can't work that fast."

Terrilee sighed heavily. "Oh, Lucia, couldn't you just *once* call in to work sick for a couple days?"

"I couldn't do that!"

"Why not?" Terrilee asked for about the hundredth time. "Why do you hang on to that dull little job? You could make more money doing gowns. Your designs are great. If you would just quit your job and hire some people to help with the sewing . . ."

"Terrilee, we've been through this over and over. I can't take the chance. If I failed I'd take Tommy's college education down the tubes with me. I have to stick with what I know. I have to have a paycheck every week."

"How could you fail? I already know a half-dozen places you could sell gowns, and you have that big house to set yourself up in . . ."

"You want me to turn my historical landmark home into a sweatshop?" Lucia cried in overdone tones of horror.

"I'll mail you deodorant spray!" Terrilee yelled, and they both started to laugh.

Even Terrilee knew when she was licked, and she changed the subject. "So what have you been doing all weekend? What's happening with your cocker spaniel?"

"He's still out of town," Lucia said vaguely, because she didn't know exactly how things were between her and Mitch. Could their encounter Saturday night be considered a date? If it was, had anything happened? Asking herself questions like that didn't help any.

So she counterattacked. "And what's your love life like?"

"Like nothing at all," Terrilee replied. "It's the trouble with being an entrepreneur. The time when I do most of my work is on the weekends. Try to find a guy who wants to go dancing on a Tuesday!"

"Somehow, you always seem to find a way."

"Listen, Lucia," Terrilee said. "I've got to have at least a couple of those rainbow things from you by this weekend. Rebecca and I are doing one of our style shows and—"

"Rebecca?" Lucia interrupted. "Is that the woman who has her store next to yours?"

"Yeah. She has this fairly regular thing she does, showing her dresses at a restaurant at lunchtime, and sometimes I take some of my stuff over. It's going to be Saturday. I need flashy things, like your rainbows."

"Sure, I'll get you something," Lucia promised. "But you don't want them the same as the others, do you?"

"They sold."

"You'd be repeating yourself. Maybe we

101

could do them a little differently. Narrower, shaped a little, maybe. How about a robe with rainbow sleeves?"

"You're the designer. Design something. Something with rainbows, anything with rainbows, but be sure to throw in a couple of those floats. The customers liked 'em and that's enough for me."

"I'll get right to work on it."

"Good girl. Gotta run now—Oh, wait a minute. Rebecca's on my back because she doesn't think it's fair she always has to supply all the models. How about modeling the float for me? You'll look terrific in it, and I don't have to pay you."

"When did you say? Saturday? This coming Saturday?"

"Say yes, Lucia. I need you because Rebecca can get out there and model her own stuff, but I can't."

"Of course you could—if you wanted. How many of your customers have perfect figures?"

"The whole idea is to sell stuff, and trust me, it isn't going to sell if I show the customer in advance that she's going to look fat in it. Oh, yeah, and Rebecca said to get somebody tall. You got any friends that are tall?"

"Somebody tall," mused Lucia, "who would just love to work all Saturday afternoon for free? Not many, I think."

"Some people think modeling's fun."

"Don't pout. I'll see what I can do."

After she hung up, there was a word stuck in Lucia's mind. *Designer.* It had a lovely ring, and sure sounded better than "the lady who answers the phone for the freight company." She was a designer. Terrilee had said so.

How charming it would be to spend her workday designing, dealing with design problems, instead of waiting it out for the day to end so she could begin the work she loved!

Lucia shook her head and strode briskly into the kitchen to begin cooking Tommy's dinner. She was foolish to be thinking, at her age, of gambling everything she had on a venture into the clothing business.

Or a new man.

Lucia rattled the pots as she pulled them from the cupboard and sent them skittering across the counters. She was thinking of a man, all right. She had only to let his image cross her mind and she could feel his impact on her almost as strongly as if he really were there. She could remember his warmth, the solidity of his character, his body, all so strongly that she imagined she could catch the masculine scent of him. She knew exactly the angle of his head, the shape of his hands . . .

"You're not foolish, Lucia," she told herself aloud. "When a person is so obsessed with a man she can smell him when he isn't there, she isn't foolish, she's sick!"

"Did you say something, Ma?" Tommy asked, prowling hungrily into the kitchen. There was a pencil behind his ear and he had that owlish look he got when he was studying.

Lucia said, "What would you like for dinner, dear?" and further startled him by giving him a swift hug.

"Oh . . . uh . . . whatever you're cooking," her son replied brightly, and she smiled as if he had said something clever. Tommy was her life, not dreams, not— What was it her mother used to say? It was a song they sang in the Depression. *There ain't no pie, no pie in the sky* . . .

Her job was to feed Tommy and see to his education, as she had done for Georgie, and she would do it.

And it would be enough for her.

When at last she got to her workroom she began at once on the robes, as they were the most interesting part of the project. She cut three, experimenting with different ways to handle the sleeves. She had assembled all three robes when she realized that it was midnight and in only six hours she would have to be getting up and preparing to go to work. She put down the sewing with reluctance and turned off the lights, thinking that it was the story of her life that she even had to hurry to go to bed.

When she got home the next day, Tommy was still studying, and he had assembled a team to help him do it. His friends were gathered around the table in the breakfast room. Craig, Jason, Glenn . . . Most of the faces were familiar, but she was a little surprised to see Debbie's mop of brown curls among the heads bent over the books. Well, of course. Debbie was in his physics class, and there was something about a test on Friday.

Lucia began cooking at once, in a hurry to get to the gowns. Maybe the kitchen smells did it; the boys took the hint and left. When Lucia peeked into the breakfast room, only Debbie was left, and she was packing up her books, chatting with Tommy as she worked.

Lucia said, "Hello, Debbie."

"Hello, Mrs. Morgan."

"We're having Swiss steak for dinner. Would you like to stay and eat with us?"

Debbie shook her head. "No, thank you, I'm going to be eating at the house."

"The sorority house? Oh, that's where you've been staying, isn't it?"

Debbie squeezed her books to her chest and grinned happily. She wore leggings and a long T-shirt. "Yes, they happen to have a room that's empty right now, so they let me stay in it while Daddy was away. I get to stay only until he gets back, though, so it's only a couple more days."

"You like being there?"

"Oh, it's so great! It's practically on campus so we can walk to school. I don't have to drive all over the place like I do when I'm living at Daddy's. I can go to the library whenever I want and attend all the functions and meetings and everything. I mean, it's so radical."

"You want a soda or something?" Tommy offered, heading for the refrigerator.

"Yeah, sure," Debbie said, and continued to talk to Lucia. "I really do like being an Alpha. That's what we call ourselves, Alphas, because it's first. All the Alphas are just great. They're all so sharp and strong and aware; they talk about politics and play bridge and everything. I could stay forever. I wish Daddy would let me."

"But you'll still be a member, even when you're living at home," Lucia pointed out.

"A commuting member," said Debbie with a moue to indicate how unsatisfactory that was.

She took the can Tommy offered her. "Thanks." With a dramatic wave that threatened to spray cola, she exclaimed, "Oh, I wish I weren't seventeen! It's not fair that I have to be younger than everybody else! It's not my fault, you know. They made me skip a grade when we came to the States because I'd been in private school in Nigeria and they'd already taught me everything I was supposed to know in the fifth grade, so I had to be in the sixth. I won't be eighteen for nearly six months, and that's such a long time! By then even football season will be over!"

"You like football, do you?"

"Actually, I hate it. Don't you? Sit out there in the hot sun; it's always hot, and watch a bunch of guys run back and forth for hours and the day's ruined because it takes forever to drive all the way over there and park and then drive back, and your hair's ruined and your nose is sunburned, but you've got to do it. Everybody does. It just isn't college if you don't go to all the games."

"I never thought of it that way," Lucia admitted.

"Football's a game of strategy and teamwork," Tommy explained. "If you study it and learn the patterns, you'd probably like it better. In a way, it's like chess. Each piece has its function, and they all have to work together."

Debbie's eyes were dark brown and thoughtful. "You mean, on some level it makes sense? That would sure make the game more interesting. Maybe sometime when we're both at a game, you can explain it to me."

"I don't have time to go to football games," said Tommy. "Or the money to pay for one of those season tickets. Maybe we could watch a game together on television."

"If I go to all the games and you don't, when would we watch? Maybe you can explain it after the season's over."

Tommy suggested cheerfully, "There's always the away games."

"Okay." Debbie took a swig of her soda and changed the subject. "This house is so radical! All these rooms and the outside with the curlicues and everything. I never saw anything like it!"

"Tommy, why don't you give her a tour of the house?" Lucia suggested.

"What's to look at?" Tommy sneered. "Moldy Manor. You want to see the place where the sewer pipe broke?"

"He's a little too close to the subject," Lucia said, laughing. "Come on. I'll show you around."

"Don't go to the third floor!" Tommy warned. "Not unless you're not afraid of bats!"

"There aren't really any bats, are there?" Debbie asked as they went down the hall.

"Of course not. However, the third floor is just an attic storeroom, and there's no point in stirring up the dust in there."

She showed Debbie the twin living rooms, one on either side of the entry hall, and explained that in the old days, one was for the family and the other for visitors.

The furnishings were stiff and formal. High-back chairs and sofas covered in red plush stood on carved wooden legs. The rug was patterned with images of jugs and trailing plants, and a maintenance-free plastic plant stood on a tall wicker stand.

"Radical," said Debbie approvingly. "It's all the real stuff, isn't it? Where did you get that big red couch? I wish I could have watched when they got it in here. How did they do it?"

"I don't know. It may have been built in here," said Lucia. "It came with the house. Most of this furniture did. You see, I actually bought the house from the heirs of the original owner. They were her grandchildren. She had lived a very long life, most of it in this house, so all her furniture was here and of course the grandchildren didn't want it, and they sold it with the house."

"I guess I see why you kept it. It just looks right in here."

"It does to me. Anyhow, I never could afford to replace that much furniture, so I never even tried. We did some repairs, reupholstered a couple of the pieces, and just kept it the way it was. It's not very comfortable, but anyway, my guests generally end up in the kitchen no matter where I start a party."

109

Debbie laughed. "Well, it figures, if you have good food in the kitchen and uncomfortable chairs in here."

"You want to see uncomfortable, try the ones in the formal dining room. I never need to worry that somebody is going to take one of them out of there and use it someplace else in the house."

As they mounted the stairs, Lucia pointed out, "All the walls in this central hall are covered in fabric. See? It isn't paper, it's silk brocade, and nearly a hundred years old."

"It still looks beautiful!"

"Unfortunately, in some places it has outlasted the plaster underneath." Lucia touched her thumb ruefully to a long wrinkle where the fabric was holding a crack together, then turned resolutely away from contemplation of the water stain next to it.

She showed Debbie the smaller bedrooms upstairs and then the big one she used for her workroom. The last of the light was slanting through the tree that filled the windows, reminding her why she loved this room. In the dusk the oak wainscoting looked properly rich, the nicks and stains on it hardly showing. The rainbow of silks on her worktable glowed under the lamp.

Debbie picked up a half-finished robe. "Oh, it's beautiful! Is this what you were talking about the other night? The things you make to sell? I love this!"

"I'm getting an order ready for a style show—" Lucia broke off, looking at Debbie. Tall Debbie. "How would you like to model some dresses this Saturday?"

"Are they dresses you made?"

"No, I make only what will sell in Terrilee's place, but Rebecca has lovely things. You'll have fun. Have you ever modeled before?"

"No. Is it hard?"

"Nothing to it. All you have to do is turn so people can see the back of the dress, and smile a lot. Wear lots of makeup and your highest heels."

She gave Debbie the address and the rest of the information. The remainder of the tour of the house was much shortened, as Debbie could hardly wait to scamper to her car and drive back to the sorority house to tell the other girls about her modeling assignment.

Tommy was left in a mood that bordered on the surly, but Lucia was not surprised. She had insinuated herself into one of his friendships, a grievous sin for any mother to commit. Lucia made no attempt to apologize. He'd get over it. And she, Lucia, had her own agenda.

Mitch called on Wednesday and Lucia dragged the upstairs phone into her workroom. With the receiver cradled between her shoulder and chin, she could sew and snip away and carry on one of those long conversations with Mitch at the same time.

He swore that his job was nearly finished and he would be back in town the following day. Lucia nodded wisely. She was already learning about the oil business.

But it gave Thursday something of a tingle, thinking that he might, just might, arrive any minute. Might call, might even be on her doorstep. But she finished her long day in the freight office and her evening with the gowns without hearing a word from him.

It was not late when she quit. For once she disciplined herself to quit while the work was still going well, before she tired and made a mistake and some mess that would have to be painstakingly picked out and reversed before she could begin again the following evening.

He called at midnight, waking her. She answered cheerfully but with a sleepy confusion that must have been obvious.

He said, "Did I wake you? I'm sorry. I just got in and I wanted to hear your voice. I didn't realize it was so late."

She mumbled, "Like always, the job took longer than you thought it would?"

"Well, not longer than I thought, but longer than I hoped. I wanted to see you tonight."

"Tonight? Oh, Mitch . . ."

"I know. It's too late. I just wanted to say good night."

Lucia looked longingly at the bed she had just vacated. "At the risk of sounding like a TV routine, good night, Mitch."

There was a little chuckle in his voice. "Good night, Lucia."

She hung on to the memory of that little chuckle, for otherwise she might have worried that he might think she was being short with him, and she didn't mean to be, of course. She just wished he understood that a person has to sleep sometime.

Tommy had already left for work when she got home on Friday, so Lucia made a sandwich and carried it upstairs. There were four unfinished gowns waiting for her to hem, and she snatched bites of her sandwich as she measured and pinned.

Cut on the bias, the floats had to be hemmed on a dress form. She was crawling around on the floor, pinning, when Mitch called.

He said, "We have a date tonight, don't we?"

"No, Mitch, it's for tomorrow."

"But we have one tonight, too, please?" he insisted. "I want to see you, and I have to get out of here on account of the dalmatian."

What had he said? Lucia had missed something, she knew, but her mind was on those unfinished hems. "I'd like to see you . . ."

"I promise I won't bother you. I know you have work to do, so I'll just sit quiet as a mouse, and—"

Lucia couldn't help laughing. "You? Quiet as a mouse?"

"Well, quiet as a rat, then. Can I come?"

"Of course, Mitch. I'll be glad to see you."

When she hung up, her concentration was already destroyed, because she was no longer just working, she was waiting for Mitch. Her hair was a mess, her lipstick eaten off, she was wearing a pair of jeans so old and well-washed as to be soft and comfortable. She should change; she should not take the time . . .

She compromised with a quick touchup of her hair and makeup. Then she went downstairs and paced around because there wasn't anybody home but her to let Mitch in when he came.

But she couldn't spare time from her work, so she went back upstairs again. She had put in a dozen pins or so before she thought she heard Mitch's car and went downstairs again. It wasn't him, so again she mounted the stairs.

She had just reached the top when the doorbell rang. She hurried down to open the door.

There he stood, right where she had seen him for the first time, underneath the dusty wrought iron lamp. He, too, wore jeans, and a rough-textured shirt. He was smiling that special Mitch smile, and their hands just naturally came together and they stood there in the hall. His warm, callused palm enveloped her hand, and she could have lost herself in those brandy-brown eyes.

He said, "Hello, Lucia," and she said, "Hello, Mitch," and they just stood there.

She said at last, "My workroom's upstairs," and he followed her to the second floor.

"So, this is your workroom?" he remarked brightly, but he was looking at her, not at the room.

"Yes, this is where I sew." She gestured around, but somehow, instead of calling his attention to the tools of her craft, she ended up in the circle of his arms. His hands slid down her back, generating sparks she could feel in every inch of her body.

He was bending toward her, his smile just inches away from hers, and he whispered, "I've missed you so much, Lucia. I couldn't wait until tomorrow."

"I didn't want to wait, either," she admitted.

Hems. Hems full of pins, and they were never going to get sewn this way. Resolutely, Lucia stepped away from him and crouched down by her dress forms. "You said something about a dalmatian, Mitch. Did you mean one of those big dogs with spots?"

He chuckled a little. "It's a spotted dog, but it's not big. It's just a puppy. The trouble with it is, it's in my house."

"I didn't know you were into pets."

"The life I lead, I couldn't have one. Debbie and two of her friends bought it for a surprise birthday present for the lady that's the adviser of their chapter of the sorority."

Lucia reached for her pincushion. "That's the worst birthday gift I ever heard of."

"They just know she's going to love it."

"How did it get to your house?"

"Debbie moved back home today. It took three cars and three, or maybe it's four, girls to do the job."

"But she was at the sorority house for only ten days!"

"Well, there was her clothes, and her bedding. . . . They supply only the sheets over there. . . . And her stereo and the television set and the typewriter and some other stuff. Lots of other stuff. They loaded up her car and the cars of a couple of her friends, and since they were the same friends who had bought the dog with her, they had to take it with them. Nobody else wants to look after it, and they have to keep it away from the house because it's supposed to be a surprise. They have to keep it a secret for another two days."

"I'm feeling sorry for that poor lady with the birthday."

"I wish she'd hurry up and have it. That pup takes more care than a baby. There're three girls putting all their time into feeding that animal, brushing it, taking it for walks. They've been at it a couple days now, and they're getting pretty sick of it. I figured if I didn't get out of there, I was going to end up dog-sitting while they all went someplace."

"So you came here?" Lucia placed a couple of pins. "How very flattering."

"Oh, you know what I mean. It was a good excuse."

She did know. Just having him there made her tasks seem lighter. The whole room was brighter and more comfortable.

She said, "I'm glad you came, Mitch, although I don't have much entertainment to offer you. All you get to do is watch me work."

"Why are you working so late in the evening? Don't you ever relax?"

"Now and then." Lucia smiled ruefully. "But not this week. If I don't have these gowns ready for Terrilee's style show tomorrow, I'll never hear the end of it."

"Debbie told me about that. Both of you going to model dresses?"

"No, I'm modeling an at-home gown."

He grinned. "Yeah? I'm glad I made a reservation."

She was astonished. "You what? You're going to be there? At a luncheon style show?"

"Why not? Got to see two of my favorite women modeling, especially the one that's going to wear a nightie."

"It's not a—Oh, you rascal! I'm warning you, you're going to feel very out of place among all those ladies with all those plates of Chinese chicken salad!"

"Don't worry about me. I'm worried about you, though. You're just going to keep going until you drop," Mitch complained. "Don't you ever take a break? Why don't you knock off for a while? We'll go for a ride someplace. Have you had anything to eat?"

"Well, I had a sandwich. . . ."

"That's not dinner. Come on. I'll buy you a steak."

Lucia put down the pincushion and stood up, astonished, even as she found a jacket and put it on, by the magic that Mitch carried with him. Suddenly the gowns, on which she had worked every minute she could for the past week, seemed unimportant. She would finish them later. There was time; it would work out. Nothing was as important as being with Mitch.

They were out the door, into his car, and away, speeding into a night that sparkled with excitement. Mitch said, "I know a place where they serve the steak on a skewer. Does that sound good?"

"I don't want anything big. . . ."

"You get to eat just as far down the skewer as you feel like," he promised.

The place turned out to be a beachside stand in Venice. Music blasted from portable radios, and spicy food smells billowed through the air. Roller skaters and bicyclists mixed dangerously with the pedestrians. Casual stands sold crafts, tourist junk, and a bewildering array of food.

The skewered beef was good, and they followed it with spears of watermelon and fresh pineapple as they strolled along the path by the beach.

"I love this," said Lucia, leaning over to let her watermelon spear dribble onto the ground. "The food is delicious and we're dressed for it!"

Mitch observed, "It's a little nippy here, but it feels good. Been hot in Bakersfield."

"Been warm here, too," said Lucia. "I don't know why I'm surprised; it's always hot in October. Makes it hard to think about taking the winter clothes out of the back of the closet, though."

"Want to walk on the beach?"

"It would be silly to come all the way down here and just walk on cement," she agreed.

They walked around the little wall and onto

the sand. It was dark there, quieter, but hardly deserted. Little groups sat on the sand, paddled in the water, or smoked in the lee of a blanket. At the first step Lucia's shoes were full of sand, and she paused to kick them off. Mitch took off his. With one accord they rolled up their jeans, picked up the shoes, and went to the water to let gentle waves wash over their feet.

The water was remarkably cold, and invigorating. It was so full of bubbles, it seemed to have a life of its own. She felt as if she were wading in champagne.

Lucia laughed and squealed as a wave came in, and Mitch laughed, too. "Does seem to wash away your troubles, doesn't it?"

"All the way to China, and I hope mine stay there," she replied.

He put his arm over her shoulders. "Somebody ought to take care of you."

"I manage."

"Yeah, I know." He pulled her around to face him and wrapped his other arm, the one holding the shoes, around her waist. She raised her lips to his kiss, standing tiptoe on the hard cool sand. A tiny wave washed chillingly against her arches. Warm lips moved gently over hers, his tongue seeking the opening she gladly gave. She felt the stir of her senses that was becoming almost familiar because she felt it every time he touched her. Her ears were full of the roar of the sea, her eyes closed against the dark.

His touch was not like anybody else's; it had a resonance like no other. He stroked her back and his free hand came to rest just at the side of her breast, and she felt it all through her body, felt it where he had never touched her. She was aware of her own flesh, of the sensitive nerve endings waiting for his touch. Waiting to touch him.

He lifted his hand from its spot near her breast and stroked down her back again, coming to rest just where her hip began to flare. Not too far. He seemed to have Boy Scout hands, too.

His broad back was toward the beach, as if to shield her from the eyes of the people up there, and they stood that way for a long time, just holding each other. At last he asked thickly, "Do you want to go home?"

She sighed. "I could just stand here like this all night."

"All night? I don't think I could."

She sighed again. "I do have to go back and hem all those gowns."

"Yeah, we'd better go."

They walked barefoot back to the car. He said, "Maybe I'd better not watch you work anymore. I don't seem to be a good influence."

"You're not," she replied with a smile, "but

I'm glad you talked me into taking a break. The work will go easier now."

He slipped into the driver's seat and tossed his shoes into the luggage space. He didn't seem to think driving barefoot would be any challenge at all. He reached for her across the map compartment and kissed her again.

She was expecting—or was it hoping—that in the privacy of the car he might go a little farther than he had on the beach. Just a touch or two . . . Her breasts felt heavy, and she knew exactly how he was going to touch her. . . .

Only he didn't. He let her go, casually, and started the car and drove her back home.

The work did go easier, but still it took a lot of time. It was early in the morning before she finished, and birds were twittering in anticipation of the coming light.

Twittering and hopping around, darn the feathered pests, fertilizing her lawn that was growing unchecked out there. It was Saturday, and her day to mow it, and she wouldn't have time to do it because she had promised Terrilee that she would be at the style show. . . .

Lucia hung the last of the finished gowns, threw herself down on the bed, and slept.

Chapter Six

She intended to get up in time to wash her hair, but when she woke there was only twenty minutes or so available for washing, and Tommy was in the shower. She banged on the door several times until he came out of the bathroom, grumbling.

Lucia dressed and rushed through the kitchen on her way out, stopping only to create a sandwich she could munch on while she drove to the Valley and Terrilee's shop.

Even as she parked in the lot, Terrilee ran out to greet her. She had her hair in rollers, and wore a suit with a fashionably long jacket and straight skirt. She was also wearing what must have been half the store's stock of costume jewelry—necklaces in a dozen lengths, bracelets, rings on every finger. Well done, Lucia thought. The long, straight lines of the suit cut Terrilee's bulk and the rhinestones would glitter under the lights when she stood up to narrate the style show.

Terrilee's harassed expression disappeared, and she grinned as she pulled open the door of the familiar station wagon. "Lucia! I was so afraid you'd be late! What did you bring me?" She couldn't wait for Lucia to unload, but climbed into the back of the wagon and pulled at the plastic wrappings, trying to see the gowns that hung there.

Lucia stood below on the blacktop and laughed. "You're impatient as a baby! Why don't you hand them to me? We'll take them inside and you can see them properly."

They carried the gowns into the shop and hung them on a rack. There were only a couple of lights on in the store and the window was obscured with a large sign that read WE'RE CLOSED TODAY, BUT COME SEE US AT THE SCUTTLED BUTT! followed by the address of the restaurant.

Terrilee whooped with enthusiasm as she pulled off the wrappings. "The rainbow sleeves are great!" she enthused. "Let me see the gown. Oh, look at that narrow little thing! I could pull it through a wedding ring. Maybe I will. Advertising gimmick."

"I'm glad you like them," said Lucia, warmed, as always, by praise from her friend.

"I want you to wear the float at the show," Terrilee decreed. "And this one with the sleeves,

124

too. You are going to put some makeup on, aren't you?"

"Sure, sure. I left home in a hurry. There's a dressing room over there, isn't there?"

"Gets a little crowded sometimes. Why don't you—" She broke off as someone began banging on the front door of the shop. "We're closed!" Terrilee yelled.

"It's Rebecca! Are you about ready to go? I have to be over there now!"

Terrilee scampered to open the door. "Yeah, I'm loaded up and ready. The last couple things just got here."

Rebecca was tall and bone-thin, carefully dressed in a fitted suit and a blouse that seemed to be one huge, dramatic blue bow. With her dark hair stiffly curled and her heavy makeup, she suggested some sort of animated doll, a marionette maybe.

Terrilee introduced them, adding, "This is Lucia, the designer I've been telling you about."

Rebecca said just a bit querulously, "Terrilee said you were bringing a friend to model."

Lucia replied, "Yes, she's coming. She's driving her own car and will meet us at the restaurant."

Rebecca said, "Well, let's get over there and get the clothes in before the models arrive."

They all rushed to their vehicles. Lucia was glad to have the chance to follow Terrilee's van, as she had not been to this restaurant before.

They parked in an ample Valley-size parking lot behind a restaurant that was rustic with stone facing and shielded by expensive underbrush. Several busboys came out to help Rebecca and Terrilee wheel their racks of clothes out of the vans and into the dressing room.

Dressing room was a grand title for what turned out to be only a small storeroom that had been cleared for this event. The clearing was not even complete, for a stack or two of cartons remained, forming a room divider and a place to put things on. A couple of mirrors attached to the wall were about the only amenities for the personnel of the style show. Lucia had to stand up, fishing things out of her purse, to get her makeup on.

Terrilee was beside her, picking the rollers out of her hair and wailing at failures of the perfect curl.

The models arrived almost all at the same time, and Lucia never did get their names straight. There were only three of them, but they chattered at such a high decibel level and made such a flurry, rushing around, fixing their hair, sorting the dresses they would wear, there seemed to be a dozen of them. Rebecca harangued them with orders and suggestions.

Debbie was last, and close to being late, but Rebecca approved of her height and handed her a couple of sports outfits to wear.

Lucia was dressed in the slinky gown and

sleeved robe she would model first, and she tried to stand out of the way, watching the models she was already thinking of as the three bimbos.

Somehow she had expected them to be more slender. One was blond, the other two brunette, and while it didn't surprise her that the blond hair looked manufactured, the funny thing was that the brunettes did, too. All of them were curvy, even just a trifle hippy. One of them was getting into a minidress that, not content with being short and cut low at the neck, had a piece cut right out of the midriff. Quietly, Lucia drifted to the door and looked out into the restaurant.

Well, she should have realized that a place with a name like The Scuttled Butt wasn't going to be a ladies' tearoom. It was a steakhouse, and it was well filled with a largely masculine lunch crowd, all having big, hearty meals and big, strong drinks while they talked in big, hearty voices.

Terrilee had finished fussing with her hair and was chattering into the microphone, giving the location of the shops and informing the crowd that everything they were going to see was for sale, a phrasing Lucia felt was unfortunate.

Even as she watched, a couple of the bimbos slithered past her and began their tour around the room. They paused at each table to show the dress and recite the price. They did it well, she had to give them that, with just the right mixture of professional distance and friendly communication.

From behind her Rebecca's voice said, "Okay, you're next. Your price is eighty-nine ninety-nine, one size fits all, pure silk and — well, I guess you know what it's made of."

Lucia glided out onto the floor, reminding herself to smile and to suck in her stomach. The bimbos didn't have to worry about things like that, they all had bellies flat as Kansas, but they weren't forty-five years old. They probably weren't half that, and sitting behind a desk all day doesn't do much for your figure, either.

Usually Lucia enjoyed these things, showing off, getting to interact with the people who would actually wear her clothes; sometimes the insights she gained were useful. But what was she going to learn from this crowd? A businessman eating his lunch was going to buy what looked good on the model, and dream that his girlfriend would wear it as well.

She recited her little spiel at each table, spreading her arms as she turned to make the rainbow sleeves ripple, handing out Terrilee's business cards. Across the room she could see Debbie wearing stirrup pants and a sweater. She was smiling at the customers, turning, obviously enjoying herself.

Lucia already had a buyer for her outfit before she came to Mitch's table. He had an enormous steak in front of him and he said, "Say, this really is a lot of fun. I've got to lunch here more often."

She made her sleeve-rippling turn. "I'm glad you like it, Mitch."

"Sure, I've always liked the way you look in a nightie."

And suddenly she was self-conscious in one of her own gowns. After all, it was nightwear. How did she get here, parading around in front of a mob of men, in the company of bimbos? Her? Lucia? She believed herself to be open-minded, but this wasn't open, it was loose.

She finished her tour as fast as she could and returned to the dressing room. She would get into the float and tell everybody it was a sundress.

Terrilee was there and Lucia told her, "The couple at the window table wants to buy it. South side, fat guy and a blond woman."

"Okay, take it off and I'll go out there and write up the sale."

Terrilee was folding the clothes into a bag when Debbie came in, stripping off her heavy sweater. "Whew! It's hot out there."

Glittering in floor-length sequins, Rebecca snatched the sweater from her. "You didn't sweat on it, did you?"

"Oh, I never sweat," Debbie replied with a hint of sarcasm.

Terrilee said, "Here, kid," and handed her a scrap of silk and lace.

Lucia asked at once, "What's that?"

Debbie held the skimpy thing briefly upright. "Babydoll."

Lucia muttered an imprecation under her breath. The atmosphere of the place had entrapped even Debbie. She said, "Now, hold on a minute! You're not modeling that."

"Why not?" Terrilee asked. "She's got good legs."

"Well . . ." Lucia hesitated. How could she put this tactfully? "She's here to model Rebecca's stuff."

"But I want to model it, Lucia," Debbie told her. "It's cute. Look, there's even lace on the panties."

Lucia winced. "You're not going to wear that."

"Well, who is going to model it?" Terrilee demanded. "You want to do it?"

"Hell no!" Lucia turned vigorously on her friend. "Really, Terrilee, I'm a little shocked at you. You said we were having a style show. This is a T and A parade. It's a burlesque show!"

"No, it isn't!" Terrilee protested. "All we're doing is showing clothes."

"So all right, let's show the clothes, not how

much skin we can put on display."

"That's not fair," Rebecca put in. "We're showing clothes, stylish clothes. If they're sexy, that's because that's what people want."

"I never noticed you designing any Mother Hubbard sacks," Terrilee added. "Your stuff is always sexy. That's what I like about it."

"I've even designed a couple of babydolls," Lucia admitted, "but I never intended them to be worn by bimbos in public."

"Maybe if you thought of it as kind of a big private party—" Terrilee began.

"All right, try this," Lucia interrupted. "Debbie's not going out there wearing that babydoll because she's under age and her father's out there!"

"Oh, yeah, throw that up to me!" cried Debbie. "I'm sorry I ever told you! Nobody would ever know I'm seventeen if you didn't tell them!"

"Sorry," said Lucia. "Terrilee, I wish you'd hide that thing so nobody will wear it."

"God, you sound like Queen Victoria," Terrilee complained. "Why don't you get yourself into the real world? All we're trying to do is make a living."

"We're all trying to make a living, but some things aren't yours to sell."

"Can't I give the babydoll to Chickie to wear?" Terrilee pleaded. "I usually sell a couple anytime she wears it."

"As a favor to me."

Terrilee reluctantly put the nightgown on a hanger and stuck it in among the clothes that had already been worn.

"I don't know why I drove all the way over here just to get pushed around," Debbie said to nobody in particular.

"Come here, I've got something for you," Rebecca said to her, and pulled a rose-red dress from the rack.

A princess would dance in such a dress. The circular skirt was waltz length and lined with ruffles, so it swirled with the slightest movement. Debbie was instantly enchanted, slipped it on, and allowed Rebecca to show her how to turn and make the skirt fly.

As she sailed out onto the floor, Terrilee breathed a sigh of relief. "Thanks, Becky. I only hope she doesn't knock dishes off the tables."

"She's got a lot of talent," Rebecca observed. "I don't suppose you're going to let her come back again?"

Lucia gave her a look.

"Are you through with your clothes?" Rebecca asked suddenly.

"No, I have one piece more to wear."

"After that, how about doing that flowered dinner dress for me? It'll go good with your hair."

"Sure, I'll model it." Lucia gave her a sly

glance. "Do I get a commission if I sell it?"

"Same as the other bimbos," promised Rebecca, and she sparkled out of the dressing room.

Lucia slipped into her float. "Sorry, Terrilee. Maybe I'm a little overprotective."

"That you are." Terrilee grinned. "Of the daughter, or the father?"

"Well, I suppose . . ."

"So go model your float already," Terrilee told her.

Lucia sold a couple of the floats, then she modeled the flowered dress. It was long, with long sleeves. Debbie was meanwhile flouncing between the tables in a disco dress of black lace. It had a handkerchief hem, so it was almost not a miniskirt.

Lucia next modeled the short version of the flowered dress, and was pleased to sell one. When she passed by Mitch's table, Debbie was sitting with him, cadging bites of food off his plate.

Lucia murmured, "Better put a bib over that dress."

"We'll be careful," Mitch promised.

Lucia made a couple of more turns and returned to the dressing room. The show was finished, and the bimbos were putting on their street clothes. Terrilee and Rebecca were getting their racks ready to load into the vans.

Lucia handed her dress to Rebecca and told

her where to find the customer.

As Rebecca was folding the dress into the bag, Debbie returned, bubbling with enthusiasm again. "This is fun, isn't it, Lucia? Working with all these pretty things."

"I always have a good time," Lucia said, and did not add that there was a somewhat sour taste to this particular show.

"I sold the red dress," Debbie reported proudly. "But Rebecca has another one in her shop and she's going to sell it to me and give me the same discount she gives the other models. It'll be just right for the fall dances."

"You do look good in it." Lucia was getting back into her reliable old everyday denim suit. She had always liked it, but somehow, in this company, she felt just a little too country-western. Defiantly, she tied a red bandanna around her neck.

When they got to the parking lot, Mitch was waiting for them. "Come back inside," he invited her, "and I'll blow you both to lunch. They make a good steak here."

"I just had lunch, Daddy," said Debbie with a grin. "I ate yours, remember?"

"It was only a couple of bites. That's not lunch."

"I can't stop now. I'm going with Rebecca to her shop. She's going to show me some dresses. You don't mind if I put them on the credit card, do you?"

"Sure, go ahead."

"You're saying that only because you haven't seen Rebecca's prices yet," Lucia warned him.

"Bye, Daddy!" Debbie rushed off to jump into her car.

Mitch gave Lucia a lopsided grin. "That bad, huh?"

"Actually, Rebecca's regular things are pretty reasonable, but she has a custom line that would make your hair stand on end."

He rubbed the top of his head ruefully. "I'm probably in for it, then. Want some lunch?"

Lucia consulted her watch. "It's far too late for lunch. And we're going to dinner in a few hours."

"You've got to eat something."

"I'll grab a snack when I get home. Thanks for the invitation, anyway. I'll see you at six."

He let her go with reluctance, and as she drove away she could see him in her rearview mirror, still standing there in the parking lot, alone and somehow forlorn.

Chapter Seven

By the time she got home it was too late to mow the lawn. It was too hot, besides, not to mention how tired she felt. It is surprising how much energy it takes just to model a few outfits, she mused. Or maybe it was because she had skipped lunch.

Lucia ate an apple while wandering around the breakfast room. She was surrounded, as usual, by chores that ought to be done. She didn't even want to remember that Terrilee had sold all the rainbow gowns and she was expected to supply new ones. Lucia curled up on the padded window seat and went to sleep.

When she woke, the light was gone. She had a date with Mitch and she still had not washed her hair. Lucia rushed upstairs, feeling disoriented from the repeated disruption of her sleep schedule, and was searching around for towels when she caught sight of the clock. It was already six, and Mitch was always on time. Lucia reached for her new peacock-blue dress. What a hectic day! Well, at last now she would have some enjoyment and peace. Soon she would be basking in Mitch's presence.

She was dressed and combed and ready, and he was at the door right on time. He came in frowning, but she figured her pretty new dress would cheer him up, and she waited for his compliments.

He said, "Well, are you proud of yourself now?"

A little startled, she said, "Hello, Mitch, how are you?"

"I trusted you!" he continued bitterly. "I never thought you would do anything to hurt my child. Putting your silly notions into her head . . ."

Lucia could only say, "Huh?"

"What do you use for a brain? All you can think about is your business, selling your gowns—"

"What in the world are you talking about?"

"I figured you knew, since you're the one behind it. Debbie is dropping out of college. She's going to model."

"You're kidding."

He took an impatient little turn around the entry hall. "You would think it's funny! That girl is intelligent, she could have a real future in science, and instead she's going to waste herself parading around in clothes like a show horse!"

Lucia shook her head to clear it. "Debbie has decided to drop out of school? Since lunchtime today?"

"And I have you to thank for it," he growled.

"Well, just a minute, now. It's an idiot decision all right, but what makes you think it's my fault?"

"You're the one who took her down there to model! She never gave it a thought until today. You're the one who told her it was fun, and she had talent, and ought to do it."

Lucia lifted a reproving finger. "Hold on right there. I told her it was fun; that it was something you do for fun. I never told her it was a career! I never would have told her anything like that!"

His scowl only deepened. "Well, then I'd like to know who did, so I could break him in half. I've paid her tuition, bought all her books, paid the initiation fee to that sorority, and now everything's down the drain. She's going to go out and be a clothes rack!"

"She can't possibly have any idea what this entails. Have you talked to her? Did you tell her that modeling is a dog's life? Did you point out that she's one of the lucky ten percent who even get the opportunity to go to college?"

"I told her there was no way she was dropping out, and grounded her for a month."

"Oh, that ought to do it. Mitch, I want to talk to her. She's at home? Let's—"

"I'd just as soon you two didn't have any more conversations. The last one was a little bit of a disaster."

Lucia was trying to adjust to his sudden negativism, his coldness. How could a person change so fast, be so different from the Mitch she knew? She asked in a faint voice, "Well, what do you suggest we do?"

He stuck his hands grumpily into his pockets. "You wanted to go out to dinner, let's get going."

Lucia could almost have laughed, it was so unexpected. She folded her arms and said firmly, "Mitch Colton, I would not set foot outside the door with anybody as grouchy and unreasonable as you are tonight! What in the world would I want to do that for? I can't even imagine a dinner in this mood. It would ruin our digestions." She stepped to the door and opened it. "Good night, Mitch."

"Hey, wait a minute! We've got a date!"

"No, we don't. I'm glad I found out you have this ungovernable temper before we got involved!"

"But we *are* involved!" he protested.

"No, we're not. Please get out of my house."

139

"Now, wait a minute—"

"Out!"

He went through the doorway, but turned and went on arguing. "Look, I may have said some things. . . . It's because I'm angry . . ."

"You did say some things. And you are not getting the chance to say any more. Goodbye, Mitch." She closed the door quietly but firmly and went into the kitchen.

In the room where she always took her wounds, Lucia hauled pots from the cupboard, vegetables from the refrigerator. She was sniffling just a bit, but she was damned if she was going to cry over that unreasonable, autocratic, male chauvinist . . . hunk.

Soup, she thought. Something hearty and comforting with beans in it.

She immersed herself in the cooking, creating a stock, peeling vegetables, chopping, snipping up herbs. The kitchen was smelling the way a kitchen should, when she heard a knock on the door.

It was so timid, she thought for a moment that Mitch had returned to apologize, but it was Terrilee. She had a baker's box and a sheepish expression.

She said, "I brought us a cheesecake, so we can talk."

She had returned her beads and bangles to the glass case in the store, but she still wore her style-show suit with the long jacket. It made her look like somebody who might chance a slice of cheesecake.

"Come in, Terrilee! I'm glad to see you."

They trekked into the kitchen and Terrilee put down her box. "I can't believe we quarreled today, Lucia. We never fight. I can't even remember what it was about."

Lucia smiled at her. "I can't either. The soup will be ready pretty soon, or do you want to eat the cheesecake first?"

"Well, maybe we'd better, and then I'll go."

"Oh, it's Saturday night, isn't it? You probably have a date."

Terrilee sat down at the table, her miserable expression already dissipating, just to be in the company of a friend. "No, but you're all dressed up, I figured you did."

Lucia scooped up the box and tucked it into the refrigerator. "We have time to wait for the soup."

"What's going on? Don't you have a date with the cocker spaniel?"

"Don't you have a date? You, Terrilee?"

Terrilee moodily pushed the condiment jars around on the table. "I'm not dating much these days. It's scary out there, you know that? One little misstep and you're dead! Not even just sick, dead! All you want is a roll in the hay, and you've got to think, hey, is this going to be worth dying for? You don't meet many guys who can pass that test."

Lucia said thoughtfully, "Surely there's some way of relating to a man that doesn't include sex."

"Yeah? Like what?"

"Well, there must be something." Lucia sat down opposite her friend. "Give me a minute, maybe I'll think of it."

"How come you aren't going anyplace tonight?" Terrilee persisted.

"I'm open. We can eat cheesecake and have old home week the whole evening if we want."

Terrilee leaned back in her chair and raised her voice. "Okay, Lucia, that's enough weaseling! What's going on?"

"Nothing! Nothing! Mitch and I are . . . we're past tense, that's all."

"What happened?"

"He turned out to have a terrible temper. Nicest guy in the world until he gets mad, and then—" Lucia ducked her head, remembering the sting of Mitch's words. "Then he's just plain vicious, the things he says."

"He didn't hit you, did he?"

"Nothing like that, but he sure doesn't care who he bawls out!"

"Everybody's got a temper," Terrilee philosophized. "But men can't handle it. They just blow in all directions."

142

"It's normal to get angry," Lucia agreed, "but a grown man goes after the person who's making him mad. He doesn't take it out on whoever happens to be standing nearest."

Terrilee pushed the condiment jars some more. "Well, I'm sorry it didn't work out for you, but maybe it's a good thing you found out about him before you got in too deep. You didn't get in too deep, did you?"

"I liked him a lot," Lucia admitted. "But I guess you could say I escaped getting deep. Change of subject. I think—"

"Wait a minute! Don't change the subject yet. I want to hear about—"

Lucia interrupted. "I want to talk to you about this afternoon. I feel like I need to apologize for squaring off at you. When it comes to the kids, I guess I get overprotective. And really, Terrilee, the sort of thing you were showing in that restaurant . . . Well, it's tawdry. It's not you."

"I know. I've been thinking about what you said, and I guess it is sort of scuzzy. I didn't mean it that way; I just sort of drifted into it. All I wanted to do was sell clothes, and the models were squabbling because they all wanted to wear the really revealing stuff. That's because it always sells and they work on commission."

Lucia said, "Let's give them something to

wear that sells because it's beautiful. Can you imagine what a woman must feel like when her guy comes home with one of those things he bought off a model? A teddy or a bustier and he calls it a present?"

Terrilee laughed. "She's probably got a few extra pounds on her and some cellulite and the darn thing's small enough to fit a model . . ."

"And she probably hates the color . . ."

"And she has to wonder where he's been . . ."

It felt good, laughing with Terrilee again. Lucia was smiling as she said, "Did I remember to tell you that suit is becoming to you?"

"You probably did. I've been wearing it everywhere and I'm already tired of it. I wish I could wear pretty things."

"Well, you can. Why not? They just have to be big pretty things."

Terrilee sighed. "Try to find any. I'd love to have something I could wear out to dinner that doesn't look like I'm going to a business meeting instead."

"Something like a long dress?"

"Out of style."

"How about a caftan?"

"That'd be okay, only most of them look like you're on your way to the marketplace and ought to have a bunch of bananas on your head."

Lucia was thinking aloud. "Something in a

144

subdued print, asymmetrical, like a bordered fabric, used sideways . . . oh! I have one I'll bet you'll love! Come upstairs and I'll show it to you."

They went to the workroom and Lucia began searching the closet shelves for the print she could see in her mind.

Terrilee stared at the stacks of fabric. "What is all this? You've got more cloth than a fabric store!"

"No, I don't, and I have to have supplies. This is my business."

"Isn't this pretty!" Terrilee pulled down a bolt of hot pink satin. "Hey, make me a caftan out of this!"

"Of course not. Here's a bordered print you might like."

Terrilee carried the fabrics to the workroom, where the light was better, and held them up in front of the mirror.

Lucia cried happily, "Here it is. This is the one I wanted you to look at," and brought a third piece of cloth.

She found Terrilee posturing before the mirror. Lucia had her take off the jacket, and she draped the fabric she had chosen over her shoulder.

"Yeah, that's pretty." Terrilee picked up the hot pink and slung it across her other shoulder. "Maybe it could have inserts of this pink."

She was clowning and Lucia laughed. "Then you really would need a bunch of bananas on your head."

Terrilee grabbed another length of fabric and wound it around her head. "No, I think this look is more North African. I see myself as a harem girl, a helpless sex slave."

They both laughed as Lucia draped the hot pink around Terrilee's body and made loops over both her arms. "No, it's not Arab, it's Ziegfeld. You're a showgirl, ready to walk down a giant flight of stairs."

"Lead me to the stairs," Terrilee demanded dramatically, and she went to the staircase, trailing fluttering ends of fabric, swags of it hanging from her outstretched arms.

The doorbell was ringing, and Lucia went past her, down the stairs to answer it. It was Mitch, his hair rumpled, his tie awry. She would have closed the door on him, but somehow he was inside, saying frantically, "Debbie's gone! She's not at home! Is she here?"

"No, she's not, Mitch. Why would she come here?"

"I don't know!" he shouted. "Maybe to get some help landing that modeling job! I grounded her, and as soon as my back was turned she packed a suitcase and left! She's run away from home!"

"Come into the kitchen, Mitch," Lucia invited him. "Let's sit down and try to decide rationally what we are going to do next. Terrilee, you come, too."

Terrilee made a small, strangled sound as Mitch looked up, noticing for the first time that she stood in the middle of the staircase in a showgirl pose, swathed in lengths of mismatched fabric.

Lucia said, "I don't think you've met Mitch. Mitch, this is Terrilee."

The two stared at each other for a moment and then Mitch raised his hand, a brief wave, and said, "Hi."

Terrilee made the strangled sound again and pulled off the fabric that was slipping from her head.

Mitch said, "That was your style show, wasn't it? Do you know where Debbie is?"

"Why would I know?" Terrilee asked.

"Because she's run away from home to model, that's why!"

Terrilee whistled her surprise. "I thought she was a college girl."

"She said she was going to drop out. And model."

Terrilee was unwinding herself from the fabrics. "Well, she wouldn't come to me. I don't pay my models. It's against my principles."

"I'll make some coffee," Lucia offered, and Mitch followed her to the kitchen. Terrilee trailed along behind them, folding fabric as she walked.

Lucia went at once for the coffeepot. "Sit down, Mitch. My guess would be that after quarreling with you, she would go to her mother."

Mitch thumped himself down in a chair. "I thought of that. It's an hour, hour and a half drive to Oxnard, so if she went there, she's still on the road. There's no point in calling Ione now. She'd only get all excited, and Debbie couldn't possibly be there yet."

"So what do you think we should do? Wait an hour or so, and then call Ione?"

Mitch jumped up again and paced to the stove and back. "I hope to God she did go to her mother. When I think of some of the things she might do . . ."

Terrilee chuckled evilly. "An angry young woman on the loose in Los Angeles? You got trouble, all right."

"Let's not panic," Lucia advised. "She's a level-headed person . . ."

"She was until she started modeling those dresses," Mitch corrected Lucia bitterly.

Lucia glowered at him. "I'm getting very tired of having the blame crammed down my throat just because I let her model a couple of pairs of stirrup pants. I very much doubt they're what's causing the problem. What this sounds like to me is a collision of childish temper tantrums, to which the whole Colton family seems to be subject."

"Well, I lost my temper, but—"

"Let me put it this way, Mitch. What are you going to do when you find Debbie?"

"Take her back home again."

"And insist she stay there? That's just what you did earlier. That's what made her run away."

Mitch sat down again at the table. "Well, I'll talk to her."

"What will you say?"

"I don't know. I have to find her before I can say anything, don't I? Lucia, will you talk to her?"

"I've got an even better idea, Mitch. Will you listen to her?"

Mitch did not answer, but he sat for a time in silent thought. Lucia finished loading the coffeepot and put it on the stove.

Mitch shook himself as if clearing away thoughts, and said, "Most likely she's still here in town. She might be with Tommy. Where is he?"

"Tommy's at work, and will be for another couple of hours. But it's a public place. I suppose she could be sitting there, eating hamburgers."

"Let's go check it out."

Lucia turned off the fires under the coffee and the soup. "Come on, Terrilee. We'll take the station wagon; there isn't room in the Porsche for three."

Mitch suggested, "She can sit in the back—"

"No, she can't, and I want to drive. You're in no state to be behind a wheel."

The fast-food place was not far away. They went inside, where the smell of frying meat filled the place. Tommy stood behind the counter, wearing his white shirt and brown pants, the old-fashioned cap covering his hair. He was gamely damping down his astonishment at seeing the three of them.

They told him their errand, and he said, "Gee, no, I haven't seen Debbie. Why don't you try that sorority house of hers? That's where she mostly is."

"Good suggestion. Thanks, Tommy." Lucia blew him a kiss as they hurried back to the station wagon.

At the Alpha house they buttonholed the first member they encountered and asked for Debbie. The girl went agreeably to the bottom of the stairs and bellowed to the floor above, "Debbie Colton! Visitors!"

When Debbie came down the stairs, Mitch did not even greet her. He had his head turned away and was pretending to cough.

Lucia said, "Debbie, I'm so glad to see you!

150

You had us all quite worried."

The girl replied, "And now you've come to persuade me to go back to school, I suppose. Well, come on in and sit down. We can't all stand here in front of the door. There's no point in this, you know. I've made up my mind."

They moved into a cavernous living room and clustered together on a chintz couch. Mitch found voice at last. "I didn't come to argue. I came to take you home."

Debbie pointed a stubborn chin at him. "Well, I don't want to go home. I'm tired of being the little child everybody bosses around. I'm going to get a job and have my own money and do something for *me*."

"You're enrolled in college . . ." Mitch began.

Lucia laid a hand on his arm and he stopped talking. "Have you thought this through, Debbie? If you quit school, you'll have to quit the sorority, too, and then you can't live here. Then where will you go? What kind of a job will you get?"

"I'll find a place of my own, and get a job modeling. That's fun to do, more fun than spending all your time with dusty books."

"Modeling!" Terrilee snorted. "You can't pay the rent with that."

"Of course I can. Top models earn two hundred dollars an hour. Everybody knows that."

"Christie Brinkley does," Terrilee agreed, "but I think her job's already filled. You want to know about modeling, you came to the right place. I tackled it myself once, about fifty pounds ago."

Terrilee sat forward, ready to lecture. "First you got to consider the numbers. Everybody wants to model, and there's Brinkley and about fifteen others doing all the photography work. Then there's a couple of hundred women doing clothes for the top houses. Most of them are in New York. They don't have clothes shows here, and when they do, the designer generally has plenty of friends who'll model free."

Terrilee hopped up from the couch and spread her arms, warming to her subject. "If you push hard, you can probably get some work in the wholesale houses. It pays minimum, and probably they'll use you a couple of weeks and drop you. They like new faces all the time, and there's plenty to choose from. You know what girls like Chickie get, and she's an experienced model? Commission only. She sells something worth two hundred dollars, she gets twenty. That's what she earned today."

"She worked only a couple of hours . . ." Debbie began.

"Right, but she's not getting paid by the hour. That was her wage for the day. Most of those girls have somebody to support them, or a day job. You know how to type? Sometimes you can land a steady job with a small company, a retail outlet or something. You do the typing and model their clothes when they need it. You don't get paid as much as a girl would who did just the typing, and you have to put up with a lot more passes and pressure from the guys. That's because guys always figure a girl who models has got to be easy. It's a living, anyhow. Of course, you'd have to lose about ten pounds. The way they like 'em these days is skinny and athletic."

Debbie looked thoughtful. "Well, maybe I'll get some other kind of job. I just don't want to live at home like a baby anymore."

"What kind of job?" Terrilee persisted. "Type and file? That's about what's available for a woman without an education. Look at me! Well, maybe I'm not a good example. Look at Lucia. She's been at that job she's got for ten years and still she earns peanuts. She can't be promoted to anything better, because she doesn't have the education."

Terrilee waved her arms, indicating the elegant proportions of the Alpha house living room. "Look at this place! Look at the building, look at the furniture! Class, that's what it is! You've got all this and you want to go live in some rathole and put in your hours at minimum wage and be stuck with it forever? Well, maybe not forever. Maybe you can work your way into something better, like five, six dollars an hour, in a couple years. You're in college now. You've got the chance to make something out of your life. You can be a scientist, and you want instead to go flip your boobs around on some runway for starvation wages?"

"Terrilee! Calm down!" Lucia took her arm and gently led her back to the couch.

Terrilee sat reluctantly. "Well, I hate waste."

Mitch said, "Debbie, you have an opportunity that not everybody gets, and you're going to take advantage of it. You're staying in college."

Lucia said, "Mitch, she has said about three times that she doesn't like being ordered around. I think you should respect that. Can't you talk to her as one adult to another?"

He grumped, "She's my kid, and she's not an adult."

"She will be soon. What are you going to do, start treating her like a reasonable human being on her eighteenth birthday, maybe at two o'clock in the afternoon?"

"It'd be a shock if he did," Debbie grumbled.

Lucia rose. "There's a compromise here, and you two can reach it if you'll just communicate instead of having mutual temper tantrums. I think you'll be best off talking it over alone. Terrilee and I have a cheesecake to take care of. Come on, Terrilee."

Mitch protested, "Hey, wait a minute. You're driving."

"My house is only a couple blocks from here, and anyhow, Debbie is an adult with a car and she can take you where you want to go, if you are in communication."

"Lucia . . ." But she was on her way out the door, Terrilee hurrying along behind.

Chapter Eight

The following morning, when Lucia got home from doing the errands that hadn't gotten done on Saturday, Tommy helped her carry the groceries into the kitchen. Then he burrowed through the sacks, searching for fresh snacks.

He asked, "Did you find Debbie at the Alpha house last night?"

Lucia was putting things away, and she paused long enough to give him a glance. "Yes, that's where she was. How did you know she'd be there?"

"It figured. She's always there." He held up a package of luncheon meat. "Okay if I make a sandwich with this?"

"That's what it's for."

"I was sure surprised when you all came to the hamburger stand. What was going on, anyway?"

Lucia explained. "Debbie and her dad had a fight, so she ran over to the Alpha house and

156

didn't tell him where she was going. They got it straightened out, I guess."

Tommy slapped together bread and meat. "He scares her."

Lucia was startled and paused again to stare at him. "What? She's afraid of her own father?"

"She says he's unpredictable."

"Well, he does have a temper, but he adores that child."

Tommy sprinkled hot sauce onto his sandwich. "She can't figure him out."

"I have to sympathize. I don't understand him, either."

"Maybe it's because she isn't used to him. She's usually with her mother, you know. She can handle her mother and her stepdad, but he's different."

"I guess that's about par for the course between parents and children," Lucia observed. "He can't figure her out, either. Maybe they're going to come to a better understanding; they were really talking to each other when I saw them last. I wish I knew how it came out; maybe he'll call me."

"Oh, he's been calling all morning; I forgot to tell you."

She threatened him with a mock snarl. "Tommy, how would you like a parent who is having a temper tantrum?"

"Sorry, sorry! I'm going!" He ducked out of

the kitchen, but he didn't forget to take the sandwich with him.

The least she could do was return Mitch's calls. She dialed his number and he came on the line at once. "Lucia! I've been trying to get you all morning. Where have you been?"

She was starting to think the man was a control freak. Since when did she have to account for her activities to him?

She said, "That's a very interesting opening, Mitch. Suppose I say it's none of your business?"

He was so taken aback that there was a moment of silence on the phone line. "Well, I suppose it isn't, but I've been trying to get you."

She relented. "I ran some errands. I appreciate your calls. I did want to talk to you and find out how things came out last night."

"With Debbie? We talked for a long time. I guess we came to an understanding."

"You guess?"

"Well, it was like this," he said. "She agreed to stay in school if I agreed she could live at the Alpha house. Then she made me take her back to my place and we loaded all her stuff into the truck, the bedding and the stereo and the dresses and all of it, and drove over to the Alpha house and put it into her room. Took us until nearly midnight. That's why I never got a chance to call you."

"But, Mitch, that's wonderful! It's a giant step in your relationship! You talked, you reached a compromise, and then you acted on it!"

The tone of his voice turned a little sour. "Yeah, and this morning I found out why she was in such a hurry to get moved. When her mother found out she'd moved into the sorority house, oh, boy! The you-know-what hit the fan. She's still saying that Debbie's too young to be living by herself."

"She is, actually," Lucia said.

"What she's too young for is to go out on her own and try to support herself at some job. I'm glad you and your friend were able to convince her of that. Your friend really helped a lot."

"Terrilee does have a certain crude eloquence, doesn't she? She'll be glad to hear that Debbie decided to stay in school."

"I wish I had somebody like her to talk to Ione. She wants to pull Debbie out of school and take her back to Oxnard. I've got both of them yelling at me until I'm about ready to pull out my phone."

Lucia managed to suppress a delicious picture of Terrilee dealing with Ione, but she couldn't help laughing. "Oh, you poor man! Sounds like what you ought to do is go fishing for about a week, until they work things out between themselves."

"Fishing? That's where I just was."

"What? You said you were in Bakersfield, on a job."

"Oh, you mean fish fishing! I've never been into it. I prefer a steak anytime."

"What other kind of fishing is there besides fish fishing?"

"When we're fishing in the oil business, we've lost something in the hole and are trying to fish it out. It's kind of like trying to screw the lid on a jar that's a couple of city blocks away."

"Well, maybe it's a good thing you don't like to fish fish. You'll be staying around and you can stick up for Debbie."

"I don't know that she needs anybody to stand up for her. She's smart enough to manipulate you and me; she can probably handle Ione."

"Manipulate?" Lucia repeated. "Do you think she did that? It was all a scam to get you to let her live on campus?"

There was a shrug in his voice. "I don't know, but it sure came out that way, didn't it?"

"I'm shocked." Lucia thought about it a moment. "Shocked that she would do that, shocked that she felt like she had to create all those dramatics to get her own way. Maybe it's true that you intimidate her. Maybe she was afraid to approach you directly."

"What makes you think I intimidate her? I'm

a pushover, a wimp. Everybody knows that."

"Oh, yes, sure you are."

"Well, if I'm so scary, how about letting me frighten you into dinner tonight? Looks like otherwise we're going to be on the phone the rest of the day."

Lucia reminded herself that this was the same man she has tossed out her front door the night before. "I don't think so, Mitch. I have a lot to do."

"Oh, come on, Lucia. We didn't get to go out last night, so you owe me one."

"I don't owe you anything, and I resent it when you put it that way. We're not going out tonight or any night."

He asked, still half amused, "Hey, are you mad about something?"

"I can't believe you're asking that, after the way you insulted me last night."

"Insult? Aw, come on. I don't do insults. I was angry about Debbie; I was never mad at you, not really."

"I wonder how I got that impression," Lucia said sarcastically. "You said that I was encouraging Debbie to run away from home, and of course, I wasn't. You said I suggested she model as a career, and I never even discussed such a thing with her."

"I always knew you didn't. I was mad."

"That's no excuse, Mitch. You're far too old

for these childish temper tantrums. I don't blame you for being upset, but flying off the handle and taking out your anger on me doesn't help. It just turns you into part of the problem."

"What do you want me to do?"

"Learn to control your temper," she replied shortly. "Do you remember bragging to me that you were so good at that? You meant only that you can control yourself physically; you have to realize that you can hurt people with words, too."

His voice sounded sincere, impressed. "You're the last person I wanted to hurt. Let me make it up to you. Come out to dinner with me."

"You still don't get it, do you? I've been hurt, I've been insulted, I need to cut out some new gowns. . . . No, that's got nothing to do with it. I am not going out with you anymore."

"We've been on this telephone an hour so you can say you don't want to talk to me?"

"I don't want to argue with you, and it looks like the only way that can be accomplished is not to see you. So goodbye, Mitch." She hung up the phone firmly.

Then she wished she had invested in a machine that would screen her calls, because the phone started ringing right away and it wasn't fair to ask Tommy to answer it for her.

She picked it up and asked, "What does it take to get you to stop calling me?"

"What does it take to get you to give in and have dinner with me?" he countered.

"I'm not going to, Mitch. Not tonight or any other night."

"I don't understand you, Lucia. Last night you helped me find Debbie, you drove me around, and today you're glad I phoned, but you're not talking to me because of something I said before any of those things happened."

"Last night you asked for my help to find a lost child, and of course I gave it, and of course today I'm interested in how it came out with her, but none of that excuses the way you talked to me. I don't need insults, I don't need someone in my life who squares off at me for no reason; I won't put up with a man who frightens his own daughter. That's enough to scare me, and when I'm scared, I move on. So I'm saying goodbye, Mitch, and this is really the last time."

She hung up before he could say anything more, and decided that if he called again, she would take the phone off the hook. However, he didn't call and she didn't have to do it.

It was a great relief, she told herself firmly, to have that all over with, and a whole week ahead of her with all the evenings free. She could work on gowns every day and have them finished for Terrilee by the end of the week, or maybe even sooner.

It was good to have work. She sewed until late, working furiously, making sure she thought about seams and sizes and colors, and not about Mitch. She did not want to think about him, about the warmth and strength she had felt from him during the good times, or about the hopes she had. It had all come crashing down and she had been foolish to think there would be any other kind of ending. She wasn't going to waste any of her time regretting the loss of what was only dreams in the first place.

The next night at dinner, a snag appeared in her plans for making many gowns quickly. Tommy said, "Help me think up a good costume for Halloween."

She loved dreaming up costumes, and he knew it, but she also knew she was going to end up sewing something, and there were all those gowns to be finished. She asked, "Don't you still have the Davy Crockett suit you wore last year?"

"Aw, Ma, you remember what happened to that. That shirt with all the fringe on the sleeves was so cool that I wore it all winter and now it's done for. Besides, the pants would be too short by now anyhow."

"Well, let's see." They had played this game

since he was tiny, and both of them always enjoyed it. Lucia began at once. "Would you want to be a pirate? A telephone lineman, a forest ranger, a Transylvanian, a transvestite?"

"Ma!"

"Baseball uniform. Football? I could make you a cute little red devil suit. Are you going to a party?"

"The Alphas are having a dance, with costumes."

"When will it be?"

"Thursday. Pretty neat for me, having Halloween fall on Thursday, huh? Guess they knew I have to work weekends."

"Pretty silly, throwing a party on a school night," Lucia grumped. "It doesn't give us much time. Maybe we had better start by looking at the fabrics I already have on hand. That's where we found the Davy Crockett Ultrasuede last year, and we don't have time to shop for anything."

"Jeez, Ma, mostly what you have is silk."

"Silks!" Lucia cried. "Jockeys wear silks. How would you like to go as the world's tallest jockey? A silk shirt in two bright colors, tight pants . . . Don't you have a pair of tan bicycle pants in stretchy fabric? Some kind of boots . . ."

He was grinning. "I know where I can borrow a pair."

In the workroom they hauled bolts of silk out of the closet and tested outrageous color combinations for the shirt. They settled on fuchsia and blue, and Lucia began the work at once, while inspiration was hot. The shirt was easy, and finished so quickly that she went on to create a beaked cap in matching fuchsia and blue.

She had lost a day, but she was back to work on the gowns by Tuesday, and that was when Mitch called.

He said at once, "Are you going to let me apologize?"

She said, "Yes, Mitch. I would be very glad if you would do that."

A smile appeared in his voice. "Are you going to let me come over there and apologize?"

"I think you can manage on the phone."

"I do it much better in person."

She said carefully, "Mitch, I really would like to . . . to explore the possibility of resuming our friendship, but it's going to take more than just asking. You can't just say you're sorry and have everything snap back to where it was before. And you haven't even said it."

"I'm sorry. Now, what else do you need me to do?"

He certainly could be annoying. She said, "And next time . . . next time you blow your stack, are you going to be sorry, or are you going to make some changes so there won't be a next time?"

He began to sound more serious. "I can't promise I'll never get mad again. How could I do that?"

"I don't expect you to promise that. I want you to think about alternative ways to handle anger."

"All I have to do is think about it, and you'll go out with me?"

Well, maybe she had better exit from this argument before it got really silly. She allowed, "I might. Do you still have the tickets for the Shubert on Saturday?"

"Sure I do. Do we still have a date for Saturday?"

She tried not to sound coy. "Well, I wouldn't want to miss the Shubert."

"We're on, then?"

"Yes, Mitch, we're on for Saturday. But we're going to have to do some talking."

"I'll come over right now, and we can get started."

"No, don't come now. I'm working, and it's already late. I'll talk to you Saturday."

He finally hung up, and Lucia returned to her sewing.

It went so well that she finished a couple of gowns that night, and the next morning she hung them in the wagon. After work she drove directly to Terrilee's.

It was one of Terrilee's early days, and she was just closing up when Lucia got there. They put the new merchandise on the racks and went into Terrilee's apartment for coffee. Lucia knew from experience that Terrilee made poisonous coffee, but coffee is a social drink. That means you don't necessarily have to drink it. Just handling the cup is sufficient for its purpose.

Terrilee poured the coffee. "So what's with Mitch? Did you make up with him yet?"

A typical Terrilee opening, assuming so much. Lucia protested, "What makes you think I'm going to make up with him? I said we were through."

"You didn't mean it, did you?"

Lucia had to laugh at herself. "Am I that transparent? We're going to the Shubert on Saturday."

"Good!" said Terrilee. "Don't give that guy up. Hunka, hunka! He's even cute when he's mad."

Lucia cradled her cup and turned serious. "I like him a lot, Terrilee, and he seems to like me. But I won't put up with that temper of his, and I want to make sure he knows that I won't."

"Okay, but don't be careless. Guys like that don't come around every day. I don't know

168

where you ever got off calling him a cocker spaniel."

Lucia grinned at her. "I don't think I ever did. And I'd say I'm being very careful. I'm not really mad at him for the things he said that night. I understand how frantic a person gets when it's one of the kids. But Mitch has to understand that he can't just go around blowing his top at everybody. And I certainly don't want him to form the habit of taking it out on me when something goes wrong."

"Okay, but watch what you're doing. He's a real catch."

"So am I," said Lucia smugly.

That made Terrilee laugh. "I never thought of it that way. We never do, do we? But you are a great catch, and so am I."

Lucia consulted her watch. "I've got to get back to town soon. I want to be there when he calls, well, the second time he calls."

"That's right! Keep your lure in the water, and don't give up the Shubert!"

It was after eight when she got home, and Tommy's friends were already gathered around the breakfast room table. Tonight's project was not to study, however. They were arranging a camping trip and the notebooks were laid out to receive an elaborate series of lists.

Lucia had made a stew before she went to work and left it bubbling in the Crock-Pot. She thought she had made an ample amount for herself, Tommy, and something left over, but the friends must have come over hungry. The pot was empty and still turned on, heat turning the morsels in the bottom to cement.

She unplugged the pot and carried the liner to the sink. Tommy came into the kitchen. "Hey, Ma."

"Hello, Tommy."

"We have to get a lot of stuff together and we need someplace to put it. Is it okay if we put it in the garage?"

"Oh, I think that's a fine idea," said Lucia. "You'll need space to do that, so you'll have to straighten out the garage. Maybe the other guys will help you. When you stack the lumber, put it all against one wall."

"Oh, and one more thing." He was scuffing his toe; this was obviously the crux of the matter. "Nobody's got a car big enough. Is it okay if we take the station wagon?"

"My station wagon? I wouldn't have any transportation all weekend?"

"You can drive my car."

"Well, okay. That makes sense."

"Thanks, Ma!" Tommy rushed back to the breakfast room. He said to his friends, "Okay, we got it. Now, what about the food?" At that point a new idea struck him, and he hollered to Lucia, back in the kitchen,

"Debbie's dad has been calling again."

"Thank you, Tommy."

When the phone rang she picked it up, and of course it was Mitch. She didn't know, until she heard it, how she had been looking forward to hearing his voice again. How much she wanted to see him. If it was a game she had been playing, she had been caught in it herself.

He said, "Are we friends again?"

"I guess so. I'm going to see you Saturday, aren't I?"

That well-remembered chuckle. "Yes, we're still on for Saturday at the Shubert. But what about tonight? I was hoping we could get together for dinner. Have you eaten yet?"

"No, and I'd love to have dinner. It's a bit late, but we could do something simple. There's a great Mexican place on Western."

"Pick you up in twenty minutes."

He arrived, driving the Porsche but wearing jeans, which was fine because she was still wearing her office clothes, a good pair of pants and a particularly nice velour shirt. They went to the restaurant and found they both loved tortillas, *ropa viejo*, and Mexican beer.

"Maybe it's not what the gourmets eat," Lucia said, "but it's good."

"Fills you up, too," Mitch agreed. "I sure got a funny phone call today. Guy wanted to talk to Debbie. It was an agency! She had actually contacted a modeling agency!"

"When? When did she contact them? Surely not in the last few days!"

"No, she'd called them Saturday afternoon. And it was Rebecca who recommended her to them. I told 'em Debbie isn't interested anymore."

"She isn't, is she?"

"Studying hard and happy as a clam to be in school. But Saturday afternoon, when I thought she was scamming me, she was so serious about modeling, she was calling up agencies! I sure don't understand kids."

"Nobody does. The whole time my kids were teenagers, I had this weird feeling there was something they wanted from me, some big thing, and they weren't getting it. Nothing is enough for them. They look at you with that accusing glare and refuse your offers of affection, food, small gifts, services. What? What is it they want? They can't tell you because they don't know, either."

He put down his fork with surprise. "Really? You feel that way, too? All my kids give me that look, but I figured it had something to do with the breakup; it was something about me. You say it's universal?"

"I'm sure it is."

He picked up the fork again. "That's really a comfort to me. You know, I've been doing

172

some thinking the last couple days and . . . Well, I'm sorry about the things I said when I couldn't find Debbie."

"I think I can understand how you felt, but maybe next time you need my help, you can ask without yelling."

"Well, I'll try." That Mitch smile. "We've got to figure out the right way to talk to each other, because we've got a future together."

Lucia raised an eyebrow. "We do?"

"You know we do. I don't feel this way with anybody else. With you it's just like . . . like everything fits in. Everything's right when it's you and me."

Lucia dipped a tortilla chip in the salsa. "It's all very right as long as nobody's yelling."

"It's always right, and we have a future because I'm going to keep after you until you admit it."

Lucia only smiled, and dipped again into the salsa.

They were easygoing in that restaurant, and didn't mind a bit when Mitch and Lucia monopolized a table and talked until midnight.

Chapter Nine

Even as she woke she knew it had only been a dream, but her cheeks were wet with tears and the terror remained, tight in her gut, sending adrenaline rushing through her system. There would be no more sleeping that night.

Lucia stared into the familiar darkness of her bedroom and sought comfort by fingering the elaborate border of a pillowcase. Years ago she had made them, all those borders for all the linens in this room. She had sewn all the lace pillows and the ruffled curtains. She had moved furniture, painted walls, hung pictures, overdecorated the room until it was feminine, girlish. Anything to make it different from the bedroom across the hall that she had once shared with her husband, George.

That room was the big one in the front of the house, and she had turned it into a workroom because she couldn't sleep in it, not anymore. Not alone.

And now, after all these years, she had dreamed of George again. She thought she had long since gotten over those dreams, those nightmares. She would dream that she was asleep, dreaming in bed, and George was beside her. Then she would see the bloody mess that was all that was left of him after his car was hit by a jackknifing semi on the freeway.

Lucia got up, slipped on her robe, and a pair of warm slippers to protect her feet from the bare wooden floors. She headed for the kitchen. It would soon be time to get up. Maybe, after a cup of coffee, she could use the extra hour that had been involuntarily added to her day to get some kind of work done.

She didn't, though. She sat at the kitchen table over her coffee, and she felt sad and almost as depressed as she had been so many years before at this same table, drinking coffee and wondering what on earth she was going to do, how she was going to survive and take care of her children.

George was gone. He had kissed her goodbye cheerfully and left for work, in a hurry like every other weekday morning, and minutes later he was gone forever. They phoned her to come to the hospital, but by the time she got there he was dead. He was dead and she was alone, with two children and a mortgage. She had no job, no money, not even a car. She had sat at this table and cried into her coffee.

Only at night, though. In the light of day she smiled, confident and competent, because she had to. She had to make her boys believe that nothing had changed, nothing would change. The picture had never left her mind of those sad, frightened little faces, the day of the funeral, when Georgie had asked in his high, still boyish little voice, "Who's going to take care of us now?"

George had carried no life insurance. Why would a man still in his thirties bother with life insurance? The only thing that was insured was his car, and she used that money to make a down payment on a station wagon, the same wagon she was still driving.

She had always wanted a station wagon, and so had her boys. She put a mattress in the back and they wrestled on it, their own personal mobile arena. Their own way of easing the incredible boredom caused by even the shortest trip.

Tommy always started it. Georgie would have been content to lie on his back and enjoy the luxury of watching the world go by while he was horizontal, but Tommy always started a fight and Georgie, older and bigger, always won. Tommy always ended up crying, "Mom!

He's sitting on me again!" But George was not there to laugh with her at the antics of their boys.

She had told herself she had to have a car in order to get to her job when she got one. You can't have a job without a car. You can't even look for a job without a car.

Everybody just loved the station wagon, the room, the novelty, the convenience. But it took Lucia a long time to learn to regard it as just a car, to get over the feeling that she had bought it with blood money. George's blood.

How grateful she had been to land the job at the freight company! The salary was low, she realized that from the start, but she had no useful work experience and they were taking a chance on her. She loved the feeling that she could pay the mortgage, make the car payments, feed the kids. Her loyalty to the freight company had a solid foundation.

She remembered those long, dreary years while she tried to be mother, father, breadwinner, comforter, and teacher to her sons all at once. The thousands upon thousands of decisions she had made, some of them boneheaded, but she had made them all.

Sometimes she felt that God had personally sent her Terrilee. The helping hand, the shoulder to cry on, the dispenser of advice and love and support . . . Terrilee was always there to hold her up. Terrilee had driven from the Valley every day that first summer to check up on the boys while they were out of school. Terrilee had taken her to the movies, had her over for dinner, tried to fix her up with a brother of her ex-husband's. . . . Well, Terrilee did boneheaded things, too.

Lucia went to the cupboard and hauled out a mixing bowl. Tonight was Halloween and she would need cookies for the children. She would need two kinds of cookies. One with raisins and one with chocolate chips. They always wanted chocolate chips, and two kinds of cookies would eat up the hour before she had to get ready to go to work. She began to mix.

She knew the reason for her bad dream. Of course she knew why all these old, buried memories were coming back to her today.

For George, there would never again be joy. He had lain cold and still in his grave now for ten long years. He had not watched his boys grow up. He never had the chance to be proud of their accomplishments, the scholarships, the athletic trophies, even the little day-to-day triumphs of the lives of his children.

George never got to do any of the things he had planned, the restoration of the house, the getaway cabin he had wanted in the mountains someday. Who could know what he might have wanted to do? He might have gone skiing or sky diving or taken up vegetable gardening, but he never got a chance at any of those new adventures.

Or a new love.

And that was why Lucia was mixing cookies before dawn in a chilly kitchen. She had intended to spend her whole life with George; she would have done it willingly, but it hadn't happened, and now she was ready to begin something new.

She was going to have a new life; all sorts of possibilities were opening up in front of her. She was moving at warp speed away from her old life and her old love, and she knew it was right that she did so, but that lingering little regret remained, a bad dream to remind her that save for a wrong decision on the freeway, she would have been about to celebrate her twenty-fifth anniversary.

She whispered into the cookie-smelling warmth that was beginning to rise from the oven, "I'm sorry, George."

That evening she packaged the cookies so they would be ready for the children, should any come to the door. Even while she wrapped the cookies she knew there probably would not be any visiting children. The custom of trick-or-treating on Halloween had almost died out.

It was sad, she thought, but the children could not be sure the treats were safe, not even from neighbors. It was not safe just to be walking around the streets after dark.

She decided to bring some hand sewing into the breakfast room so she would not have to run downstairs should anyone come to the door. She collected her work, a pincushion, thread, needle, scissors, and went into the breakfast room, and there was Tommy at the table, his head bent over his books.

She said, "Oh, hello, dear. If you are going to be here for a while, would you mind answering the door? If the children come, there are cookies for them in a basket next to the door. I'm going to be working upstairs."

He muttered, "Yeah, I'm going to be here."

"Let me know when you leave. You are going out later, aren't you?"

He snarled, "No. I thought I was going to a dance, but I didn't get invited."

"Oh. Debbie?" She felt his pain as if the wound were hers. What could she say that would not add to his hurt?

He nodded grimly. "She's really gone Alpha."

"Alpha? Is that something that's catching?"

"You know what I mean. That sorority she belongs to. No Alpha can date a chemistry major. It's against the rules, or they've got it in the sorority charter, or something."

180

"That's really sad," said Lucia. "I didn't know you had to get all new friends when you joined a sorority."

He shrugged. "Some do, some don't."

"I'm sorry. I didn't think she was so superficial."

"That's the way it goes." He picked up his book, dismissing her, and Lucia went upstairs to sew.

She cooked dinner for all the boys on Friday night and fed them a hearty pot roast with potatoes and vegetables. Considering their skills at cooking, camping, and procurement, she feared they would be very hungry before the end of their two-day campout.

They would leave at first light the next morning, heading for Castaic Lake, and loading of the station wagon was in progress. Their gear was spread all over the garage floor and spilled out into the driveway. The boy who was in charge of the food was doing his packing up in the front hall. Lucia suspected he had chosen that location for its nearness to her kitchen, and the items that might be supplied from there.

She was trying hard not to interfere, or even to make suggestions. The boys saw the project as a test of their independence and inventiveness and they resented offers of help. She knew they had forgotten the salt, but she wasn't going to tell them unless they asked for her advice.

She was delighted when Mitch called. He said, "I'm not doing anything. Are you doing anything?"

Of course she was. She was going to mix up some yeast-rising dough for rolls in the morning, and there was a new batch of unfinished gowns on her worktable, but she replied airily, "Nothing much. Terrilee has a check for me and I thought I'd drive over there a little later and get it."

"How about I ride along with you?"

"It would be nice to have some company, but it's in Tarzana, and you don't need to—"

"Just for fun. Just for the company."

"Well, okay. Do you want to go now?"

"I'll be right over."

Well, the heck with the yeast-rising breads. She'd make muffins for the boys in the morning. Lucia trotted upstairs to comb her hair.

After she had fixed her hair she decided that the robe on her table was close enough to being finished that she could get it ready and take it to Terrilee, as long as she was going anyway. She went into the workroom. The robe needed only a little finishing on the hem and it would be ready. Lucia sat down to her machine, keeping one ear cocked for the doorbell.

When Mitch arrived, the boy with the food

packages let him in. Lucia went to the head of the stairs and called, "I'm here, Mitch. Come up for a minute."

He came up the stairs smiling. He wore his usual jeans with a blue shirt and he looked fresh and clean and shaved. Lucia glanced down and the food-package boy was watching them, open-mouthed. What could possibly be so astonishing? Well, no reason to give the kid any more surprises. She stepped inside the workroom, out of sight, and waited for Mitch to follow her.

He did, and took her promptly in his arms. His kiss was warm and exciting and she leaned joyfully into it, meeting his ardor with her own.

When she broke the kiss he still held her, and she asked, "Can't you even say hello?"

"Hello," he replied, and kissed her again.

He murmured against her hair, "I've missed you so much all week, Lucia. I couldn't wait until tomorrow."

"It was only a couple of days ago that we had dinner . . ." she began as heavy adolescent feet thundered up the stairs and Tommy's voice called, "Mom? Where are you, Mom?"

Lucia stepped gracefully back, a little away from Mitch. "In here, dear."

Tommy poked his head in. "Mom, do we have any . . . oh, hello, Mr. Colton. Mom, do we have any rope?"

Mitch nodded hello, smiling grimly. Lucia asked, "What sort do you need, dear? I believe there are a couple coils of clothesline in the storeroom."

"That'll do fine." Tommy rushed out.

Lucia sat down and began feeding fabric into her machine. "I'm almost finished with this robe and I want to take it with me when we go to Terrilee's. I'm afraid this isn't going to be a very exciting evening for you."

"Wasn't looking for excitement. Just a little company. You know, we can't hang up anything in the Porsche. We'll need the wagon if you're going to take that robe along."

"It can be folded up. These things don't really wrinkle; hanging them is only for convenience."

They chatted while she finished the robe and then she packed it carefully in paper. They got into the Porsche and drove to Tarzana.

Terrilee's shop was still open, although there were no customers and she was only sitting behind the counter, watching television. She offered coffee. Mitch had been warned, but he accepted a cup anyway, so Lucia had to also.

"We can go sit in the back room," Terrilee offered. "The chairs are more comfortable, and I'll hear the bell if anybody comes in."

But Mitch was still wandering around the

store, his coffee mug in his hand. Terrilee had so many rainbow floats, she was able to display them as she had planned, pinned to the wall like a color wheel. Posed before that dazzling display, a manikin wore only a pushup bra and bikini panties.

Mitch regarded the plastic curves with amusement. "You sure do have an interesting line of merchandise here."

"What I put out there is what I think is going to sell," Terrilee said. "And that Goldie Hawn lingerie moves just fine. But the manikin's only to attract attention. I'm not trying to complete with Frederick's of Hollywood. We're not really in the same business. Most of my stuff is real clothes—lounging pajamas, nightwear, hostess dresses."

"Yeah? What's a hostess dress?"

She gave him a saucy grin. "A long one when long isn't in."

They settled into Terrilee's living room, leaving the door open to the shop. The chairs were all of wicker and creaked ominously when sat upon. Mitch kept looking down between his legs to see if the furniture was buckling under his weight.

"Don't worry about it," Terrilee said. "It's strong enough, just sort of springy. Lucia, you've got to give me a recipe for stuffing. What I made last year came out of the turkey looking like wet cement and tasted about like it, too."

Lucia said, "You either put in too much liquid or didn't cook it long enough. Maybe both. Is it time to be planning Thanksgiving food already?"

"A couple weeks off yet, but my family's coming, so I've got to get ready."

"I'll give you a recipe with measurements, so you won't have problems," Lucia promised. "How big is the turkey going to be?"

Mitch asked, "Do you have children, Terrilee?"

"Ten, twelve pounds, and I have grandchildren," she replied proudly. "I dropped out of school to get married when I was sixteen, so I've got a son who's almost thirty. He's a career army man. Any of your kids old enough for the army? That's the place for 'em. Mothers never can make them stand up straight or keep their rooms clean, but the army can. My kid loves it. After seventeen years of my cooking, he even likes their food!"

He chuckled a little. "No, neither of my boys is in the military."

"Were you in the army, Mitch?" Terrilee asked.

"Navy Construction Battalion. And I have to tell you the truth about that, we had a great time. I really enjoyed the whole thing, except they didn't have any drilling rigs."

They talked and laughed together and forgot to close up the shop for so long, Terrilee sold a peignoir at eleven o'clock to a slightly drunk man who hoped a gift would make his wife forget how late he was getting home.

Chapter Ten

The next morning Tommy and the rest of the campers filled sacks full of blueberry muffins and went off in the station wagon, and Lucia used his hatchback to run her errands.

She discovered at once that the squeal in the brakes was because he needed new linings. She knew he had no money and she also knew that she would pay for the repairs rather than have her Tommy riding around on dangerous brakes. The thought didn't depress her much, but she did feel blue while contemplating what boys do with their gym clothes.

Probably they had to take them out of the lockers for the weekend, but the clothes got no farther than the back seat of the car, where they ripened in the heat until they were carried back to school on Monday.

Lucia shuddered as she picked up Tommy's

shorts and shirt and carried them, at arm's length, into the laundry room. She found plenty of towels to make up a load; there always was a good supply of dirty towels.

Of course she could not begin her bubble bath until the washer had finished its cycle. There wasn't enough water pressure in the house to supply two faucets at the same time. But it all worked out. By the time she had the groceries put away and the kitchen straightened up, she could throw the towels into the dryer and go for her bath.

A luxurious bath, as long as she wanted, because there was no Tommy in the house to need the bathroom. She washed her hair and put it on rollers to dry. She painted her toenails and primped luxuriously until it was time to dress.

She took extra care with her makeup, darkening her thick eyelashes, touching her high cheekbones with a trace of blush. The blue dress slithered on, silkily outlining graceful curves. When she took the rollers out, her hair fell, of course, right back into its usual waves. Well, what of it? Mitch seemed to like it just the way it was.

She was ready on time and waiting, so alert for his arrival that she heard the car pull up in front. It would scarcely do to open the door at his first ring, as if she had been standing behind it, waiting for him, so she counted to twenty first.

He was wearing one of his splendid suits, smiling, lips stretched tight against his teeth. It was surprising that nobody ever noticed, when he smiled like that, that she had melted into a small puddle at his feet.

She said, "Oh, hello, Mitch."

He answered, "Are you ready, Lucia?"

"Just let me get my coat. It might be chilly later on, don't you think so?"

He came inside and smiled some more. "You look lovely, Lucia. I like your dress."

"Thank you." She didn't mention it was the same one she had been wearing for last Saturday's disaster. She took the coat from the closet and let him hold it for her.

She slipped her arms into the sleeves and somehow continued slipping right into his arms. He pulled her against him and touched her ear with warm lips. He whispered, "Its seems so long since I've seen you, and it was only yesterday!"

He turned her so she faced him and brought his lips down to hers for a kiss. She leaned gladly into it, opening to him. She lifted her arms and put them around his neck, caressing the soft, thick hair at the base of his skull, tasting the velvet of his tongue. The feeling of being enveloped in his warmth had become so dear to her that she nestled into it, careless of how she would feel the cold when he was gone.

They ate at the place under the Shubert. Mitch liked the fettucini and veal but complained of the smallness of the portions. At every intermission he reiterated that he was starving, so after the show they found a place that was still open and he ate again, while Lucia nibbled fruit from the salad bar. She enjoyed watching him eat. Like her sons, he needed a lot of fuel for a big, hardworking body.

She complained that Terrilee pressured her, trying to get her to open her own business. Not much to her surprise, he agreed with Terrilee.

"I've seen some of your things," he said, "and you have a lot of talent. You ought to be doing what you want to do."

"That's what Terrilee always says." Lucia changed the subject. "What's Debbie doing? Have you seen her?"

"Oh, sure, she's at my house a lot. They were there when I left."

"They?"

"She and a couple of her friends. They wanted to make cookies, and the sorority won't let them do stuff in the kitchen, so they came over to my place. I felt like I ought to be staying around and keeping an eye on them, but that's dumb, when she's on her own and living someplace else. It's just that it makes me feel like I've given up on all my responsibilities toward her."

"That's it! You've got it!" Lucia applauded. "When you feel like a rejecting parent and are sure your child is being neglected, you've reached the right balance for living with a teenager."

Mitch laughed his big, healthy laugh. "Hold her with an open hand, I guess that's what it's called. About the only good thing about having teenagers is the chance to commiserate with other parents about it."

It was late when they reached her home, and the street was dark and quiet. Water swished under his tires as he pulled to the curb. There seemed to be a lot of water about. Lucia saw it fanning across the sidewalk, cascading into the gutter.

"It seems wet around here," she remarked. "Somebody must have left the sprinklers on too long."

Mitch observed, "The somebody seems to be you."

"Me? Oh, my stars!" Lucia jumped from the car and stood staring in stupefaction. From a spot near her porch steps water was spouting wildly, a fountain tossing up as high as the second-story windows. It sprayed straight up, then turned into a feathery top that shimmered

The Publishers of Zebra Books
Make This Special Offer
to Zebra Romance Readers...

AFTER YOU HAVE READ THIS
BOOK WE'D LIKE TO SEND YOU
4 MORE FOR *FREE*
AN $18.00 VALUE

NO OBLIGATION!

TO GET YOUR 4 FREE BOOKS WORTH $18.00 —MAIL IN THE FREE BOOK CERTIFICATE T O D A Y

Fill in the Free Book Certificate below, and we'll send your FREE BOOKS to you as soon as we receive it.

If the certificate is missing below, write to: Zebra Home Subscription Service, Inc., P.O. Box 5214, 120 Brighton Road, Clifton, New Jersey 07015-5214.

4 FREE BOOKS

ZEBRA HOME SUBSCRIPTION SERVICE, INC.

YES! Please start my subscription to Zebra Historical Romances and send me my first 4 books absolutely FREE. I understand that each month I may preview four new Zebra Historical Romances free for 10 days. If I'm not satisfied with them, I may return the four books within 10 days and owe nothing. Otherwise, I will pay the low preferred subscriber's price of just $3.75 each; a total of $15.00, *a savings off the publisher's price of $3.00.* I may return any shipment and I may cancel this subscription at any time. There is no obligation to buy any shipment and there are no shipping, handling or other hidden charges. Regardless of what I decide, the four free books are mine to keep.

NAME

ADDRESS _____ APT

CITY _____ STATE ___ ZIP

TELEPHONE ( )

SIGNATURE _____ (if under 18, parent or guardian must sign)

Terms, offer and prices subject to change without notice. Subscription subject to acceptance by Zebra Books. Zebra Books reserves the right to reject any order or cancel any subscription.

4 FREE BOOKS

FREE BOOK CERTIFICATE

GET
FOUR
FREE
BOOKS
(AN $18.00 VALUE)

ZEBRA HOME SUBSCRIPTION
SERVICE, INC.
P.O. Box 5214
120 BRIGHTON ROAD
CLIFTON, NEW JERSEY 07015-5214

white in the pale moonlight like a monument.

Lucia breathed again, "Oh, my!"

Mitch came to stand beside her. He seemed to be with difficulty smothering a chuckle. He asked, "Do you have any tools? I don't carry anything much in this car."

"I have a roomful of tools, but I think I had better send for the plumber. Look how big it is!"

"Probably isn't as bad as it looks."

"More likely, it's worse," she countered. "Maybe I should call the Army Corps of Engineers."

Mitch did chuckle. "Looks like you popped a valve. Can you find me a wrench?"

"Really, can you fix that?"

"Of course I can fix it. What's a rig but a big bunch of plumbing?"

"I'll show you where I keep things." Lucia started up the walk but it was flooded. She stopped, looking for a way around the flowing stream that was cutting into her lawn.

"You'll wreck your shoes if you walk in that," Mitch warned, and picked her up.

She was so startled that she squealed and thrashed at first but he only squeezed her against his chest. His arms were strong and the chest . . . She nestled cooperatively against it and put her arms around his neck. As he sloshed toward the house she nuzzled his neck and whispered, "Now you're wrecking *your* shoes."

The water was running away from the house and it was dry at the top of the drive. Lucia led the way to the back of the house and opened the door to the storeroom. It was a windowless hole under the kitchen, and there she kept the equipment she needed for the maintenance of the house.

The tiny room was lined with shelves that were crammed full of tools, lumber, and bits of pipe. Mitch was impressed. He said, "You sure do have a lot of stuff here."

"Takes it all for this house."

He found a wrench. "This looks like it'll do."

"Oh, Mitch, let's call the plumber. You're going to ruin your clothes."

He said, "Oh, yeah," and put down the wrench. Shrugging out of his coat, he handed it to her, then rolled up the sleeves of his shirt and loosened the collar. He took off his tie and handed that to her also. The thin fabric of his dress shirt was stretched tight over the muscles of his chest, his hair was tousled, and she could feel his nearness in the little room, feel him although they were not touching. Like a naughty child she wanted to forget everything—the disaster outside, all her responsibilities—and hide in the storeroom with Mitch. Something in his look told her that he felt it, too, but he picked up the wrench and went out.

Lucia carried his coat upstairs, hung it up, and changed into jeans and rubber sandals. Now she was better dressed for the job at hand than Mitch was. She went downstairs and found him rummaging in the storeroom.

"Your valve is okay," he announced. "It's the pipe that feeds into it that's rusted out. Trouble is, it's on the street side and you don't have the tool that turns off the water at the street. I can fix it, though. Most of the pipe is above ground."

"It is?" questioned Lucia, a little confused.

He grinned and added, "Well, it wasn't before all that water started to run." His hair was wet and clinging to his forehead and his grin made him look like an endearing little boy.

"Can I help in some way?"

"No, don't you go out there. You might send Tommy, though. What's he doing, anyway?"

"Tommy isn't home, Mitch. He's gone for the weekend. He and his friends went camping."

Mitch looked far more surprised than the information warranted. After all, he had seen the boys packing up last night. "Camping? Tommy? I didn't know he was the outdoor type."

"It's sort of an experiment. They just decided to try it. Trouble was that all his friends have weekend jobs and for them all to get off at the same time took more planning than Operation

Desert Storm. They've been working on it for months."

Mitch gathered up tools and pipe joints. "Why don't you go into the house and open a few faucets. It will help relieve the pressure when the water starts running through those pipes again."

Lucia did as he said, and when she returned to the front porch, the water was still spouting. Mitch sat under it, patiently allowing water to pound down on his back while he worked unhurriedly with the pipes. It was the chilly time of the night, and Lucia was sorry she had not put on something more substantial than her tank top and jeans, but she remained on the porch, feeling illogically that she should, since it would be so much colder under that waterfall on the lawn.

At length the water stopped spurting. For a space it turned into a stream that ran briskly into the street, then that, too, stopped. Mitch called out, "Okay, it's hooked up. You can go turn off the faucets in the house. Look around for any leaks while you're doing it."

Lucia found everything in order, turned off the faucets, and went looking for Mitch. He was putting things away in the storeroom. He was soaked, of course, dripping streams of water onto the floor.

She said, "Oh, Mitch, you're the wettest thing I've ever seen!"

"Guess I am," he agreed. "I'd better not go into your house; I'd leave a trail like a snail. I'll just get into my car and go home."

"You'll do no such thing!" Lucia cried. "Do you want to ruin the seats in your car along with your pants and shoes?"

"What else can we do?"

"Go up on the service porch and take off your things," she ordered. "I'll find you something dry to wear."

He followed her up the steps to the service porch but asked, "Where are you going to get any clothes my size? I don't think I'd fit into anything of yours."

Lucia opened the dryer and handed him two large towels. "With any luck, you won't have to. My son Georgie is almost as big as you. I'll find something that fits him loosely, and then I'll make you a hot drink.

He took the towels gratefully and rubbed one over his hair. "That sounds good. Aren't you cold, too? You don't have much on."

"I'll get something in a minute. Give me your shoes."

When she upended a shoe, water flowed out. Lucia said, "Oh, I could cry! They're spoiled!"

"Stuff them full of paper towels," he suggested. "It might save them. That's what my grandmother used to do when we walked in mud puddles."

Lucia went to the kitchen for the paper towels, and when she returned, Mitch had taken off his shirt and was toweling himself. The towel flicked across his chest, riffling the dark, curly hair that grew in the shape of an arrowhead, the point below his belt. He held out the dripping shirt. "Mind if I just drop this in the washer?"

"What a good idea!" said Lucia. "Put the rest of your clothes in there, too. I'll spin out the water and hang your pants to dry and maybe tomorrow the cleaner can save them. Give them to me."

He said, "Well, Lucia . . ."

"Oh, come on, don't be shy," she said, and her glance was suddenly full of mischief.

She was standing between him and the washer. He caught her look, picked up the challenge, and tossed it back to her. Their gazes locked. He unfastened his belt, zipped down the trousers, and lowered them. With some difficulty he stripped them off his wet legs. He handed her the dripping garment and she turned to hoist it into the washer.

When she turned back, he was handing her a pair of soggy white briefs. One of the towels was wrapped modestly around his waist. Naked except for the towel hugging his narrow hips, he was all magnificent male, from the strong, sun-browned neck and arms rounded with muscle, down the extra-broad chest, and all the way down his long legs corded with muscle.

She put the briefs into the washer and pushed the spin button, and suddenly it was hard to turn around again to face Mitch.

She didn't have enough on. What had possessed her to wear this tank top, too skimpy to have a bra under it? Her breasts were clearly defined under the stretch fabric. They felt heavy, the nipples tightening, all on their own. She had seen the leap of desire in Mitch's eyes; when she turned, would he as easily be able to see the hunger in hers? She could feel his hot brown gaze on her. She was bending over the washer, and she knew the jeans fit tightly over her rounded derriere. She turned quickly and his eyes rose slowly, past her breasts, her bare shoulders, to her eyes.

She couldn't meet that honestly-questing look, and she dropped her gaze. She was looking at his chest, at the two smoothly-muscled mounds that were his male breasts. He was breathing heavily, the mounds moving slightly apart and then together again. . . .

She said breathlessly, "I must get you some clothes." As she moved toward him her hand came up, an oddly jerky motion, and she laid her palm on one of those fascinating mounds of muscle. "You're cold as marble. You're going to catch pneumonia."

He pulled her, unprotesting, against him. "I will for sure, unless you warm me up," he promised, and brought his mouth down on hers.

He had kissed her before but never with such purpose as now. His tongue briefly admired the curve of her lip, then plunged deeply, assertively, with a meaning plain as words. She responded, wrapping her arms around him, feeling his smooth, cold skin and the strength of muscle and bone underneath. His icy hands caressed her back, seeking the warmth under her top, against her skin.

Under the towel she felt his hardness and knew, even as she felt it, that she had become aware of it too late. She was pressing herself against him and she had lost her last chance of hiding her feelings, of looking cool and controlling the situation.

She tried anyhow. She broke the kiss and would have slipped gracefully out of his arms, but he only held her more firmly.

She gasped, "I'll fix something hot. Soup, or would you rather have a nice hot grog?"

He growled, "Baby, you have already fixed something hot." He kissed her lightly, first on the lips, then along her jaw and under her ear, his face buried in her hair. Electricity crackled through her. She had disappeared; she existed only where he touched her, his lips, his hands.

He whispered, "You know how I want to be warmed up, Lucia, and you want it, too."

"Oh, Mitch, I do want it, only . . ."

His lips moved lower on her neck, his hands higher under the tank top. "Only what?"

Her breath was coming in short gasps, but she managed to whisper, "I do, but oh, my dear, I don't think I can remember how!"

"Nothing to it. You don't forget; it's like riding a bicycle." But she thought she heard him add, almost under his breath, "I hope."

She hoped he had said "I hope." It made her feel more at home with him, quelled a little of her nervousness and her fear that in some compartment of his mind he was about to test her for a rating.

She pushed him away with a laugh that was more of a nervous hiccup. "Well, not on the service porch. Let's go upstairs."

"Show me the way. Is the front door locked?" Like a good householder, he checked all the locks before he followed her upstairs, the towel still firmly tucked around his waist. She led the way to her bedroom and turned on the small bedside lamp.

And there hung his coat, right where she had put it earlier, quite as if she had expected all along he would spend the night in this room.

She tried to explain. "I brought it with me when I came up here to change my clothes. . . ."

"It's okay. Relax." He closed the door and locked it; the world was outside, but she went on babbling. "I wouldn't want you to think I put it in here so you'd have to come in here to get it and—"

Long arms reached for her, pulled her to him. "Shhh, Lucia, you're spoiling it. I was hoping you'd planned all along to seduce me."

She leaned against him and looked up into his dear face. "Oh, I did, but this isn't exactly how I dreamed it. I really didn't rust that pipe out on purpose."

"Must have been fate, then. It picked just the right time to go. I don't know how much longer I could have waited. I've been wanting you since—" He broke off, smiling quaintly. "Since I don't know when. I can't remember when I didn't want you."

"I can't remember back before you, either. Isn't it funny? It's as if we had a history, or as if we knew each other before we ever met."

He stroked back her heavy hair. "Just man and woman history, that's all."

"You mean men and women have been getting together like this for some time now?"

"Something like that." He dropped light kisses on her face, her hair. "It'll do for now, anyhow."

"For now?"

"Until we have a history of our own. We're going to have a real long one, you know. I'm not ever going to let you go."

She said, "I'm glad you're here with me now." She was filled with joy that he was, that he was in her bedroom, her own private space. She had made this room her own, with her favorite things, with curtains, spread, and even pillows she had made herself, and now Mitch was here, large and solid.

His hands had become warm; she quivered as he stroked her, as the rough skin of his palm caressed her breast. He pulled the shirt off over her head and held her, his hands on her shoulders, his eyes loving her. He whispered, "You are very, very beautiful."

"You are, too," she replied, and to her he was. There was beauty in his strength and masculinity and passion. Her whole body responded to it, to the force of desire she saw in his eyes. The fire behind those eyes, the hunger in them, filled her with a wondrous sense of her own femininity, her power to give him what he longed for. She pressed herself against him, her bare breasts against his chest. Her marauding hand found its way under his towel and searched down the surprisingly smooth skin of

203

his belly to the interesting curve of the groin.

With firm fingers he positioned her a little away from him so he could reach her zipper, and pulled it down. He tried to push the jeans down over her hips, but they were tight, or his hands had become unsteady; he couldn't do it. She pushed him gently and he backed up, losing his towel as he sat on the edge of the bed.

Lucia pushed down the jeans and stepped out of them. She moved slowly toward him, looking at his eyes. They were dark with passion and his voice shook as he said, "Luci, my Luci!"

He put his big, hard hands on the backs of her naked thighs and drew her gently toward him, bent his head, and pressed his lips to the taut curve of her belly.

Even at this point she was unprepared for the strength of desire that rocketed through her. Her loins were drenched with heat, her legs would not hold her. She sank down against him, whispering hoarsely, "Kiss me, Mitch."

She had to have his kiss, for only then was she able to bear her volcanic longings for his touch, for the feel of his skin against hers, for the weight of his body pressing hers to the bed.

He swung her onto the bed and under him, then broke the kiss long enough to mutter, "I think it's all coming back to me now."

She panted, "If it doesn't, I'm in trouble, big

time." She pulled his head down until their mouths met, for they needed no words.

They spoke with touching, with caresses that fired them both with passion. They came together quickly, impatient with preliminaries. His strength became hers, her heat melted him as they joined for that journey that needs no map. They took what they longed for, the union, their moment of being ultimately together. The moment when they each were, at last, no longer alone.

Chapter Eleven

Lucia loved cooking breakfast. The center of the cooktop on her ancient range was a griddle, so long and wide she could prepare whole meals on it, organizing her ingredients and moving them about like a general marshaling armies. She made sausage and eggs and her own special recipe for hash browns. She tossed freshly-grated raw potato on the grill until it was faintly golden. Then she put down a pat of butter, piled the potato on top of it, and pressed a heavy saucer over the mound. When everything else was ready, a swish of her spatula lifted the hash browns, sizzling in their saucer, and flipped them over, ready to serve, the crisp golden crust now on top.

It was a soft morning, already warm, with the air as fresh and bubbly as new cider. She sat across from Mitch and watched him eat, almost forgetting her own food in the pleasure of watching him, her man with the heart-stopping smile.

She was reflecting that she had done every one of the things Terrilee had warned her against. Especially, she had fallen in love.

Well, what of it, and how could she have helped it, anyway? The process was begun the first time he ever smiled at her, the first time she had seen him that night when he had been so worried about Debbie.

Lucia forked up a morsel of sausage and tried to eat it. Why did the sunshine fade when she thought about Debbie?

And Darryl.

And Jared.

And Ione.

Somewhere there was a paper that said Mitch was free, but it was only a paper. How could he be free of his children? How could he be free of the marriage that still lived in those children? How could he be free of Ione, who was as close as her telephone? She could call him anytime and ask him anything, make any request, even if it was silly, and he would comply.

Lucia felt suddenly restless and got up to freshen the coffee in the cups. Foolish Lucia, she told herself. You have fallen in love by yourself. Fallen for a man who is still tied to his ex-wife. Still in love with her. He must be, for if he were not, wouldn't he love Lucia? They had wonderful times together. Last night they had shared ecstasy, but never had he said that he loved her. Not even in the heat of passion had he said he loved her.

She picked up her coffee cup and touched the hot rim to her lips. She was almost startled when Mitch spoke.

He was still smiling, full and content, leaning back with one large bare foot hooked over the rung of the chair next to him. He wore a shirt of Georgie's and cutoff jeans. He said, "That was a good meal, Lucia."

"I'm glad you liked it."

"It was a great breakfast!" he enthused. "It's so great being with you, I don't ever want to go home. I'm even getting so I like this funky old house."

"It's not funky," Lucia protested. "It's historical."

"I like this funky, historical old house," he corrected himself. "Lucia, I'm appallingly lonely and nobody has cooked for me in a long time. Let's get married."

She stood up, unpleasantly jarred. Why did he have to say that? Couldn't he have left bad enough alone? She said, "That's not very funny, Mitch."

"I'm not trying to be funny." He was still

smiling, confident. Lucia began clearing the dirty dishes off the table.

He waited, but Lucia only went on stacking dishes. He asked again, "Well, what do you say?"

Lucia carried the plates to the sink. Falteringly, she managed to say, "I don't know, Mitch. I hadn't thought about it."

"Well, think about it." He pretended to consult his watch. "That ought to be long enough. Yes or no?"

The arrogance of him! He thought she'd jump at the opportunity, snap at the chance to marry a man who didn't love her, who didn't care, who needed only a cook and a bedmate and somebody to help him cope with the children.

Lucia said clearly, "No, Mitch. I do not want to marry again."

"You don't want to?" His voice was loud with astonishment. "What do you mean, you don't want to?"

"The way things are . . . well, right now I have everything my own way. I don't have to justify my decisions to anybody, or account for the money, and nobody, nobody tells me how to raise my children. Why should I want to change things?"

It was obvious that he, too, had been unpleasantly startled. He stood up and his voice was almost angry. "Dammit, do you like living on the thin edge of poverty? You haven't got anything, not a decent car or a real house to live in or time for anything but working. If you were sick or out of work for three weeks, you and your kids would starve. That's what you call having your own way? I could do a lot for you, and for Tommy, too."

She filled the sink and automatically began washing dishes. "You know I would never marry for money."

"You mean you are going to refuse just because it might be a financial advantage to you? That's dumb."

"Maybe it is, but it's also honest. You want me to marry for money while you marry for cooking. We'd be like a couple of stockbrokers arranging a merger."

"So what's wrong with being practical? You have the silliest objections I ever heard!"

Lucia crashed the rinsed dishes into the drainer. "Okay, if that strikes you silly, how's this for something you can get your teeth into? I can't have any more children."

"What? Children?"

Lucia attacked the grill with a scrubber. "That's right. I had to have some surgery. A terrific guy like you, with money, could marry anybody. You could marry a young woman, one who could give you children."

He sounded bewildered. "I *have* children."

"You could have a second family."

"Oh, God, no!"

She smiled at his vehemence, but just a little sadly. "Don't you ever feel like starting over, correcting the mistakes you made the first time?"

"Never!" he replied fervently. "Jared and Darryl and Debbie are my kids. They aren't replaceable with new models. Besides, it wouldn't work. You might not make the same mistakes, but there'd be new ones to make. You don't want another family, do you?"

"Bite your tongue! I couldn't manage a baby, not again. Maybe if it were a grandbaby and I had to do it for only a weekend at a time . . . maybe."

"You're too young to be a grandmother."

"It's not my age that counts, you know, but Georgie's. He's quite old enough, and now that he has a job and is solvent, some girl is very likely to grab him."

"I'm solvent and I'm not having a bit of luck," Mitch complained. "Why won't you marry me?"

"Oh, Mitch, you're in such a hurry! We've known each other only a few weeks. How do we know we could make a go of a marriage?"

"I'm used to making decisions and implementing them, and I've decided on you."

"That decision takes two."

"So what are we going to do?" he asked impatiently. "Shack up together like the kids do these days?"

"Certainly not!" Lucia gave a final wipe to the stove.

"Then what?" he pursued. "Go sneaking around to motels?"

"I've never gone to a motel, and I do not intend to start."

"Bribe the kids to go camping so we can have some time together?"

"Last night just happened," Lucia said defensively. "It just happened that Tommy was away. We were discreet. I will be discreet, but I will not stoop to deception."

He folded his arms with an expression of mild disgust. "You're the one who said you didn't like games, and that's a word game."

"Maybe I am just playing with words," Lucia admitted miserably. "Maybe I'm just playing with this whole idea. I do want to be with you, Mitch. Really, I want that. Maybe I'm just resisting the idea of marriage because I'm not used to it, and because it isn't romantic."

"Romantic?" He spoke the word as if he thought it ought to be handled with tongs. "You mean poetry and flowers and moonbeams?"

"And kisses and heavy snuggling and being

just a little bit crazy." She leaned back against the empty sink. Everything was clean.

"Getting married at our age is the craziest thing I can think of right now."

"Exactly! It's crazy, so why aren't we acting like it? Let's do something totally mad! Let's shock everybody!"

He thought it over and then he smiled. "Okay. Let's fly to Acapulco."

"What?"

"This weekend's no good; it's almost over now. How about next weekend? We can leave Friday night and be back in time for a night's sleep before work Monday morning. How does that sound?"

"Oh, Mitch! You are romantic!"

"Practical, too," he bragged. "The only way we can be together is to go someplace, and Venice Beach sure wasn't the place. Is it okay? You'll go?"

She had planned to defrost the freezer, and there would be laundry to do, and the yard work, and could she finish the rainbow gowns on time? She shoved it all resolutely out of her mind and agreed, "Yes, Mitch, I will go to Acapulco with you next weekend."

"All right!" He gave her a smile and a hug but not a kiss, for his mind was already elsewhere. "Give me the key to that storeroom," he commanded. "I'll get a shovel and clean up some of that mud we made last night."

"You mean when the pipe burst?" Lucia had forgotten all about it. "Oh, look at the time! I ought to get out there and mow the lawn."

"I guess you can find enough of it left to mow," he allowed. "Come on. We'll work together."

She protested, "Oh, Mitch, you shouldn't spend your Sunday working in the yard."

"So what else am I dressed for?" He laughed and they went to get the tools.

He filled the holes the water had made and mowed both lawns for her and cut back some bushes that were trying to take over the driveway. She weeded and edged until she was tired and then suggested knocking off for coffee. He agreed, but when the coffee was ready he was nowhere in sight.

She went looking for him and found him sitting on the bottom step of the staircase, admiring the classic proportions of it. He said, "You know, that balustrade is beautiful."

"Mahogany," she said.

He scratched at one of the spindles with his thumbnail. "The varnish is all cracked."

"Has been for twenty years."

"Sure would look pretty if it were refinished. Shiny and smooth."

"There's no easy way to do that job. Each spindle has to be stripped separately, by hand.

Paint on the stripper, scrape it off, use steel wool on all those little grooves and turnings . . ."

Mitch fingered the bulge of a spindle. "A man could do a few of them at a time. A couple each day and the job would be done before you knew it."

Lucia watched his hand caress the wood, and the feeling that stabbed through her was almost like jealousy. She didn't want to see Mitch toiling, night after night, over cracked varnish on the woodwork. She wanted his attention for herself. Suppose he finished the staircase, then there would be the window frames, and the crown moldings . . . This house could absorb any amount of restoration, swallow years of one's life.

Well, every mother knows how to veto the wild project her child is getting into. You distract him, preferably with something he likes better. She leaned over and rubbed his cheek. "You've a spot of dirt there."

He chuckled. "Probably I've got several. It's about time I went home and cleaned up." He kissed the fingers that lingered near his mouth.

She sat down close to him on the step and stroked back his hair. "You're a little dirty, but it's cute. You smell like cut grass."

"I probably have some of that on me, too," he admitted comfortably.

She leaned against him and he put an arm around her. His legs were white; he must not be accustomed to wearing shorts in the sun. She touched the surprisingly smooth skin of his thigh, sliding her fingers under the frayed edge of his cutoffs and he stirred, laughing. "Don't do that, woman, unless you want to be made love to by the lawn man."

"Why should I mind that? I've been slogging through the grass, too."

"You? You look fresh enough to go to a tea party." He tugged at the knot that held her shirt together, tied high up under her breasts. "How do you do that? What does it take to get you mussed up?"

"Somehow, I think you're about to find out."

The knot pulled loose and he reached inside the shirt. She pushed halfheartedly at his arms. "Hey, not right here on the stairs!"

"What have you got against stairs?"

She got away from him and scampered up the stairs, laughing. He caught her in the upstairs hall, as she was running very slowly, caught her in his arms and moved her backward into the bedroom.

When he laid her down on the bed, the unfastened shirt fell open, baring the smooth, compact rounds of her breasts, and it made him suddenly very serious. He lay down beside her and pulled her to him. His lips were warm and sweet on hers. Sparkles of excitement darted through her as he explored her body with his free hand. He stroked her thigh and slipped his fingers up the leg of her shorts. The air went out of her lungs in a rush.

"Oh, Mitch, stop!" she gasped. "This is something kids do, and ruin their clothes!"

"You're not really worried about the clothes we've got on, are you?"

"Of course not, only—" He touched her again, and a long shudder ran through her body. She closed her eyes, unable to meet his. How could she admit that it felt strange, almost frightening, to be making love in the bright afternoon daylight?

Lucia had married young. Young and innocent, married to a boy as young and nearly as innocent as herself, they had taken up the burdens of householding and children almost at once. They had never thought to idle away an afternoon in this fashion; seldom would they have had the time. She didn't know how to respond, what might be expected by a man as experienced and forceful as Mitch.

Between kisses he whispered, "Don't fight me. Just let go."

She opened her eyes, looked at him, and knew that he meant to let go of fear and doubt. To trust. Slowly, watching his eyes, she took his hand and pressed it against herself.

She abandoned herself to him, let him lead, let him explore the rhythms of her response.

The long shadows of afternoon crept along the walls as they lay together, the murmur of their voices scarcely louder than the drone of bees in the garden. Playing, testing, teasing, sharing, allowing unhurried climaxes that came as they would, some wild, some so soft and unexpected that she cried out with surprise.

Love and passion were shared, and a feeling of confidence and belonging. Whatever might be missing in the rest of their relationship, their bodies knew they belonged together.

Chapter Twelve

They had dinner at a place in the Valley where the lights were dim. They blew out the candle so they could hold hands over the table. Lucia ate hungrily. All that activity had given her an appetite, and she felt strong and able and somewhat larger than life.

As she unlocked her front door she could hear her telephone ringing. Mitch followed her as she hurried toward it, pausing only to turn on lights as she went through the rooms. It went on ringing until she reached it and picked it up.

Tommy's voice called impatiently, "Hello? Hello?"

"Tommy, is that you?"

"Mom, where have you been? I've been trying to get you for hours!" her son complained.

"I was out, dear. Has something happened? Where are you? Why aren't you home?"

"Now, Mom, don't get excited—"

"What is it? Is anybody hurt?" Lucia realized she had to stop asking so many questions. The boy could hardly get a word in edgewise. She felt Mitch's presence, and it steadied her; she could feel his support like a helping hand. She took a deep breath and listened.

"Don't get excited, Mom, but it's your car. The clutch is out. Gone. Finished. Done for."

Lucia let out her held breath. "You're all right, then? Everybody's all right?"

"Mom," he explained patiently, "we're in Castaic. The car had to be towed. They towed it here but they can't fix it until tomorrow. Nobody's working this late and anyhow, they have to send to Los Angeles for the parts. We're sitting here in Castaic and we all have eight o'clock classes tomorrow morning. Will you come and get us?"

"Yes, yes, of course." Lucia found a pencil in the clutter on the breakfast room table. "Tell me where you are."

She wrote hastily as he described the coffee shop where they were waiting. He added, "Hurry up, will you? We used about all of our money for the tow and we've already been sitting here drinking coffee for hours and we're about to float."

"You'll just have to sip slowly," she returned. "It's at least an hour's drive. I'll be there as soon as I can."

"It's cool. Thanks, Mom."

She hung up and found Mitch dancing impatiently. "What?" he demanded. "What's going on?"

She giggled a little, mostly from relief. "Nothing earth-shaking. They had me frightened at first, but it's only that the car broke down and Tommy and his friends are stuck in Castaic. I'm going to go and pick them up."

"Castaic? That's fifty miles!"

"A little more from here, I think."

"I'll go with you," he said at once.

"Mitch, that's kind of you." She was checking out the contents of her purse as she spoke. Keys, credit cards, a few dollars in cash. She should change her clothes, put on more comfortable shoes. "There's no need for you to lose a night's sleep just because I have to."

"You shouldn't be out there on the highway alone at night."

She smiled, touched by his concern. "All I'm going to do is drive. Besides, as much as

I would like your company, there isn't room. I'll be picking up four boys and their equipment. They took my station wagon because they needed the room, and now I have to go get them in Tommy's hatchback. It's going to be crowded with the five of us. We couldn't fit you in."

"Four kids! Don't any of them have parents? Why do you have to do this?"

"Well, Craig's mother is sick and—never mind. Take my word for it, every parent of every one of those kids has a good reason why he or she can never do anything. It has to be me. I'm the only one. Give me a goodnight kiss, Mitch. I'll look forward to seeing you next week."

He stubbornly refused her upraised lips. "Well, I'm going with you, and forget that baby hatchback. We can take my truck. It has a camper shell on the back. They'll all fit into that."

Mitch's truck was a big, new four-wheel-drive pickup, the shiny new shell on the back outlined with a festoon of red lights. He parked the Porsche in the garage under his condo and they climbed into the truck and soon they were on the I-5, heading north toward Castaic.

It didn't seem a long trip at all, nestled

against Mitch in the cozy cab of the truck. They were higher than other vehicles, and it gave her a wonderfully superior feeling that she was floating over the humming traffic on the freeway. She felt pampered, cosseted, loved. Caring is close to love, and Mitch cared for her, so thoughtfully, so helpfully. It's a kind of love, she felt.

Castaic was a tiny place, but spread out, and they searched for miles before they found the right coffee shop. The boys were wild with impatience and hunger, so everybody took a break and everybody ate, the boys gobbling hamburgers and pie. Mitch paid.

Tommy and his friends had taken most of their gear out of the ailing station wagon and they were dragging it around with them, bags and sacks and, for no reason anybody ever got around to explaining, a giant cooking pot.

When they had finished eating, the boys loaded it all into the truck, made nests for themselves among the sleeping bags and jackets, and immediately went to sleep. Mitch got behind the wheel again and drove everybody back to Los Angeles.

Each boy had to be driven to his home, of course, where his belongings had to be sorted out and unloaded, and then new nests had to be created for the remaining boys to sit in for the trip to the next place. It was after two when they got to Lucia's.

Mitch helped Tommy unload his things and then, to her astonishment, she heard Mitch firmly inform the boy that Lucia would drive the hatchback to work the next morning. Tommy could either walk to school or find himself a ride. Further, Tommy was instructed to find a friend with a car who could drive him to Castaic after school so he could pick up the station wagon. Apparently overwhelmed, Tommy agreed to everything.

The one thing Mitch didn't mention was how Tommy was going to pay for the new clutch when he got to Castaic, but that was already covered. The intelligent boy had put the wagon into a service station for which he knew Lucia had a credit card.

It is a long week that starts with a tired Monday. Somehow Lucia got through the day at the freight office, so she could begin the struggle to catch up.

Tommy had brought home her station wagon, and with it a shocking bill that was now on her credit card. Lucia put it resolutely aside and said, "It's all right, I'll pay it somehow, but, Tom, you've got to get your car into the garage and have the brakes fixed."

"I'm going to soon as I get the money," he promised.

"No, I mean it. That squeal you were hearing is a lot more than just noise. Your brakes are dangerous and you are to get them fixed tomorrow."

"Mom, don't sweat it. It stops okay if you pump the pedal."

"I'm telling you to get them fixed tomorrow while you're still alive to have it done, and don't ever let them get that bad again. I'll pay for it. Put it on the credit card."

"You're going to have an awful big bill," he warned, "and I can't help out much with it. I'm broke. I spent money on the camping trip and I lost a whole weekend of work and a paycheck."

"Put it on the card," Lucia repeated. "It's cheaper than paying your funeral expenses."

"Okay, Ma."

She then called Terrilee. She confessed to weariness and burnout and begged for additional time to deliver the gowns she had promised.

Terrilee agreed at once. "It's okay. I didn't sell a lot over the weekend; I still have most of your pieces left."

"Aren't they selling?" Lucia asked worriedly.

"It's not the gowns. They're fine. Nothing's selling. It's just the way it is sometimes; I guess all the customers spent the weekend at the beach. They sure weren't here."

"Do you think we should go back to the floats?"

Terrilee brightened a little. "They sold."

"Okay, you were right, Terrilee, and I'll make you some more floats."

Terrilee was pleased and Lucia didn't mind deferring to her opinion. The floats were easier to make than the robes and fitted gowns she had been working on. She could almost make them with her eyes closed, or half asleep, which was about how she was going to have to approach them.

She had three gowns well under way by Tuesday, but she had let most of the household chores slip, and on top of everything, she had to cope with Tommy.

It wasn't just that he was also tired and cranky and had too much to do; she could deal with all that, but she knew she had to tell him about her coming weekend in Acapulco, and she couldn't even find a way to bring up the subject with him.

What gentle way is there to drop a bombshell on your son? When she had blithely said she wanted to shock everyone, the very last person she was thinking of was Tommy, but he was the first one who was going to have to absorb the jolt.

She even considered lying, but besides her distaste for untruths, she could not think of any story to tell him that was not so transparent as to make her ridiculous. Tommy knew she could not afford to fly to an expensive resort for a weekend, and he was old enough to understand what it meant when she allowed a man to pay for her trip. How would Tommy react? She didn't even want to find out.

She was washing dishes on Wednesday night when the doorbell rang. It was Mitch. His truck was at the curb and he stood on her porch wearing jeans and a khaki shirt. His large black boots had buckles on the outside edges of the high tops.

He was smiling. "Hello, Lucia."

"Mitch, how nice to see you! Come in. There isn't anything wrong, is there?"

"Nothing wrong. I was just coming back from Commerce and I had to go through this part of town. I thought I'd drop in and see how you were."

"Commerce, hmm? You're a bit out of your way."

"No, I'm not. When I see the Harbor Freeway, my car just naturally gets on it and heads for the Hoover off ramp."

"How nice of your car to come and see me," cooed Lucia. "Have you eaten yet?"

"No, I just came from work." He followed her into the kitchen.

"Really?" She frowned at his clothes. "Is that how you go to work? In jeans? I thought you were a big, important executive."

"Oh, I am, I am! The oil business is a little different. We have to be prepared for anything."

"Well, you're not exactly prepared for a board meeting," she pointed out.

He laughed. "No, although I have turned up at a couple of them dressed like this. I'm what they call a hands-on executive. That means I'd rather be in the field with the machinery than in the office with the paper and the personalities. Machinery is what I handle the best."

Lucia put a fire under the pot that was still on the stove. "I'm afraid what we have tonight is only stew, but there's plenty of it." She sighed. "I can't get used to cooking for just two people. I'm still making enough for Georgie, too."

Mitch sat down in his usual chair at the

table. "You miss him, don't you?"

"Sure do."

"I came over only to say hi. You don't have to feed me. But I love stew. What kind is it?"

"I call it Instant Replay, because it's a review of everything we had for dinner last week. It came out pretty good."

"Sounds like my favorite kind."

She served him a bowl of stew and some of the fresh bread she had brought from the bakery. He relished it.

Mopping up the last drops of stew with his bread, he said, "This is good food, Lucia. I really didn't come over here to eat. I wanted to check with you about this weekend. Is it still on? Are you going to go with me?"

Lucia answered, "Yes, sure I am."

"That's good. Not going to have any trouble getting away, then?" There was a knowing look in his eye as he added, "Debbie's going to be visiting her mother for the weekend. What's Tommy going to be doing?"

"Oh, I don't know. Just hanging out, I guess."

The knowing look increased, and she had to admit the truth. "I haven't talked to him about it yet."

"I kind of expected that. Lucia, it's

Wednesday. We leave the day after tomorrow. You have to talk to him."

"Yes, I know, but it's hard to find a way to bring it up. It just isn't a subject that often comes up in our conversations."

"What's so hard?" he demanded. "Just tell him you're going to be away. That's what I did with Debbie."

"Easy for you," she scoffed. "You're always on business trips. You take off for Stavanger on a few hours notice. The last time I left town was three years ago, when I went to a wedding in Santa Ana. There's no way he's not going to know that something's up, Mitch. I have to level with him."

"Well, you'd better do it soon. Where is he tonight?"

"He went to a friend's house to study. I'll talk to him, really I will."

She had to get to the gowns, but it was tough putting Mitch out the front door. He didn't want to go, and she didn't want him to, and the kisses grew warmer every time somebody said, "Well, good night, now."

"I don't know if I can wait until Friday," Mitch whispered with a light little kiss to her nose. "We'll be alone together, just you and me."

"No families, no work, just us," Lucia

agreed. "It's not long now."

"Seems like forever. Can't we . . ."

"No," said Lucia.

"I know, but can't we just—" His kiss was urgent, his hands sought the secret places on her body that were well remembered.

Lucia broke from him with an effort. "We are going to have to close this conversation right now. Good night, now."

It was a mistake to use that phrase. Their exchange was long and ardent, and she was disappointed to the center of her being when he lifted his hands reluctantly and said, "You're right. I've got to quit this. Until Friday."

He was off down the walkway and her gowns awaited her and Tommy would be home any minute. But there was nothing but deprivation in her voice when she called after him, "Good night, Mitch."

It was late when Tommy came in and Lucia had already put away her sewing things and was almost ready for bed. So nearly ready that, by hurrying just a bit, she was able to slip between the sheets and turn off the light and tell herself that it was really too late to have serious talks with her offspring. It would have to wait until tomorrow.

Tomorrow would be better, for it would be

her last chance. She wouldn't have a choice anymore and therefore would get the job done.

It started pretty well. She was preparing dinner and Tommy drifted into the kitchen to take a soft drink from the refrigerator. He seemed relaxed and the meal she was cooking was something he approved of. She took a deep breath and began.

"Tommy, if I were to be away for a few days, would it bother you to be here all alone?"

He popped the top of his can. "No, it's cool, Mom. Where're you going?"

"You can have a friend stay over if you like. I'll leave you some ground meat and things in the refrigerator."

But he was looking at her, watching her evade his question. She said quickly, "I'm going to spend the weekend at the beach."

Astonished, he repeated, "The beach? You?"

"Tommy." In her abstraction, she realized, she had grated the carrot and put the potatoes on to boil. Well, she could mash the potatoes and drop the grated carrot into the salad. She found herself saying, "Tommy, Mr. Colton has asked me to marry him."

"Who?"

"I am considering it very seriously."

Tommy put down his soft drink, rejection in every line of his lean young body. "Colton? You mean Debbie's father? I thought you were just making up to him because he has that big truck."

"That's not a very nice thing to say."

Tommy seemed to be trying, in his own frame of reference, to absorb the information. "You mean Debbie would be my sister?"

"And Georgie's, too, I suppose. Then there's Debbie's brothers, Darryl and Jared. They would be your brothers, too."

The thought gave her pause. "Five kids! Thank the saints most of them are too big to live at home!"

"You've got to be kidding!" Tommy's arms waved wildly, like a mechanical doll. "Mr. Colton! You got to be kidding! He's tall as a telephone pole and he's old and he's Debbie's *dad!*"

"There isn't any law against being tall," she protested. "Not the last I heard, anyway."

"What do you want to do it for?" he demanded.

Lucia made a last try for the effective approach. "I see it upsets you to think that I might marry again. . . ."

"Yeah! Again! That's it! You were married once, what do you want to do it for again?"

"I loved your father very much, Tommy, but I'm not dead. I'm a very long way from dead, and it is possible for people to fall in love again."

"So you just go ahead and pick some old guy—"

She interrupted. "Tommy, that will do! I'm trying to talk to you like an adult, and you're acting like a two-year-old."

His eyes were wide with outrage. "Well, I don't mind having an adult conversation with you, but does it have to be X rated?"

"That's enough! This subject is finished! I am leaving tomorrow evening and I will return Sunday afternoon. I'll leave the phone number posted on the refrigerator in case of an emergency, but it had better be a real emergency if you use it."

He quieted his arms by putting his hands into his pockets, his shoulders hunched. "Yeah, Mom."

"There's plenty of groceries around, but if I get back and find the slightest evidence that there has been a party, you will be in a lot of trouble."

A little gleam started far back in Tommy's troubled eyes. He said, "Party?"

"Slightest evidence."

He didn't smile but he straightened a little. "You won't find any," he promised.

He went upstairs and Lucia returned to the meal she was preparing. It wasn't much, but some communication had been established, at least. Tommy loved a party and his friends loved the pure spaciousness of hanging out in Tommy's big house. And they would clean up carefully. When it is called concealing evidence, cleaning up becomes quite glamorous.

Chapter Thirteen

Mitch wanted to leave for the airport at seven although the plane took off at ten.

"The restaurant's good," he explained. "We'll eat there. There's no way you can miss your plane if you're already at the airport, eating dinner. You've got the luggage checked in and the car parked and you can't get caught in traffic or lost on the freeway."

"I don't even get home until six-thirty," Lucia had protested. "I won't have time to pack."

"You should always have your bag packed a day ahead," he lectured.

"Toothbrush and everything?"

"The experienced traveler always has two toothbrushes."

"Not being an experienced traveler . . . I guess I could buy another toothbrush," Lucia allowed. "You know, if I'm going to be all packed, there's no point in going home at all. I could have the suitcase in the car and leave for the airport from work. There's no reason for me to go home. In fact, going home is asking for trouble. There's always a drain stopped up or something when you're in a hurry."

"It's a good idea," he agreed, "but let's not line up a meeting at the airport. There're no good places to meet; everything's too big. We'll end up waiting around for each other and looking for each other and parking two cars. Why don't you come over to my place when you finish work? It's just up the hill from your office. We'll take the truck to the airport and leave your station wagon in the garage at my place."

Lucia packed the little weekender bag that was nearly new. The only place it had ever been was Santa Ana. She put in all her best things: the blue silk dress, a colorful caftan, a couple of swim suits, and one of the slinkiest nightgowns she had ever designed. Also a new toothbrush.

She dressed herself in a practical knit suit that could take a beating and never whine or wrinkle and she kissed Tommy goodbye before she left for work. It made the workday very long, for she had felt as if she were leaving on vacation when she got into her car in the morning, and it was an anticlimax to find herself sitting behind the familiar desk. Same old office, answering the same questions on the same phone.

She was delighted when Georgie called. He came in on the eight hundred line, for her son had discovered how to phone his mother from San Jose without paying a charge.

"Georgie! How nice to hear your voice!" And how nice to talk to a son who wasn't sulking. She didn't have to tell Georgie about her plans for the weekend.

"How you doing, Mom?"

"Just fine. Everything okay with you?"

"Great! I got a new car! Turned in my old Beetle."

"Turned it in? Oh."

"You didn't still want it, did you? I needed it to trade in and anyhow, it was up here and I couldn't figure out how to get it down there so you could have it."

"Hold the wire, I have to take another call." She had planned to make some sort of a deal with Georgie for his old car when he was ready to sell it. The tough, frugal Beetle was more economical to run than her station wagon, and more reliable, even though it was somewhat older. Well, too late now.

She finished the other call and got Georgie back. "How are you getting along?"

"Great, but it's cold! Boy, does it ever get

WINGS # 606
82 SOUTH LUMINA AVE.
WRIGHTSVILLE BEACH, NC 28480
919-256-2696
505 CASH-1   1515 0606 002

INVENTORY	MDS 1	3.99
ITEM # 1		
INVENTORY	MDS 1	3.99
ITEM # 1		
INVENTORY	MDS 1	9.99
ITEM # 1		
INVENTORY	MDS 1	9.99
ITEM # 1		
SUBTOTAL		27.96
"6%N.C. TAX"		1.67
TOTAL		29.63

CASH TENDER   50.00
              CHANGE   20.37
THANK YOU FOR SHOPPING AT WINGS
PLEASE COME AGAIN!
RETURNS MUST BE MADE WITHIN 30 DAYS
OF PURCHASE!!
THANK YOU FOR YOUR PATRONAGE!

6/12/94 10:45

cold early up here! Will you send me my ski sweater? You know the one I mean, with the reindeer on the front?"

"Sure, Georgie." Why couldn't it wait until he made his visit home, only two weeks off? Well, two weeks is a long time to be cold, and it was just possible that Georgie wanted to impress somebody. A gorgeous hunk was her Georgie, and he looked terrific in that bulky sweater. Or maybe he had changed his plans for coming home?

She asked, "You are going to be here for Tommy's birthday, aren't you?"

"Wouldn't miss it. I'll be there Friday, two weeks from today. Is everything okay, Mom? You're still my best girl, you know."

"Oh, that's too bad!" said Lucia. "Look, I have another call coming in. Write me a letter, will you?"

She had her desk cleaned up early and was out the door on the moment of quitting time. She drove up the hill to Mitch's home and was so prompt that they arrived at the same moment, Mitch's truck following her up the last section of the road. They both parked on the street across from the garage entry and Mitch jumped out of the truck.

Lucia started to laugh, for Mitch was not ready to go anywhere. He had obviously just finished some messy job and his clothes were covered with greasy black blobs. Even his face was dirty. Crude oil? Something crude, certainly.

She leaned over the wheel, helpless with laughter. He ran over and stuck his head in her window. "Don't kiss me," he warned. "I'm dirty."

"Are you? I would never have noticed. About that dinner at the airport . . . Can we have separate tables?"

He laughed his easy laugh. "I just got back from Long Beach. We had some pipeline trouble. It won't take me long to clean up. Put your car in the garage, slot eighteen."

He returned to his truck to push the secret button that opened the garage gates, and then he followed her in on foot. The sun was almost down, and she had to turn on her headlights to find her way in the dark and cavernous garage.

She parked in the slot and Mitch led the way to the staircase. "Watch your step in here. It sure is dark. They ought to turn the lights on earlier. A person could trip over a Volkswagen."

As they entered the condo he asked her, "Can I get you a drink?"

"No, I don't think so, yet."

"I'll go shower, then. Be ready in twenty minutes."

"Okay." Lucia picked up a magazine and began thumbing through it as Mitch left. She would have liked to follow him and see the rest of the condo and Mitch stripping for his shower, but she knew she had better stick with the magazine. To let her thoughts run along the line of being in Mitch's bedroom while he undressed could lead to missing their plane.

The magazine was boring. Probably something of Debbie's; it had a hundred and fifty pages and most of them seemed to be about painting fingernails. She could hear water running in the bathroom that was on the other side of the downstairs bedroom. Then the phone rang. And rang. And rang.

From the bathroom, Mitch called, "Get that for me, will you?"

She would have protested, but she didn't think she could shout loud enough. Probably he wasn't listening anyway, but had his head back under the water. He would never hear her. Besides, the nonstop ringing was getting to her, too.

She picked up the receiver and said, "Hello?"

A breathless, girlish voice said immediately, "Who's this?"

"Lucia. Who's this?" she countered.

"It's Ione. Let me talk to Mitch."

Ione. The ex-wife. The children's mother. Now, what was she going to say? It would hardly do to blurt out, "Sorry, Mitch is in the shower, getting ready for our flight to Acapulco tonight."

She also discarded, "No, Ione, this isn't how it looks. I came over here only to park my car."

Very briefly she was tempted to say, "No spik English. Am coming to cleaning house only."

What she did was answer carefully, "Mitch isn't available right now. Can I take a message?"

"Will you see him soon? This is important. Write it down. He has to get over to the Medical Center at UCLA right away. Darryl's there and they keep calling me to sign something so they can operate."

"Darryl? Is that your son that goes to UCLA? What's wrong?"

"He's not sick," Ione insisted, "but if he is, he ought to be with his mother. You tell Mitch to get him and bring him to me right away."

"He's not sick, but he's in the hospital?" faltered Lucia, trying to figure it out.

"I've been trying to get Mitch for hours. He's got to get over there; they don't listen to me."

"I'll tell him, of course. Do you have any names? Who is calling you?"

"Poconasky. Dr. Pocosinsky."

"Poco—How do you spell that?" Lucia was

making distracted squiggles on the pad by the phone.

"I can't spell it, but that's what it is. Please, will you tell Mitch right away?"

"Yes, of course I'll tell him."

"And have him call me as soon as he has straightened Dr. Pocosanasky out."

"Okay, Ione. I'll do that."

She was still scribbling on the pad when Mitch came up the stairs, drying his ears with a towel. Another towel was wrapped around his waist, exactly as one of hers had been on Saturday night. She wished he hadn't done that. It brought back so sharply her memories of Mitch on that night, the urgency of his body, the sweetness of his mouth on hers, that her fingers grew nerveless and the scrap of paper she was holding fluttered to the floor. She felt almost as if she were back on the service porch at home and Mitch was about to take her in his arms and his kiss would be insistent . . .

He bent and picked up the paper. "What was that all about?"

"It was Ione. She says your son Darryl is in the hospital and he isn't sick but somebody has to sign a paper so they can operate. That can't be what she said; I must have gotten it wrong."

"Probably not. Sounds like a pretty typical Ione conversation. What else did she say?"

She said the doctor is named Poconasky or Pocosinsky and you had to get right over to the UCLA Medical Center and straighten them out and bring Darryl to her if he's sick."

"Well, I can't do that; we have to catch a plane."

"But, Mitch, maybe something is happening to Darryl. She can't be just making the whole thing up. It sounds as if he were the prisoner of fiends."

"Oh, probably somebody did call her, but it's hard to say what it would be about. Ione's a little excitable."

"But what if it really is something?"

"I guess we could look into it," he said reluctantly. "UCLA isn't far out of the way when you're on the way to the airport from here. I'll be ready in a few minutes and we'll drop in and make sure the kid's all right." He came closer and put his arms around her, tickling her ear with a kiss. "And then I'm going to have you all to myself for a whole weekend in Acapulco. I hope you don't want to do much sightseeing."

"I want to see everything," she replied firmly, but she put her arms around his waist, feeling his body against hers, feeling his skin, warm and faintly damp from the shower. "Do you want me to pack your shaving things for you?"

"All packed. I travel so much, I've got two of everything."

He was efficient. In minutes he had his clothes on, in a few more he had checked the locks and temperature settings in the condo, then he picked up his bag and they were on their way.

At Westwood they left the freeway and drove to the Medical Center. Mitch was easing the truck into a parking place when he asked suddenly, "Suppose he is sick?"

"Ione said he wasn't."

"Then why is he here? Dammit, I wish she would check these things before she calls me."

They got out of the truck and together hurried into the building. The receptionist recognized Mitch's name right away.

"Oh, Mr. Colton! Dr. Posanski said I was to page him if you showed up. He's in the cafeteria."

"We can go down there," said Mitch. "Don't drag him away from his food."

"No, he said to page him. Please wait here."

In a few minutes the doctor appeared. He was short and almost square, bearded and feisty. He fixed Lucia with a cold eye and said, "Well, it's about time you got here, Mrs. Colton!"

Lucia would have explained who she was,

but before she could frame a word, Mitch rose from his chair. He towered so high over the doctor that his view must have been chiefly of the little man's bald spot.

Mitch roared, "I'm Darryl Colton's father. What's wrong with my son?"

The doctor regarded him with surprise and a slightly exaggerated craning of his thick neck. He said, "Appendicitis. Very acute. He should have been operated on hours ago, but we had to wait until you came and signed the papers because he isn't of age."

Mitch's face seemed to crumple as the doctor spoke, and he whispered, "He's of age. He's nineteen."

"He is? He said he wasn't. At any rate, sign the paper now and we'll begin at once. I was going to do it as soon as I finished dinner anyway. He's an emergency."

He waved at the receptionist. "Will you bring those forms over, please?"

Mitch's face was still crumpled, but he was getting bigger and taller by the minute. "Appendicitis? Isn't that dangerous? He must be in pain. Why have you waited so long if it's dangerous? Why didn't you operate at once?"

"When the kid is under age, we have to have consent from at least one of his parents."

"He is not under age! Why did you think he

was? Why didn't you ask him how old he is?"

"We did, of course, but he's under sedation. Maybe he didn't understand the question."

"Well, why didn't you just look up his records? You must have records. Doesn't anybody keep records in this university?"

"I can understand why you're upset, Colton—"

"Upset! I'll say I'm upset! Why does my kid have to suffer for hours just because nobody here is efficient enough to look at his records? How did this whole situation get started, anyway?"

The doctor shrugged a little impatiently. "He didn't report that he was sick. He's been walking around with appendicitis for at least a week because he didn't want to miss any school."

"Sounds like Darryl," Mitch admitted grudgingly.

The receptionist handed the doctor a form, and the doctor passed it to Mitch. "Here it is. If you'll just sign right here—"

"I don't need to sign it! He's an adult according to the laws of California!" Mitch grabbed the paper. "But if it will speed things up and get you moving, I'll sign it. I'll sign anything. Just get your butt in gear and start doing something for him!"

He scrawled his name on the paper. The

doctor took it, took the pen, and offered both to Lucia. "Mrs. Colton?"

"I'm Lucia Morgan," she replied firmly.

"You don't need any more signatures!" Mitch roared. "You have mine; it's more than enough. Get on with your job!" Then he added in a lower tone, "Can I see the boy?"

"You can have a few minutes while I'm scrubbing. But he's been sedated; he might not be able to talk to you."

"That's okay. I . . . just want . . . to . . . see . . . him." Mitch hunched his shoulders, his face crumpling again.

The doctor asked, "You, too, Miss . . . er . . . ?"

Lucia declined. "I'll wait here. He doesn't know me."

Mitch followed the doctor out and she sat down to wait. She sat, she squirmed, she sighed. She struggled to get through a chunk of that particularly thick time they have in hospitals.

Her heart went out to Mitch when he returned. He looked whipped. He sank down beside her on the thin little couch.

"He looks so bad, Lucia. So pale and sick. His eyes are all funny, sort of glazed over. He opened them and said, 'Hi, Dad,' and . . ." Mitch's eyes were wide with the fear that a strong man knows only for someone he loves. "Oh, Lucia! People can die of this, can't they?"

"He won't! It's all right!" She put her arms around him.

"Why did Ione say he wasn't sick?"

"He probably wasn't when she saw him last." He rested his head heavily on her breastbone. "If anything happens to him —"

"Hush, darling. He's in good hands. This is a great hospital; these people are the best."

"I sure hope their doctoring is better than their paperwork."

"It's all right, Mitch. It's going to be all right." She cradled his head against her shoulder, crooning empty reassurances, and they sat like that for a long time, his head heavy against her, his breath warming her skin through her blouse.

At last he stirred and said wearily. "I've got to find a phone and call Ione. She ought to be here."

"Yes, you should do that."

He wandered off and she returned to looking at the magazine. It was true that Ione should be there. She should have been there several hours earlier. Ione had definitely dropped the ball, and Lucia wondered why she was constantly leaping to the other woman's defense.

It was a natural mistake Ione had made, and

Dr. Posanski's bedside manner probably irritated his patients into getting well, but there was no reason for Lucia to try to make Ione look good. She didn't even want Ione to look good. Her needs would best be served by an Ione who was a witch and a dolt, and physically unattractive besides. Lucia sighed. Being a mother is likely to cause one to be unnecessarily tolerant of other mothers.

She tossed down the magazine, which seemed to be a twin to the one she had found in Mitch's apartment. At length he returned and sat down stiffly beside her.

Lucia asked, "What did she say?"

"She figures if she starts now, the operation will be over before she gets here and she wants to know right away how it comes out, so she's going to stay home until I call her and tell her he's okay."

"I can understand that."

There was a long silence, and then he added, "While I was at the phone I called the airline and canceled our reservations."

"Oh," said Lucia, fighting down her disappointment and an irrational sense of betrayal. "Of course you had to do that. We could never catch that plane now."

"We'll go next week."

"About this time next week Darryl will be

250

getting out of the hospital and you'll have to take him home with you. He can't go to his dorm, and his mother's place in Oxnard is too far for 'im to travel. We'll have to make it the week after—Oh, no. Not that weekend. It's Tommy's birthday, and we always have a family picnic. Georgie's coming home for it specially; I haven't seen him since June. I can't be away."

"All right, three weeks from tonight. I'll take care of the reservations first thing Monday morning."

"Cross your fingers whi'e you're making them," Lucia suggested with a feeble flash of humor. "It's a well-known scientific fact that illnesses in children are caused not by germs, but by the possession of reservations on the part of the parents."

"I have observed that," he admitted with a small smile.

They talked about their plans for Acapulco in a desultory way, then sat for a while, so silent as to seem almost sleepy. They talked some more and then were quiet again.

At last the doctor strode back into the room. He wore his green operating-room suit, the comical cover still on his head, the mask dangling under his chin.

He was smiling.

He said, "Well, you almost lost your boy. It

was real close. He's doing fine now; they're taking him down to recovery."

Mitch seemed too overwhelmed to say anything, so Lucia answered for him, "Oh, thank you, doctor!"

Posanski's smile was almost smug. "You two are really lucky to still have your son." He strode away.

Mitch said to his retreating back, "But she's not his mother—" But the doctor was already out of sight. Mitch asked, "Why doesn't that man pay any attention?"

"I think he pays attention where it counts." Lucia laughed with pure happiness and hugged him. "Oh, Mitch, isn't it wonderful? Darryl's going to be okay!"

Mitch's look was bemused rather than joyous. Lucia thought probably his feelings were in confusion. If she felt this tremendous relief and gladness for a boy she did not know, whose face she had never seen, what must his father be feeling?

Mitch was starting to smile. "How long do you think he'll be in recovery? We should have asked."

"I don't know. I think it takes hours, and you can't see him until after."

"Let's go find somebody we can ask."

"Why don't you phone Ione first? She's waiting for your call."

"Yeah, I'll do that."

Lucia thought she could not bear any more of this waiting room. She said, "I'll go with you."

They went into a corridor that gleamed with cleanliness. Looking down the bright length of it, Lucia suddenly realized that the young girl walking toward them was Debbie. Debbie saw them at almost the same minute and rushed into Mitch's arms, wailing, "Oh, Daddy! What's happening to Darryl?"

Mitch caught her in a massive hug. "The operation's over and he's doing fine." Over Debbie's glossy brown curls he looked at Lucia and smiled swiftly, almost as if he were apologizing for the mist in his eye. Could he think that she of all people did not know the pure flame of love for one's own child, and how it sears the heart?

"Is he going to be all right?" the girl asked.

"Fine, just fine. Where's your mother?"

"Oxnard," the child replied, disentangling herself from her father's embrace and preparing to resume her adolescent dignity. "Didn't she tell you she wasn't going to come?"

"Yeah, but I thought since you were here, maybe she had changed her mind."

"Changed her mind? Well, you know Mother.

253

She changed her mind about eight times, until I got tired of waiting for her to settle on something and just got in my own car and came here. Mother likes to dither around until she's decided what the wrong thing to do is, and then she does it."

"Now, Debbie . . ."

"Well, why is she making such a big deal out of driving down here? It's an hour, and that's if you drive slow."

"Something you are never guilty of," he teased gently.

She seemed back to normal, and a dimple sparkled in her cheek when she smiled. "Oh, Daddy, you know I never go more than fifty-five."

He agreed firmly. "I have never known you to go faster than that in the parking garage. It's when you get out onto the street that I start to worry."

"Oh, Daddy! When can we see Darryl?"

"I'm trying to find somebody I can ask right now. Why don't you go phone your mother and I'll see what I can find out. The phones are right over there."

"Oh, well, okay," Debbie agreed, and turning, almost ran into Lucia.

Startled, Debbie said, "Oh, Mrs. Morgan! I didn't see you standing there."

She meant that she did not expect to see Lucia standing around at all. Lucia said with as much noncommittal calm as she could muster, "Good evening, Debbie."

"Go make your call," Mitch urged, "and after we've seen Darryl, we'll all go to dinner. I can't even remember when I ate last."

He got hungrier before he was at last allowed to see his son. The visit he and Debbie were allowed was short and may or may not have done Darryl good, but it definitely cheered Mitch. He reported that Darryl was groggy but entirely coherent and demanding that somebody bring him his schoolbooks.

Debbie had called Ione, and she rolled her eyes in exasperation as she reported Ione's latest decision. She had decided to drive to L.A. the following day, since, should she start at once, Darryl would surely be asleep by the time she arrived to visit him.

Lucia commented, "She's probably right. He would be asleep."

They ate in Westwood, which was lit and lively despite the lateness of the hour. The restaurant was comfortable, reasonably quiet, and apparently accustomed to families that dined at midnight.

Their mood was joyous and quickly warmed to hilarity. They laughed and teased and truly enjoyed being together. Debbie was a delight. She was funny, affectionate, and charming. Lucia thought wistfully that it would have been nice to have had a daughter.

Mitch and Lucia ordered coffee, but Debbie didn't want any and said she would go home to bed. She meant Mitch's home, for it was too late for her to return to the sorority house, and too far to go back to Oxnard. They were quieter after she left, dawdling over coffee and trying not to think of tropical skies and the weekend they had missed.

They drove back to Mitch's place, still quiet, tired, and thoughtful, her head on his shoulder. When they arrived at the condo, Mitch touched the button on the dashboard and the garage gates slid open. They drove into darkness.

"Look at that!" Mitch complained. "There's supposed to be lights down here all the time. They must have blown a fuse."

Muttering about the inefficiency of the management, he followed his headlights to his own place in the garage. It was filled, of course. He had three slots, and his Porsche occupied one, Lucia's station wagon the next one, and Debbie's compact the third.

"I see Debbie got here," Lucia commented unnecessarily.

"There's nobody around this late," he said. "I

can just leave the truck here in the traffic lane and I'll park it after you leave. Do you want to come upstairs for a while?"

Lucia shook her head. "No, it's really very late. Time we both went to bed — I mean, it's time we got some sleep. And I wouldn't want to disturb Debbie. She's had a big day, too."

He agreed, "Yeah, not much point in dragging it out now."

They got out of the truck and he followed her over to the station wagon. When he pulled her into his arms they forgot for a precious moment that the night had turned cold, forgot their disappointments and worries. His lips on hers told her a wordless story of his longing, his thwarted expectations. She laid her head on his chest and suppressed a sigh.

"Good night, Lucia."

"Oh, Mitch . . ." She had the keys in her hand, but she went on standing there, leaning her head on him.

"Yeah, I know. We would have been in Acapulco by this time. We'd already be in the hotel, in bed."

"And sound asleep," Lucia added mischievously.

"Maybe." He kissed her again, his big hands crumpling her jacket. "Lucia, I need you with me."

"I've got an idea." With swift gestures she selected a key, opened the back of her station wagon, and pulled down the gate.

"In there?" Mitch grinned in the darkness. "That's something kids do, and spoil their clothes."

"Let's spoil a few." Lucia climbed in, throwing down her purse and overnight bag. The floor of the wagon was soft with a litter of sleeping bags that Tommy had forgotten to remove.

Mitch hoisted himself in after her. "I can't believe this. I'm forty-eight years old. I'm a vice president. I've got stocks, bonds, four cars, and a condo. I've got a tax accountant, a secretary, a broker, and a tailor, and I'm making love in the back of a car."

Lucia flipped one of the bags open. "It's the best offer you're going to get tonight. Take it or leave it."

"Oh, I'll take it." He closed the gate and crept across the sleeping bags, feeling for her. He encountered a leg and groped it, then eased himself down beside her and found her face with kisses.

A chuckle rumbled upward through his chest as he nuzzled in her hair and pressed his face to her neck, drinking in her warm female scent. He said, "You know, there's something exciting about being this sneaky. Makes me feel like a kid."

"Did you do this a lot when you were a kid?" Lucia asked, mocking her own unreasonable prick of jealousy.

"Hell, no. Those days, I couldn't even afford a car."

They warmed each other with caresses, fumbling around the frustrations of their clothes, sharing the rapidly growing heat of their bodies. It was a small victory when he worked his hand under all the layers of her jacket, sweater, and blouse to touch the sensitive round of her breast.

They pulled off only enough of their clothing for practical purposes, for it was surprisingly cold, and anyhow, undressing was difficult in the confined space. Each bared such a small area that when at last Lucia's hot skin touched Mitch's, the connection was electric. They clung together, all the passion of two bodies concentrated on that one spot, that little patch of incandescent heat where they joined together.

She felt his hands, his lips, she knew the exciting, rutting smell of him, but only peripherally. Everything was secondary to the window, that one small opening where passion was free to meet passion, love could join with love. She quivered under him, sobbing his name, devastated with the force of her feelings, overwhelmed with the strength of his.

The old wagon was drafty and it was too cold for them to lie there long. She pulled herself away from Mitch with reluctance, rearranging her clothes.

He felt for his trousers in the darkness and groaned, "Lucia, we've got to be together, and I don't mean like this."

"It wasn't so bad," Lucia pouted. "I kind of liked it."

"I enjoy everything I do with you, but why aren't we ever enjoying something that's supposed to be a pleasure?"

"Our turn's coming," she promised, and prodded him gently in the ribs. "Now, come on and get out of my station wagon. I have to go home."

Chapter Fourteen

She really was tired, Lucia realized as she wrestled the station wagon down the dark, twisting road that led away from Mitch's place. The wheel felt sluggish in her hands and her eyes burned. She touched her face and felt cold tears on her cheeks, and wondered why she was crying. For Acapulco? Was she crying with disappointment, like a child?

It was only because she was tired. Tired, and, yes, disappointed. Disappointed enough to cry.

She told herself she was being ridiculous. She was a grown woman, and quite old enough to know that for good or for bad, tomorrow always comes. She would have her tomorrow with Mitch.

The wagon reached level ground, so much

easier on old brakes and joints, and Lucia sat back to drive it in her usual calm and confident manner. She would feel better when she got home. She was feeling better already, driving the easy, familiar neighborhood streets.

As she turned onto her own block, headlights flashed in her eyes. She slammed on the brakes, but the other car was not moving. It was parked on the wrong side of the street with the lights on bright.

Shaken, she lifted her hand to shield her eyes from the glare, and then she could see the light bar on top of the vehicle, flashing red and blue.

Police. Wasn't it interesting, thought Lucia, that light bars have a code of their own. Police light bars are red and blue, fire trucks are red and yellow, and an ambulance is red, with flashing red lights on the sides.

And wasn't it interesting that there were all three in the driveway of her house.

Her hands were suddenly numb and shaking, but Lucia managed to park her car at the curb and she jumped out to hurry up the sidewalk toward her home. It was, it couldn't be anything else but a fire truck under her living room windows, lit up all around the top, lights endlessly rolling and flashing. The ambulance was in front of it with a second police car straddling the sidewalk at the ramp. Radio chatter bounced from one to another, bored metallic voices in the dark.

The two police cars were pointing their lights at each other, creating a lighted space in which uniformed men milled about. There was a boy bent over the hood of the first car, his arms spread wide, his head turned toward the policeman who questioned him in a low voice.

It wasn't Tommy. It couldn't be. But where was he? Nervously, she glanced at a group of neighbors gathered on a lawn across the street. They seemed to be just standing there. Her gaze shifted to the roof of her house. No flames leaping. Then to the ambulance. The doors were closed, they had not wheeled out a gurney. Where was Tommy?

She moved toward the house and it seemed as if she toiled through molasses, her movements unbearably slow, for she was pushing through a terrible fear, pushing toward one even more terrible.

There were perhaps a half-dozen boys standing on her lawn, chatting pleasantly with a policeman. She thought she saw, yes, one of them was Tommy. Truly Tommy, his stringy body intact, his hand, in characteristic gesture, brushing back his hair as he talked.

There was a policeman standing in her way.

A big, bulky one. He said, "Why don't you just move on, lady? There's nothing to see here."

"I'm Lucia Morgan, and this is my home," she replied. "What has happened?"

She had caught his interest. "This is your house?" He pointed toward the street. "Is that your kid?"

"Of course not." Lucia forced herself to look at the frightened boy on the hood of the squad car, and she did not know him. He had the face of a stranger, but there was something familiar about the motorcycle that lay on the sidewalk near him. She knew in her heart it was the same boy who had tuned that same motorcycle under her window two Sundays before.

She said, "I never saw him before. What did he do?"

"It was a high-speed pursuit," the cop replied. "Jumped a signal on Jefferson and made us chase him all the way here. If you don't know him, why do you think he came to your house?"

"Had to go someplace, I guess," Lucia replied. "Do I have this right? This whole mess has nothing to do with me, you just happened to stop that boy in front of my house?"

"He sure acted like he was coming here," the

cop argued. "Tried to make a high-speed turn into the driveway and flopped. That's when we caught him."

Her relief was so strong, it was turning into irritation. She said sarcastically, "That must have been some high-speed chase. Jefferson isn't ten blocks from here, and he couldn't have flopped at much of a speed, or he'd be spread for about half a block. You're a real bunch of heroes, stirring up the whole neighborhood because some kid jumps a signal on his motorcycle."

"I didn't say he was on a motorcycle," the cop observed shrewdly. "How did you know that?"

"It's lying right there on the sidewalk," Lucia pointed out. "What was I supposed to think he flopped, a Rolls Royce? Or maybe a military tank, from the number of people you have turned out to catch him."

"Sure we sent for backup units," he said truculently. "We've got to protect ourselves. Don't you think we have families to look out for, too? He could have had a weapon."

"Yes, that's true." Lucia was suddenly contrite. Policemen are only mortals, and for all his overblown bluster, this one was a man earnestly doing his best with a nasty job. She asked, "Is it all right if I go to the house?"

He shrugged and she went up onto the lawn where the boys stood with another policeman. She heard Tommy's surprised voice, "There's my mom!"

The lawn cop turned and regarded her with that analyzing look that cops have. She was suddenly aware that her clothes were crumpled, her hair and makeup surely a mess. What was he seeing? Did she have the look of an alley cat just before dawn?

She restrained the impulse to straighten her jacket and said calmly, "Good evening. I'm Lucia Morgan. Are my son and his friends being detained for some reason?"

The lawn cop smiled a charming smile. "No, I was just talking to them."

"I've been with a sick friend and I had no idea all this was going on," Lucia explained. "The other man said it was only a traffic offence. Is that really true? All these vehicles?"

That charming smile again. "Just routine. When there's a pursuit, they have to send for backup; those are the rules, and they have the paramedics come in case somebody gets hurt. This time of night the paramedics won't go out without the fire truck, not in this neighborhood, anyway. It does look like kind of a lot. Sorry if it scared you. Is your sick friend all right?"

There was a sly look in his charming eye as he said this. Lucia drew herself up and reported, "The doctors at the UCLA Medical Center saved his life, I am very glad to say. May the boys go inside with me now?"

"It's okay."

"You go ahead, Mom," Tommy suggested. "We're going to stay out here for a while."

Lucia replied in a voice that was gritty with purpose, "You are all going inside because you have to get your things together, as you are all going home immediately. Move!"

She stalked toward the house, followed by a train of subdued boys. The house looked about as she had expected. Every light was on. In the breakfast room an elaborate card game was laid out on the table. The kitchen was cluttered with soda cans and sacks of chips.

One of the boys was saying, "We got to tell Jayce's folks. Somebody's got to call them."

Lucia turned blazing blue eyes on him. "That boy is a friend of yours, then? He was coming here?"

Tommy said, "You know Jayce, Mom. All he did was go out for more beer, and—"

"Beer!" Lucia's voice rose. "You bring your friends in here and drink beer when all of you are under age and then you arrange to have the lawn covered wall-to-wall with cops? Were you born this dumb, or have you had to acquire it?"

"I didn't know he'd bring the cops back," Tommy whined.

Another small voice added, "We'll help you clean up, Mrs. Morgan."

"Oh, no, you won't!" Tight and high with rage, her voice did not even sound like hers. "You're leaving. All of you. At once. And nobody's going to help me clean up, because Tommy's going to do it all. Now, get your stuff and get out!"

The boys began picking up their belongings, shambling around the room with maddening slowness. Somebody said again, "We should call Jayce's folks . . ."

"It's the only thing we can do for him," Lucia agreed. She picked out the boy who had made the suggestion. "You can do it, Craig. You can call them from your house after you get home."

"Why me?" protested Craig.

"Because!" Lucia explained. "And you're not going to phone from here, because you're all leaving right now! I don't want to see you. Just get out!" She didn't want to think about Jayce's parents. Just the idea of them filled her chest with a ball of fear, the fear that was fueling her anger. Fear of the disaster that had brushed by, so close to her. Fear, and the sure knowledge that only a fine line separated her from the mother who was about to be wakened with the news that she was going to have to go searching for a lawyer and a bail bondsman in the middle of the night.

Tommy said, "Mom, will you cool it, please? We haven't done anything. We were just playing Illuminati. . . ."

"Don't you tell me to cool it! All I did was turn my back on you and you're consorting with criminals and turning my home into a scandal."

"What did you come home for?" he demanded. "You said you were going away for the weekend. If you'd stayed away like you said, all this would be over and you never would have known anything about it."

"Never know!" she shouted. "All my neighbors are standing out there in their pajamas, watching Lucia get raided, and you think I'd never know? The police are going to have me on their list of people who ought to be watched forever, and you figure it would be okay if I never know? Illuminati! You get yourself into that kitchen, and I don't want to see a dish or a crumb—"

The phone rang. Lucia's voice ground into silence at the suddenness of it, and she remembered at once that as usual, Mitch was waiting for her to call him and report that she was home safely. He must have gotten impatient and worried and decided to call her. One of the boys reached for the phone, but she stopped him.

"I'll get it. It's for me." She picked up the receiver and snapped into it, "Forget it, Mitch!"

She would have slammed it down again, but she could hear him. She could hear Mitch's dear voice, calling her name.

"Lucia! Lucia, what's wrong?"

The concern in the voice went straight to her heart, or maybe it was her tear ducts, for tears were suddenly spurting from her eyes. She held the receiver to her mouth and sobbed, "Nothing's wrong except I'm through. I quit! I can't take this anymore!"

"Lucia, what happened? What did I do that was wrong?"

"You didn't do anything, but there's no way things can ever be right for us. I don't have room in my life for a relationship. I haven't even got time for one!"

"Lucia . . ."

"You haven't got time, either. You haven't got time for me. Neither of us has time for Acapulco. It just isn't going to work."

His voice was urgent. "Lucia, you stay right where you are. Don't do anything. Just wait for me. I'll be right over."

"No, Mitch . . ." But she was talking to the air.

It didn't matter. Nothing mattered. Mitch was lost to her. The light and joy he had given her were gone, and her life would go on without it. It was gone, her last chance for warmth and sharing.

And love.

She could feel the tears pouring down her face, and she became aware of a semi-circle of boys staring at her. They were all so similar in size, clothing, and facial expression that she had trouble picking out her own child. They looked frightened, eyes round as grapes. Obviously, they thought something was wrong. They might even have observed that she was upset.

She swallowed the tears that clogged her throat and said sharply, "I told you guys to leave; I'm sure it was a half-hour ago, and you're still here. Scram!"

The timid voice again said, "Mrs. Morgan—"

"Out!"

The boys scampered. Lucia added, "Not you, Tommy! Get in that kitchen!"

271

The boys gathered up jackets and books and trailed to the door. She followed them and looked out. The ambulance, the fire truck, and one of the squad cars were gone. The street was quiet and dark except for the dome light in the remaining squad car, which stood in the same place as before. Jayce sat in the backseat with a cop, still answering questions.

The boys climbed into a car that was at the curb, and in a few seconds it pulled away, just as Craig ran from the house, shouting, "Hey, guys, wait!"

Lucia regarded him sourly. "Craig, why are you still here? I meant for you to go with the others."

"Well, so did I!" he reported, outraged. "We all came in the same car, and they just left without me! Can I use your phone?"

Lucia held her head. "Oh, Lord!" She went inside and raised her voice to shout down the hall. "Tommy! Craig needs a ride home!"

Tommy came from the kitchen. "What?"

"Craig needs a ride home. I have to move the station wagon anyway and I'll— No, I won't. You will. You take the station wagon— It's down the street a ways . . . and drive him home and when you get back you can put the wagon in the driveway."

"What about—"

"You can finish the kitchen when you get back."

"Okay, okay." Tommy dried his soapy hands on the back of his jeans. "Jeez, it's like the army around here."

The boys left, and Lucia was grateful to notice that the police car was also gone. The neighbors had returned to, presumably, their beds, and the street was back to normal.

She was weary, so weary. She had to lift each foot consciously, first one and then the other. Lift, step, lift, step. She was in the breakfast room and could not remember why she had gone there. She wanted something. What was it?

She wanted Mitch.

She didn't have Mitch anymore, but she thought that if she could just lie down and rest, she would be able to bear it. Failing that, she could sit down. On the window seat or in the chair? She stood between them and couldn't decide. The chair or the seat? Through the miasma of grief around her head they both looked equally unattractive, and she was too tired to decide. She sank down on the floor.

What a relief! The rug felt soft and inviting and she stretched out on her back. At last she had reached a place where she could cry, and the ball in her chest demanded that she cry. Quiet tears ran down her temples and into her hair.

After a while she heard Mitch calling her name but she refused to answer. He was there, right in the breakfast room. She must have left the front door unlocked.

She said feebly, "Go away, Mitch."

"Lucia!" He dropped to his knees beside her and began chaffing her hands. "Lucia, what happened?"

"That's just it. Nothing happened."

"Then why does this place look like a tornado went through it?"

"Tommy had a few friends over," she replied in that same faint voice.

"Where is he?"

"He drove one of them home. The kid lives in Glendale."

"But what happened to you?" Mitch asked, feeling her forehead. "Did you faint?"

"No, I'm just resting."

"On the floor?"

"I'm too tired to go to bed."

He put his arm around her shoulders and pulled her up. "Come on, Lucia. You're being silly." He hoisted her onto the chair and she lolled there, regarding him with eyes sticky from tears.

"It's no use, Mitch."

"I think you need a drink. Where do you keep the liquor?"

"I don't need anything. The cupboard next to the refrigerator."

He went to the kitchen, and after a minimum of crashing about returned with a bottle and a glass. "Is this all you've got?"

"Cupboard next to the refrigerator? That's it, then."

He shoved aside some of the Illuminati tokens to put down the bottle. "I didn't even know they made plain-wrap brandy."

"I use it only for cooking. I don't want anything, Mitch. I told you to go away. It's no use anymore."

He poured brandy into a stemmed glass he had found in the cupboard. "That's what we have to talk about. What do you mean? What's happened to make you say that we're through?"

"I keep telling you that nothing's happened. Nothing's changed; nothing can change. We can't change our lives and we can't make things different."

She took a sip of the brandy and it was harsh. "We're locked into what we are: parents, householders, workers. We can't fly to the moon with all that baggage, or even to Acapulco."

"I'm sorry about what happened to our trip . . ." he began.

She finished for him, "But we'll get another chance. Maybe we will, and maybe we'll take it, but we shouldn't. Think about it, Mitch. Suppose we hadn't been here tonight? Suppose our plane had taken off at six instead of ten? What would have happened to Darryl?"

"But we were there."

She took another sip of her brandy. She felt calm. Empty but calm. Everything was so much clearer, so much easier since she gave up. Her duty was evident now, but the tears went on dribbling down her cheeks and plopping into her drink.

She went on. "Have you ever heard it said that to have children is to give hostages to fortune? Well, we have given hostages, and fortune doesn't want us to be together."

"That's nonsense."

"The truth often is."

Somehow as she was talking she had emptied her glass. It did make her feel better. She felt so much better that she smiled and would have sauntered off someplace, but when she tried to stand, her legs gave way under her. Mitch was right there and caught her in his arms.

For a moment he held her against him,

warm and cherished against his heart, then he scooped her up as he had the night of the burst pipe and carried her upstairs. She didn't kick this time, but rested in his arms as light as the fluff of a dandelion. What a luxurious way to go upstairs! She wondered if she could patent it.

He kicked open the door of her bedroom and deposited her on her bed. She lay quietly while he wrenched off her shoes and pulled the spread up over her. She was still wearing her sweater, jacket, and all the rest of her clothing, but she felt entirely comfortable. She burrowed into the pillows and said, "Leave me alone, Mitch."

"Lucia, you are overtired, hysterical, and overreacting," he pronounced. "You lie there and get some sleep—"

She interrupted, "Oh, Mitch, I loved you so much! Why couldn't it have worked for us? All we needed was a miracle. Couldn't we have had just one little miracle?"

"I'm going, Lucia."

"That's right. Go away and don't come back. It was a lovely dream, but it's over."

He waited a few seconds, watching her, listening to her breathing, and then he went out.

As he quietly closed the door, she raised herself up and yelled, "Leave the door on the latch so Tommy can get in!"

Well, that was a dumb thing to say. She burrowed again into her pillows. He would have to leave it on the latch, of course, for he had no key with which to lock the deadbolt. Even as she thought it, she heard the front door slam and knew it was Tommy, not only by the sound of his heavy feet but just because Mitch would have closed it quietly.

When her child is home, a mother can sleep, and she did. She drifted in and out at first, with the odd feeling that she could hear voices and dishes rattling in the kitchen. Of course she could not hear anything from the kitchen, which was downstairs and across most of the spacious house from her bedroom, but somehow she knew that Mitch and Tommy were cleaning up, and talking together as they worked. She wasn't really hearing it, but she felt the quiet, low-keyed tone of that male exchange.

Chapter Fifteen

She made breakfast for Tommy in the morning but they didn't talk much. She said she was sorry for yelling and he apologized for having such careless friends, but she didn't ask him about Mitch. Tommy even volunteered to clean up the kitchen. Maybe he felt a proprietary interest in it after the magnificent job he had done the night before.

She left it to him and went upstairs to her workroom where she laid out as many gowns as could be cut from all the silk remaining in her store. Terrilee had been flexible with her; the least she could do was make her a lot of gowns. She cut eight items, six gowns and two robes. She was assembling the robes when Mitch came.

She had not heard him arrive and did not even know he was in the house. It did seem that he and Tommy had come to an understanding. She was basting the elaborately-seamed sleeves of a robe, and she looked up and there he was.

"Hello, Mitch."

"Are you all right?"

"Yes, thank you." She went on basting. "You were right, and I was overtired. A night's rest has done me good. How is Darryl?"

"He's fine. Trying to get the doctor to write him a prescription for schoolbooks, since they won't let him have them."

"Oh, that's cruel! He should have them if he wants!"

"I took care of it."

"I'm glad you did."

He sat down in one of her chairs, looking big and relaxed and clean and cheerful. He raised quizzical eyebrows and said, "You said some wild things last night. Do you even remember?"

"Of course I do." Lucia went on basting. "I meant every word I said, but it was kind of you to come by and tell me about Darryl this morning. I was concerned about him."

"Aw, come on, Lucia. You said we were through and you didn't have time for me. You didn't mean all that."

She lifted her calm blue eyes and held his tawny brown ones for a minute. "Yes, I did,

Mitch. It's all true. We're not free and we're not children who can do just as they please and take what they want when they want it. As deep as my feelings are for you, I cannot and I will not neglect my duties to my children."

He stirred restlessly. "You say *children* as though you had a houseful of babies. Tommy's just one kid, and a pretty sensible one at that."

"I have two children. I didn't disown Georgie; he just got a job."

"He's taken charge of his own life, which is what he ought to do, and Tommy will be doing the same thing in a couple of years. Then what will you have if you've spent your life on your duties to your children? You were worn out last night, exhausted. You didn't mean the things you said. You don't want to change things for us, for you and me."

"Yes, I did. The way I exhausted myself was trying to keep up with my children and your children and us, you and me, all at the same time. I lost control and it was not a pleasant experience. It's not going to happen again."

"Well, what about me?" he demanded. "You know I need you. Do I get to live out my life all alone just because our kids have gotten into a couple of jams lately and it's been a lot of trouble getting them out?"

"We both have commitments to honor. Old ones. Maybe we don't have the right to make new ones."

"Lucia, I'll protect you from my kids! We've got to be together."

"I suppose I could simply ignore the needs of your children," she mused, "but you can't. What kind of together would that be?"

He got up and paced around the workroom, tiny scraps of discarded fabric squashing under his shoes. "The problem is that you're trying to do too much. You were overloaded before we ever met, so probably you can't take on anything new. But why does it have to be me that gets eliminated? You could get rid of something else. Get some help in the house or hire a gardener or—" His eyes darkened and a twist of anger flickered across his face—"or you could stop making those goddamn gowns!"

He snatched the fabric that lay across her lap and threw it down. Grabbing her wrists, he pulled her to her feet. His arms around her were like steel bands, and he pulled her to him, stifling her protests. "Lucia, you come alive when you're in my arms."

He brought his mouth down on hers, so swiftly that she was still standing there, her head thrown back and her mouth slightly open, when he caught her with that hard, insistent kiss. His lips quivered across hers in the way she remembered so well. His hand caressed her back and then dropped lower, gathering her against him, and she relaxed into his kiss, feeling his hard chest, his thighs against hers.

"This is what's real," he murmured against her mouth. "This is what matters, and it's solid enough to build a whole life on, but you have to have the courage to start a whole new life. Oh, look at us, Lucia! We take fire if I just touch you. You can't just throw it away."

She disentangled herself from him, a little surprised that he let her. "It's true I can't help responding to you," she admitted, her voice almost as calm as before. "And it's unfair of you to remind me this way."

"I don't care if it's fair or not! I want you!"

"I want you, too, Mitch." She bent and picked up the sleeve she had been working on. "But I don't know if it's right for us to take what we want. I also don't know if the gowns are the basis of the problem, but I will consider it. I am considering a lot of things. I doubt I am going to change my decision, but I am doing a lot of thinking."

"Love isn't rational," he said stubbornly. "Come on, Lucia, fly to the moon with me!"

"And we'll come down in time to visit Darryl in the hospital? Mitch, can't you see that it just doesn't work? What will it take to convince you? Do we have to have a real disaster? We brushed close two times last night. Two times, and I got hysterical. I'm ashamed of that, but I don't really think I need to apologize for it."

He spread his big hands helplessly. "Lucia, what do you want me to do?"

"Leave me alone, Mitch. I want to think about my life. I want to think about you and me. I want to think over a period of time, without pressure from you, and decide what I will do. You confuse me. Being with you is intoxicating, and this is too important a decision to make drunk. I want you to go away. You have things to do for your family, and I'm going to make some gowns."

"How long?"

"I don't know."

"Well, it better not be too long!" he said angrily. "I'm not a kid and I don't have unlimited time to wait around while you decide it's safe to love somebody!"

He did leave. He thumped down the stairs two at a time and slammed the door as he went out. After his Porsche had pulled away from the curb, the stench of burned rubber hung in the air for a long time.

She cried some, careful to wipe away the tears before they stained the silk she was working on. She wondered if he was right. She wondered if last night was just a freak, a set of coincidences that could not be repeated.

And yet, how could she take the chance?

On Sunday Tommy helped her reseed the lawn, for the burst pipe had left large bare patches and the feet of the policemen had tamped them down. Tommy was agreeable and extra helpful the whole week. He was also very quiet, hardly having anything to say. That was all right because she was quiet, too, thinking a lot and also because she had an embarrassing tendency to burst into tears. She cried the day Mitch sent flowers. She cried the next day, when he did not.

He called on Thursday and opened the conversation by saying, "Hello, Lucia. Are you hungry?"

"Hello, Mitch. You weren't supposed to call me, but since you did, thank you for the flowers. They are beautiful."

"In that case, how about having dinner with me?"

"Mitch, you know I can't do that."

His voice took on a small edge of irritation. "Why not, Lucia? A steak isn't going to kill you."

"I'm not going to see you, Mitch. How is Darryl? Is he recovering all right?"

"He's doing fine; he comes home tomorrow. Why can't you see me? Just a dinner. You have to eat."

"Darryl's coming home, Mitch. You haven't got time for me, as I haven't got time for you. Please don't call anymore." She hung up gently and cried so much that her tears must have fallen into the quiche she was making for supper, for it separated in the oven.

Tommy was working on a project and spent a lot of time at the lab, including most of the ensuing weekend. Lucia sewed.

Sunday evening Mitch phoned again. "Let me come over," he begged. "Oh, please let me come over to your place!"

"Mitch, I am getting so tired of saying I can't see you!"

"Then stop saying it and let's go to dinner. I've got to get out of here; you wouldn't believe how noisy it is!"

"Noisy? I thought you were taking care of a sick boy."

"I am, I am! And do I ever have a lot of help! Debbie is here, and so are about six of her sorority sisters. Every half hour one of them opens Darryl a can of soup. He has maybe six of his friends from the dorm visiting him to bring the lecture notes and stuff, and they're interacting with the girls and everything in the kitchen is covered with bowls of soup and please, Lucia, have mercy on me!"

She didn't laugh. She even managed to make her voice severe as she said, "You just can't take me seriously, can you? You won't believe I meant what I said. I don't have time and neither do you. I don't want the kind of relationship where we just meet now and then, when we both have the chance to put our responsibilities aside for a few hours. Just a few laughs and maybe a quick roll in the hay. If I didn't care so much for you, maybe that would be okay, but I want more from you, and I want to give you more than that."

"I can't figure out how this got to be a problem. If we both want to give—"

She interrupted. "The problem arose when I ran out of resources. I have to figure out how I can give to you, and to the rest of my commitments, without being torn apart. I need time and I need to be free from pressure."

She took a deep breath and ignored it as he tried to say something. She finished firmly, "You will please respect my wishes and stop calling me. Good night, Mitch." And she put the phone firmly into the cradle.

And cried.

She worked on the gowns every evening, and it pleased her that she seldom thought of Mitch when she was cutting and sewing. Other times, of course, she thought about him constantly. Working, cooking, driving . . . His image came often to her mind, but the concentration necessary to create her increasingly elaborate rainbow stripes kept her mind from wandering.

She finished the robe-and-gown sets and sent them to Terrilee, using a friend who had volunteered to make the delivery for her. It seemed an imposition, but Lucia had to remember that she couldn't do everything. "Learn," she told herself sternly, "to accept help when it is offered."

Later that same day, she was washing the dinner dishes when the doorbell rang. She ignored it, for Tommy was at home and it was probably one of his study buddies. She heard him go to the door.

A few minutes later there was the sound of young voices and feet approaching, accompanied by an odd scratching sound on the bare wood of the hallway. Tommy ushered Debbie into the kitchen, and she had the dalmatian puppy on a leash.

His coat was shiny white, the black spots standing out as if backlit. He was yanking at the leash with puppy enthusiasm at the opportunity to explore a new place.

Lucia knew immediately what the problem was. No great mental feat; it wasn't hard to figure out.

Debbie said, "Hello, Lucia."

"Hello, dear." Might as well get right to the point. Lucia added, "What a charming little dog!"

Debbie brightened perceptibly. "Do you like him? It's the one we bought to give to our adviser, but it turned out she couldn't keep him. Her apartment building doesn't allow pets. So she gave him back to be the mascot for the Alpha house, but all he does is go around chewing things and spoiling the rugs and I have to get rid of him."

Lucia went on washing dishes. "That's too bad. What are you going to do?"

"I thought you might like to have him, since you've got this big house and all. . . ."

"He's very cute, but I decided years ago that I can't keep pets. It isn't that I don't like them, but it's wrong to have an animal if you can't take proper care of it and I don't have the time. It would be a prisoner, not a pet."

The dog scurried about, tangling his leash in the table legs and the legs of the chair where Debbie sat. Her expression was turning sulky. "Okay, that's your answer. Does Tommy get to say what he wants?"

"Don't look at me," Tommy said.

She did, anyway, big melting eyes holding his. "Oh, Tommy, won't you take him? I've asked practically everybody I know."

A look like that has ruined stronger men than Tommy. Lucia said quickly, "If you need any help making your decision, Tommy, be advised that I will accept no responsibility, not even temporarily, for the care and feeding of anything that's not of my own species."

"Even if she won't help you, you could take care of him, couldn't you?" Debbie asked.

There was bitterness in Tommy's voice. "You just don't get it, do you? My mom doesn't have time for a dog, and neither do I. I'm carrying sixteen units, and if my grades go down, I lose my scholarship. I have to work two nights a week at least to support my car. You wouldn't know anything about that, would you? Your dad bought your car for you, he pays for the insurance and even the gas. Well, I get to do all that for myself."

Lucia murmured, "I really don't do it to build his character. It's not the principle of the thing, it's the money. If I could, I'd do exactly what Mitch does."

"We don't have time for puppies," Tommy repeated. "Take him back to the house and let the Alphas look after him. None of them have to work their way through school."

A tear formed at the corner of one of those melting brown eyes. "You don't need to talk to me like that, Tommy. It's not my fault my dad has money."

"No, I guess it isn't."

"I only thought you might help me."

"Help you? Sure, I'll do that. That's what friends are for, isn't it? Just don't expect me to take him myself."

Debbie smiled, sunshine after the rain. "You will help me?"

"I'll help you, and we'll find a good place for him."

Lucia suggested, "Why don't you take him back to the kennel where you bought him, Debbie? They might even refund some of your money."

"I tried that, but they said they couldn't take him back because there was no way of telling where he'd been and what germs he'd picked up and what awful things I'd been feeding him. He might be coming down with something that doesn't show yet."

"They could take him back. They're just trying to get more money out of you."

"You could put an ad in the paper," Tommy

said. "Say you'll give him to a good home."

"What will I do with him until somebody answers the ad?" Debbie asked. "I can't take him back to the house. The girls won't let me."

"What about your dad's place?"

"I just came from there. Dad said if I ever brought that dog back inside, he'd wring its neck and maybe mine, too. That was right after it ate a hole in his Italian leather couch."

"I think I know somebody," said Tommy. "Come on, we'll take your car."

"Can't we take yours? If you go very far, he throws up on the seats."

"Yours."

The kids had barely left when the phone rang. Of course it wasn't Mitch. She had told him not to call and she would be very annoyed if he did. It was Terrilee.

The booming voice filled the receiver. "Lucia! I got the gowns you sent over with that friend of yours. She going to deliver regular for you now?"

"No, but I didn't have time and she owed me a favor," Lucia murmured. "Didn't you like the gowns?"

"They're fine, fine!" Terrilee shouted uncertainly. "Only—"

"Only what, Terrilee?"

"Only I've got so many rainbow gowns,

they're starting to call me the rainbow lady! Stop already! No more rainbows! A customer came in today, looking for a present for a bridal shower, and I lost the sale because I didn't have enough to show her that's white. Make me some white things like you used to, Lucia! For brides! That's where my business is."

"Brides? Okay, Terrilee. I'll make you some white things, but please don't hold me to a deadline. I'm planning a big weekend."

"You are? Doing what?"

"We're having a picnic. Georgie's coming."

"Georgie? Your son Georgie? That's not a big weekend. That's a family weekend. Are you sure you know the difference?"

"To me there isn't a difference. What have you been doing, Terrilee?"

They were laughing together by the time they hung up, but something about the conversation reminded her that she missed Terrilee. They had always used the delivery of Lucia's gowns as an excuse to have a visit, and Lucia regretted sending the last batch with a proxy.

Well, there was a way to fix that. She put together a couple of white gowns, liquid satin in a classic pattern. They were finished by Thursday evening, so she hung them on the rack in the station wagon, picked up a cheesecake at the bakery, and drove over to Terrilee's.

She caught Terrilee just closing up, as usual, and they hung up the gowns in the store, all as usual.

But when they opened the door to Terrilee's living room, a spotted streak attacked Lucia's ankles. She exclaimed, "It's the pup!"

Terrilee picked up the dog and it wiggled in her arms, frantically trying to lick her face. "Cutesy itto t'ing!" she cooed. "Mustn't jump on Lucia and spoil her stockings!"

Lucia put down the bakery box, pushing it to the center of the table. "The kids gave that dog to you?"

"Wasn't that thoughtful of them? He'll grow up to be a fine watchdog, and I really do need one around here at night. I don't know why I didn't think of it before."

Lucia observed the cuddly thing that was frolicking in Terrilee's lap. "Oh, he looks like he's going to be lots of protection."

"Even Arnold Schwarzenegger was a baby once."

"What's his name?"

Terrilee ducked her head and Lucia could almost have thought she blushed. In a small voice she admitted, "Spot. It wasn't my idea, the kids named him. I couldn't change it because he already answers to it. See?"

She put the dog on the floor, held out her hand, and said, "Here, Spot." The puppy playfully attacked the outstretched hand, and Terrilee said again, "See?"

"He'll be ready for obedience trials in no time," Lucia assured her.

Terrilee gave up patting the dog and said only a little sarcastically, "Okay, tell me about this big weekend."

"Georgie will be here Friday sometime," Lucia related, sliding the cheesecake out of its box. "He's taking the day off to drive down. Saturday we'll have the picnic at the beach and Sunday he drives back to San Jose."

"The beach? Good God, woman, it's November!"

"It's still nice at the beach. We've always gone there on Tommy's birthday. It's sort of a tradition."

"Tradition to freeze your butt off? Sometimes I wonder about you, Lucia."

"The water's cold, but it's nice on the sand. Nobody goes swimming."

"Oh, I see. Just a tradition to have sand in your food. What about you and Mitch?"

"That was a quick change of subject."

"Not really. Isn't Mitch what you came over here to talk about?"

Lucia pushed cheesecake onto a pair of

plates. "Oh, well, to tell the truth, we had a falling-out."

"Yeah, I know."

"You do?"

"Mitch told me when he took me to dinner Sunday night. So why were you keeping it a secret?"

Lucia rose, looking dangerous. "You have been dating Mitch? You, Terrilee? Why would you do such a thing to me?"

Terrilee shrugged, looking not the least bit guilty. "So, one dinner. He did it only because he knew if he took me out, it would get back to you. I knew that. He knew that. You know that."

Lucia was not mollified. "You rat! You sneak! Behind my back you go out with Mitch?"

"Lucia! Calm down! You want a cup of coffee?"

"No! I want an explanation!"

Terrilee began forking up her cheesecake. "Sit down, Lucia. I'm not trying to steal your guy. What do you think? He called me up and said, 'Let's go to dinner, I'm hungry and I need a friend.' And told me you had just turned him down. So why wouldn't I go? He was a perfect gentleman. He even agreed we could meet halfway, in Van Nuys. That's what a smart woman does, you know. Then if the guy gets pushy, she's got her own car right there in the parking lot. I made him take me to Shain's. Why not? He can afford it."

Lucia snapped, "I don't care if it was harmless. It was a low thing to do. You know how I feel about Mitch!"

"So why aren't you dating him? He's nice and he's got money and he's single and he's really cute. What's wrong with you?"

Lucia sat down slowly. "What's wrong with me? People seem to be asking me that a lot lately. What's wrong is, I feel pressured from every side. I know I can't stall forever. I have to make a decision soon. I just don't know if I can do it all."

"All what?"

"All the adjustments. All the compromises. I haven't been a wife for ten years. I guess I did okay with it the first time, but can I do it again? Now? Starting all over when I'm forty-five years old? How can I give a marriage the attention it deserves? Where would I get the time?"

"You, Lucia, you're saying you've got no time for love? Give me a break. You make time for love, that's where you get it."

"I don't know, Terrilee, I just don't know about marriage, and I just don't know about Mitch."

"Well, you'd better decide pretty quick. There's plenty of women around, and they aren't all perfect ladies like me."

"I appreciate it that you were a perfect lady," said Lucia, "but I still don't know. I just don't know."

Chapter Sixteen

Georgie's new car was red and had a number instead of a name. The upholstery was charcoal, the windows black, and wind dams under the bumpers gave the whole thing the outline of a flying saucer or of a machine for vacuuming the streets. Tommy and his friends went wild over it, exclaiming, admiring, begging for a chance to sit behind the wheel. It was the chief topic of conversation throughout dinner and most of the evening that followed.

Lucia had created a menu that incorporated all Georgie's favorite dishes, and cooked everything ahead so it would be ready when he arrived on Friday afternoon. With careful planning, when she got home she had only to warm things up and serve the meal.

There was a crowd for dinner, for Georgie was already holding court among his friends and Tommy's, all of them hyperactive with delight at having their prince among them again.

She was delighted with him herself. Georgie was handsome and big, bigger than his brother, bigger than his father had been, as if he were some modern achievement, a triumph of science. His hair was black and wavy and his eyes were as blue as Lucia's and it was so good to have him home again. To a mother, the return of a child who has been away is more thrilling than a visit from royalty. Lucia knew for certain that it was better to see Georgie at her door than, say for instance, some prince of the blood or even the Queen of England herself.

On Saturday they drove to Zuma Beach and held the picnic in celebration of Tommy's birthday. It was a warm day, although the evening would probably be chilly.

Georgie went ahead in the red car, crowded with friends and, of course, his brother. Lucia followed in the station wagon. It was loaded with food and the coolers of soft drinks and a couple of boys who couldn't be crammed into the sports car. They viewed parents as they would visitors from a far country; except for a few phrases of greeting they had no common language.

The day was fine but the water was cold and rough and only a few hardy souls swam in it. The boys clowned around for a while, then tore into the picnic lunch she had prepared. It was remarkable how swiftly they could demolish her hours of careful preparation.

Georgie initiated a game of Frisbee that involved throwing the Frisbee toward the water and the guy who failed to make a catch had to go in and fetch it. Lucia joined the game for a time, and even waded after the only throw she missed. But she was wearing shorts and a shirt and she did not want to get wet, and somebody had to clean up the remains of the feast, so she went up the beach and started packing the picnic things.

Craig was still eating and she gathered a few remaining treats for him to finish off. Craig's home situation was enough to make the angels weep, but there wasn't anything she could do about it, except maybe feed him. His most endearing quality was his steady appreciation of her cooking. He would eat anything if Lucia cooked it. Leftovers were never a problem when Craig was around.

Lucia emptied the water from the coolers and packed the rest of the equipment inside them, ready to be carried to the cars. Then she sat down to watch the boys run around. She was nursing a little feeling of being left out, of being the person who came to the party for the purpose of bringing the food.

Well, they could have bought sandwiches at the delicatessen and left her at home; they knew how to drive themselves to the beach. She had planned the party and volunteered the food, but she had no real function at this affair, and she found that she resented it.

She felt uncharacteristically sullen, annoyed at the boys, the fun they were having, their exuberance, the very redness of Georgie's car.

For sixteen years she had worked and kept Georgie in school. She had struggled, sewed, pinched pennies, helped and encouraged him, fed him, all with one goal in mind — that he would complete his education and qualify for the kind of job that would enable him to afford some of the goodies of life, like a red sports car. And there he was, healthy and solvent and laughing as he chased the Frisbee through the foaming surf. Why did she resent that? It wasn't his fault that she had to worry about the funny sound in the engine of her station wagon and wonder how much it was going to cost her.

She was tired. She had worn herself out again, staying up late, on her feet in the kitchen preparing the picnic that probably would have been just as good from the deli.

Why was she here at all? She could be in Timbuktu, for all they would notice.

Or Acapulco.

She shook away the thought. Of course, the whole point of the weekend was to spend some time with Georgie. He had driven five hundred miles to see her and would drive five hundred back the next day. He could have taken a plane, of course, but maybe it was more fun to drive the distance in a new car while listening to a stereo that alone had cost more than she earned in a month. Yet somehow she had pictured this visit as a little more personal than watching Georgie thunder by in pursuit of a Frisbee. She had imagined talking to him about Mitch and the decisions she must make regarding him, and getting fresh ideas, her grown-up son's up-to-date slant on her situation.

To her surprise, Georgie broke away from the game and came up the beach to her, almost as if her thoughts had summoned him. He rubbed a towel over his ebony curls as he thumped down on the blanket beside her.

"I'm telling you, that water's cold!" he said, laughing. "You're smart to stay up here out of it. Are you having fun?"

"Of course," she replied automatically, but then decided she didn't need to create social

303

lies for Georgie. He had always been a perspicacious boy, his sensitivities scraped raw by the early death of his father. She had tried to let him have a childhood, but always she had sensed that he felt responsible for her and Tommy.

She amended, "I confess I'm finding it a bit slow up here." Lucia reached out and smoothed his hair, ruffled by the wind and the towel. "You could do with a haircut."

He moved closer to her and began massaging her shoulders as he always used to. "Boy, are you stiff! Why do you get so uptight when you're fixing food?"

She leaned into the pleasure of strong fingers soothing tired muscles. Georgie had always been a cuddler. She thought of the fat, smiley baby he once had been, and the joy returned in her heart, the fierce joy of loving one's child.

He was older now than his father had been when he and Lucia first met. He was like his father in some ways, but more like her side of the family. Actually, his resemblance to one of her cousins was striking.

She was getting sloppy and sentimental, Lucia told herself, mooning over those long-gone days when she was the mother of babies and the wife of someone who cared for her and looked after her.

She said, "I miss you since you went away, Georgie. Your brother is a dear boy, but there are times when a person really needs an adult to talk to."

"Boy, do I know what you mean!" His body was glowing with warmth from the exercise and still damp with cold salt water. He had finished the massage, but he kept up a pretense of rubbing her back, just to maintain the contact.

"Do you need somebody to talk to, too?"

"Sure do!" he replied. "Being in a place where I have to make all new friends is the pits! I've made friends, of course, and some of them are great, but they aren't my old friends, you know what I mean?"

"Are you sorry you took that job and went so far away?"

"No, not really. It's exactly the job I wanted and pretty soon I'm going to be at the place where I can level with my new friends, but that hasn't happened yet. Sometimes I get so lonesome, I wish I were back here, where I could talk to you!"

Lucia smiled, warmed by even so mild a compliment. "I miss talking to you, too, Georgie. You've always been understanding. Maybe I have asked too much from you, but I always

305

felt we could be honest with each other, even when you were just a little boy."

He grinned at her. "Yeah, we've got something special. Most guys can't talk to their mothers, but you're different."

Well, that was even better. Lucia said, "Maybe we were too satisfied with each other. Now that you're away, I find myself lonely at times and I think it would be nice to have somebody to talk to. Do you know what I mean?"

"Do I know! A guy has to have somebody to talk to. A guy needs a girl, and the girl I need is a sexy little bundle named Ellen."

"Is she somebody you met up north?" Lucia asked hopefully.

"You know Ellen," he replied impatiently. "You met her . . . oh, a couple of times."

Lucia tried desperately to remember. Ellen, Ellen. Was that the one with her hair in spikes, or the one that wore lace mitts with her leather jacket? Or was that the same girl? Maybe Ellen was the one with all the dirndls. She murmured, "Oh, yes, Ellen."

"I come all this way and she won't even see me. Says I'm G.U."

"G.U.? Is that catching?"

"Stands for geographically undesirable," he explained. "Wouldn't you think she'd think

306

enough of me after all this time to make a few allowances? You aren't here to take a girl out every Saturday night, she forgets all about you."

"Maybe I can relate to how she feels," Lucia allowed. "It isn't any fun to have a romance with a man who isn't in town very much. Out on the rig, like—"

"Well, it isn't like it was just something minor!" her son interrupted indignantly. "I was almost going steady with Ellen!"

"Almost? Did you have some sort of an understanding?"

"That's a good word for it. Understanding. I thought she understood that if everything went along okay after we both got out of school, we'd be engaged to be engaged."

"Oh, that's very serious stuff!" said Lucia. "You were thinking about thinking about getting married?"

"Sure I was! I thought probably someday we'd get married, and now she won't even talk to me. She's never home when I phone her. She can't stick to anything for a minute!"

"Maybe you're lucky. Who'd want a wife who can't concentrate?"

"Aw, Mom!"

"You know, there are occasions when I think about marrying myself."

Her understanding son agreed. "Yeah, it sounds so great. Having somebody to talk to, somebody who's always with you and shares with you and cares about you . . . And then the girl says you're G.U.!"

Lucia leaned her elbows on her crossed legs. "You know something, Georgie? You blew it."

"What?"

"You had your chance and you blew it. What's-her-name . . . Ellen liked you fine when you were here in town, but you were so afraid of commitment that you ran all the way to San Jose without asking her to marry you. You went away to a place with a million new possibilities and forgot that you were leaving her here with just as many. If you want something, son, grab it when you have the chance. If you are in love, grab that person you love and don't let anything on earth stop you."

"Well, gee, Ma, I don't know if it was all that flaming an affair. I kinda thought we were in love, but maybe we weren't, not enough."

"Enough! Enough? If you have to wonder if it's enough, of course it isn't. How fortunate that you are out of the whole thing!"

He put his chin on his knees. "Maybe so, but I feel like I lost something. How are you going to know when you've met the right person?"

"You just know. You just know that you have to be with that person because nothing else is ever going to make you happy."

The afternoon wind had begun to blow and the boys were coming up the beach to search for towels and shirts. Lucia stood up and began handing them things to carry to the station wagon.

She said, "You know, Georgie, this has been a very instructive conversation. It certainly is good to have an adult to talk to!"

She pushed the old station wagon unmercifully on the way back to town. She could hardly wait to get home, where her telephone was, so she could call Mitch.

She got Debbie, who put down the phone and disappeared for what seemed like a very long time. She could hear music and voices in the background. At last Mitch picked up the phone and cried, "Lucia!"

"Hello, Mitch."

"Lucia." His voice dropped as if he were trying not to be overheard. "Lucia, I'm glad you called."

"I called for a purpose," she said. "I have to tell you that I've been a dolt. I should have listened to you; we belong together. I don't know how we're going to work it, or when, but I need to be with you."

309

"Hold everything," he said. "Don't move a muscle. I'll be right over."

"No, don't do that, Mitch. This house is full of boys, and the way I feel about you, I'm afraid I'd set them a bad example."

"This place is full of boys, too, and girls and a dog and I don't know what all else."

"Surely you didn't get the dalmatian back?"

"No, this is another dog. I'll be there in five minutes. We'll take a ride."

"Five minutes! Don't drive that fast!"

"Five and a half, then. Wait for me!"

Lucia put down the phone, feeling familiar pressures. She ought to put on some fresh clothes. She ought to straighten the house a little if she was going to have a guest. She should tell the boys that Mitch was coming. . . .

Ought. Should. Lucia looked at the crowd of boys milling around her breakfast room. Whom was she kidding, to think she could get them to straighten up the place? She would be lucky to get their attention long enough to tell them anything at all. They were planning a snack of toasted cheese sandwiches with bacon, a project that always left the kitchen a shambles.

She called gaily, "I'm going out for a while, guys!" and hurried out the front door.

Her timing was about right. She had waited only a few minutes before Mitch drove up. He was in the truck, she was surprised to note, not the Porsche. Whatever. She jumped in.

"Drive, Mitch, drive!"

He chuckled and put the truck in gear. "Do you feel like getting away from the kids for a while, too?"

"They're like the ooze from outer space. I know I'm going to be swallowed up by it any minute. Drive faster! I can feel it nipping at me!"

"You want to hear something wonderful?" he asked her. "Listen!"

"I don't hear anything."

"That's it! No kids yelling, no dogs barking, no music. Especially no music."

She agreed. "Isn't it funny? I used to like music."

"I still do. I just don't like what the kids play."

"I don't think they do, either. They just play it because it grates on our nerves."

"Oh, that couldn't be true, Lucia. An industry worth billions with no purpose except to annoy parents?"

"Exactly. Where are we going?"

"I'm not locked into anything. Just driving. You hungry?"

"No."

"I've got just the place, then." He turned the truck swiftly and headed for Hollywood. At the next stoplight he turned to her and said, "Lucia, it's so good to see you."

He was smiling, that smile that was so right, because it was exactly the way Mitch smiled. She thought it must be engraved on her heart. He bent his head and kissed her, but she pulled back and said, "The light just turned green."

"Just wait," he chuckled, and put the truck in gear. He turned up a steep street beyond Hollywood Boulevard.

Lucia asked, "Are we going to your place?"

"It's in the neighborhood, sort of. It's a little road running off Nichols Canyon. The view is great."

It was, too. The road dead-ended on a mountain and all Hollywood was spread at their feet, a million lights glittering in orderly rows.

Lucia marveled, "Look at that! Somebody even has searchlights up! It looks like a postcard!"

"It is one," he deadpanned, and put his arms around her. "Lucia, I've been half-crazy waiting for you to change your mind. Is it really true? Are we on again?"

She kissed him briefly, just long enough to feel the sweet familiarity of his mouth on hers. "I don't know how we're going to work it or what we're going to do about the kids, but yes, we're on. Life isn't worth anything unless I'm with you."

He held her against him, kissed the side of her neck, and whispered, "I never canceled our Acapulco reservations."

"Well, you were sure of yourself!"

"More like I didn't give up hope."

"Really, can we still go? We can go next weekend?"

"I'll have you to myself for two whole days."

"I hope they don't have any telephones there."

"They don't, I promise."

"Oh, I wish we were there now!"

He squirmed guiltily. "Well, I hate to suggest this, but it does seem to be the most tactful thing when we're in town and so are all our kids. . . ."

"The back of your truck? Let's go. I hope you have a sleeping bag or two back there."

"Oh, I thought of everything," he promised, and when she crawled through the tailgate, she discovered that he had.

He had had the camper shell carpeted. The sides and roof were covered with shag, the truck bed was soft as a mattress. From the truck he used to haul equipment to the rig sites, he had created a cushy boudoir. The windows were one-way glass and didn't even have to be opened for ventilation, as there was a sunroof on the top.

She laughed as she sank into his arms. "All this and Acapulco, too! I'm glad you kept hoping!"

She felt safe in the upholstered darkness of the truck. Safe and free from the danger of interruptions. Safe in Mitch's embrace, for surely he loved her, to upholster for her. Is carpeting a sign of love?

She was still wearing the shorts she had put on for the beach, and he slipped his fingers up the leg opening, because he knew how it excited her. In the years ahead, how many such tricks might he learn, what power might he gain over her? Moreover, she thought as she tugged at his shirt, what might she do to him? What might they do together, two powers in tandem?

All she had to do was trust. She knew he could bring her to ecstasy and knew she could trust him to give her fulfillment, even before his own. She arched herself back to receive him gladly, her moans of pleasure swallowed by the heavy carpeting around them.

314

Afterward she clung to him, her face pressed against his neck. He smelled excitingly of himself and of the secrets of love. She murmured, "What a wonderful truck. I wish I could ride in it forever."

"After a trip to the moon and back," he mused, "I wonder if I should have it lubed."

"It doesn't take engine grease to sail on magic seas," she chided.

He said wistfully, "I wish we could run away together. Just take the truck and drive."

"I'd be good at that," she sighed, for he was reminding her of the real world. "Running away is what I'm doing right now."

"How about Alaska?" he pursued. "We'll follow the pipeline as far north as it goes."

"Maybe we could get snowed in," she said hopefully.

"We could go someplace where it's absolutely certain, like the North Slope."

"Just you and me, alone together. The Garden of Eden, with icicles." The wheelwells bulged into the bed of the truck, and, upholstered, they made perfect backrests. She sat up and leaned against one of them, stretching long, bare legs in front of her.

It felt so good to be with Mitch again. He had been so patient while she sulked. She didn't count his dinner with Terrilee; after all,

315

patience wasn't his thing.

Or was it? How patient he was with Ione, who had treated him so badly!

He moved to sit beside her, a strong, hairy leg nestled against her smooth one. He whispered, "I probably will have to go to Alaska on business in a month or so. . . ."

"Practical again!" she groaned. "You even have practical fantasies!"

He stroked her gently, his fingers remembering the beloved curves and hollows of her body. "The most practical thing of all would be for us to get married."

She shifted, a little uneasy. "That's what I meant about running away. I not only ran away from the kids, I've run away from what I was supposed to be doing, which was thinking about you and me, and our future."

"Why don't you just stop thinking and do it?"

"You put that rather well," she observed dryly. "I'd have to be not thinking to marry you."

"What's so bad about it?"

"I'm not sure I want to join the band to play second fiddle. Your family comes first with you."

"Your family comes first with you," he countered.

"It's different."

"How?"

She shrugged off his hand, annoyed with his persistence. "I don't mind sharing you with your kids, but I'm damned if I'm going to spend the rest of my life with Ione!"

"What makes you say a thing like that?" he demanded.

"You're still in love with her; that's why you can't love me."

"That's the dumbest thing I ever heard you say!"

"Dumb, maybe, but it's true. When she says frog, you jump."

He put his hands on his own knees and rubbed them thoughtfully. "I didn't know you thought that."

"Well, why do you do everything she tells you to?"

He mused silently for a moment before he answered. "Remember what you said about people dying? About the phases you have to go through to get over it? It's sort of like that when a marriage dies, and I've been through all the phases. I was mad for a long time, and then I was down and sorry for myself and felt like I must be less of a man than what's-his-name, but all that's behind me now."

He turned and looked at her, leaning close

so he could see her eyes in the dark. "I still wish it hadn't all happened, that Ione had given me a chance. I wish I'd listened to her more. But it's all done and I've learned to live with it. There were good things about that marriage and the kids were the best part. The kids are still here, and what good would it do them if I weren't considerate to their mother?"

She put her arms around him, drawing his head onto her breast. "I'm sorry, Mitch."

"Why are you fretting over this old stuff? We're here, together, now. I don't have any ghosts."

He slipped his arms around her and nestled closer, increasing the exciting contact of skin against skin. She wove her fingers into his hair as they kissed, pressing him close, and still she wanted him closer.

He whispered against her mouth, "Was that all that was bothering you? You never needed to worry about Ione. Can we go ahead and get married now?"

She laughed a little. "Is there such a thing as saying no to you?"

"It's been done."

"Well, I can't do it."

Somehow he managed to move even closer to her. "In that case, shall we try for two trips to the moon between lubes?"

She agreed readily, for her passion, like his, was only on simmer, and needed little to come to a boil. But still the word she was waiting for, she did not hear.

She could get him to say that he loved her, she knew. In this sexually-heated atmosphere he would probably say anything, but that was not what she wanted. She knew enough about men to know that they do not consider what is said in an hour like this one to be a real lie.

Chapter Seventeen

After he got home he phoned her. "You know something funny?" he inquired. "There's nobody here."

"Nobody at your house? Where did they all go?"

"Darryl decided he was well enough to go back to his own place. He left a note. Debbie is driving him to his dorm and then she's going back to hers. I'm alone!"

"For the moment, so am I. The boys all went cruising. They are convinced that Georgie's new car guarantees success with women for all of them."

"Might work. You want to come over here?"

"Yes, I want to, but I won't. I'm making brunch for the boys in the morning and I'm expected to come downstairs and start cooking. It just wouldn't look right if I drove up instead."

"You wouldn't be alone," he promised. "I'd come with you. You make great breakfasts."

"That's a good idea," she said. "Why don't you come over for brunch? It will be your only chance to meet Georgie; he has to leave about as soon as he has eaten."

"I'd like that, Lucia."

The hitch in her plans turned out to be that both of her sons were reluctant to get up the next morning. After she had stirred up the muffin batter and set the table and arranged the garnish of blueberries over the melon slices, she went upstairs and rapped at Georgie's door. He mumbled something in a sleepy voice.

A little later she rapped again, and knocked on Tommy's door, too, but both boys were still upstairs when Mitch arrived.

She let him in and he looked around. Having assured himself that they were alone, he gave her a furtive kiss. "Good morning, Lucia."

"Now what am I going to do?" sighed Lucia. "They're both still in their rooms. You'll have to sign an affidavit that you spent the night in your own home."

"You worry about these things too much."

Lucia went to the foot of the stairs and called, "Come down now, boys! Mitch just got here!"

Tommy appeared at once, yelling down the stairs, "Hi, Mitch! Have you seen Georgie's new car?"

"Is that the red Z in the driveway?" Mitch asked, and Tommy hurtled down the stairs to relate all the details.

Lucia went into the kitchen to put the fire on under the grill, and they followed her. Tommy was still talking, but what everybody really was doing was waiting for Georgie.

She had made up her mind exactly how she would introduce them when he got there. She absolutely refused to identify Mitch as her "boyfriend."

Or her posslq.

Or the er . . . a . . . uh.

When Georgie finally drifted into the kitchen, she was ready. "Mitch, this is Georgie. Georgie, Mitch."

She rather enjoyed the baffled look in Georgie's eye as they shook hands. After all, he could have listened when she had tried to tell him about Mitch.

Mitch may have been enjoying it, too, for he just waited, relaxed and friendly, for Georgie to take the lead.

Georgie tried, "Oh. Did you come for brunch?"

Mitch said, "Yeah."

Georgie hazarded, "You're one of our new neighbors?"

Mitch took pity on him. "I'm a friend of your mother's. A very good friend, I hope."

Georgie said, "Well, come and sit down, then."

Mitch observed the table, set with china, silver, and with blue napkins to match the berries in the melons. "Hey, that looks nice. I thought we were going to have breakfast in the breakfast room."

"Oh, I never serve breakfast in there," said Lucia from her place at the griddle.

"Why not? Isn't that what it's for?"

Lucia plied her spatula a bit impatiently. "Why are you making me think up excuses for not doing something that never crossed my mind?" she demanded. "I never serve breakfast in there because the kitchen is big enough."

Mitch took a chair, as did Georgie, and Tommy poured the coffee. Mitch remarked, "It is about the biggest kitchen I ever saw. This is quite a house. What kind of historical significance did you say it had?"

"If I ever knew, I've forgotten," Lucia answered carelessly. "Grover Cleveland slept here or something. They wanted to put in a plaque, but I wouldn't let them. I figured, no matter what they said, some way it was going to cost me money."

Georgie was sipping his coffee and regarding Mitch with an expression somewhere between puzzlement and calculation that would have been comical if he hadn't been so earnest about it. He asked at last, "What do you do, uh . . . Mitch?"

"I'm a tool pusher," Mitch replied as usual, and added helpfully, "I'm in the oil business."

Georgie was not enlightened. "I don't know much about oil."

"I don't know a lot about computers, either. That's what you work with, isn't it?"

"I'm a mathematical programmer," said Georgie with an abstracted air. "When you're a tool pusher, do you work, like, regularly?"

Tommy broke in, "He's rich, Georgie! He drives a Porsche and a big four-by."

"Sounds like some things have been going on while I was away," said Georgie.

"Nothing's going on except your meal's ready," grumped Lucia. "Come and get your plates, please, all of you."

They came eagerly for their food, and Lucia handed them each a plate with the sausage, eggs, and hash browns. She arranged the hot muffins in a basket and joined them at the table. The conversation became general, and everybody was relaxing nicely until Mitch's children were mentioned.

Georgie dropped his fork and stared at Mitch. "You're married?" he demanded.

"Well, I was once, but I've been divorced for a number of years." Mitch gave Georgie a long, almost reproving look. "You know, you're coming on like your own grandfather."

"Well, I—" Georgie began but Mitch interrupted him.

"To forestall the rest of your questions, grandpa, my intentions toward your mother are honorable and I can well afford to support her. She'll be better off with me than she ever has been by herself."

"Well, she has to be the one to decide," Georgie admitted.

"I'm hoping she will soon," grumbled Mitch, but Lucia only looked at her plate and said nothing. How like men, to natter on and on about money, when the question was love!

It was already late for Georgie to start his long drive home, and he had to go almost as soon as he finished eating. Lucia walked out to the car with him and tried not to sound anxious as she said, "I hope you have a good trip back."

Georgie demanded, "Are you going to get married?"

"I haven't decided yet, but if I do marry again, it will be Mitch." She squeezed his hand affectionately. "The vibes I'm getting from you are kind of . . . . lukewarm. Can vibes be lukewarm?"

"He's okay. Seems like a nice guy, but couldn't you have picked somebody we know?"

She gave him a motherly kiss. "Georgie, you've got a lot to learn about love."

Tommy came running from the house to say goodbye one more time, and Lucia went up on the porch. She waved as the little red car scooted out of the driveway, carrying away her beloved son to his new life, his life, in which she had no share. She thought it would be easier to bear if she knew what his new home looked like, if she had been inside and touched his things, so she could imagine him there.

She went back into the house sniffling a little, because she missed him. He was probably, right now, waiting at the stoplight on Hoover, but she already missed him. She filled the sink with soapy water and started doing the dishes.

Mitch was still sitting with his coffee. He asked, "Well, did you finish raking me over the coals?"

326

"We didn't mention you," she lied.

"You sound like you're mad at me." His tone was close to reproof.

She admitted, "Well, I did rather resent that remark about how much better off I'm going to be if I marry you. I've been doing all right. I may not have cars and money-market accounts, but I'm raising two kids who are functioning, healthy-minded adults, and that's an achievement I'm proud of."

His head came up sharply. "Are you saying my kids aren't?"

"No, of course not. You have fine children." He was glowering, so she went on. "It's just that I don't think you ought to throw it up to me that you raised the children and made a financial success, too, and I didn't. It wasn't my fault, it was the times."

He cocked a skeptical eyebrow. "The times were against you?"

"That's more truth than cop-out," she insisted. "You'd know if you ever had to look at the world from my angle. There's a lot of talk these days about all the wonderful opportunities that are open to women. . . . Well, there are some, but they're for young, educated, unattached women. Especially unattached. Who's going to give a responsible position to a woman who always has to leave the office before the day-care center closes? A woman who can never work a weekend or take a business trip? I made my choice and I'm happy with it."

"I'm happy with the way my kids came out, too," he grumped. "I did the best I could for them. It wasn't my idea to break up their home."

"I know that, Mitch."

He brought his coffee cup over and stood beside her at the sink. "I was only trying to reassure your nervous son. And tease him a little."

"He was pretty funny. The infant Dutch uncle."

"I only wanted him to know that you won't have to worry about money when you're married to me," Mitch added, trying to catch her eye.

She concentrated on the specks she was scraping from the frying pan. "Don't push me, Mitch. I still think we are both hauling too much freight to be able to consider marriage."

He moved impatiently away. "Why are we always having serious conversations while you're washing the dishes?"

"Why do you always bring these things up right after breakfast?"

"Why do you always bristle up every time I

say something about money?"

"Why are we playing Twenty Questions?" she asked. It was like Twenty Questions, she thought, because the one question she was forbidden to ask was the one that would tell her what she wanted to know.

"The game we seem to be playing," he said slowly, "might be called Questions That Don't Get Answers."

She looked up and smiled ruefully. "We're supposed to be adults. Do you know what we're fighting about?"

He smiled back. "The way I see it, we're fighting because your son has just left and I'm still here for you to pick on."

"Do I do that? I ought to be ashamed, and I am. I couldn't wait for him to leave so the house could get back to normal, and now I'm heartbroken because he's gone."

He chuckled and took her into his arms. "You're normal. I always feel like the kids ought to go, but not today. What you need is to get out for a while. Let's go to the swap meet."

"To the what?"

"They have this big swap meet in the Valley. It's a great show and you don't have to buy anything unless you want to."

Lucia said firmly, "A swap meet is exactly

329

where I want to go today."

Where she really wanted to go, of course, was anywhere at all with Mitch. She left the dishes draining and they went.

The swap meet resided in a vast warehouse far out in the Valley. Acres of booths sold everything that could be dragged inside the building: furniture, clothing, crafts, jewelry, pictures. It was fun, a shopping adventure with the unexpected around every corner. Lucia bought some lengths of antique lace that she could incorporate into the white gowns she was making for Terrilee.

They strolled along, her hand tucked into the crook of Mitch's arm. She wasn't really afraid they would get separated, she just liked the feel of that arm, with the heavy bulge of muscle on the upper part almost touching the rock-hard forearm. She paused at a booth of ceramics and said, "Oh, look, Mitch! It's a dalmatian!"

He laughed. "Take it away!"

But Lucia was charmed with it. The figure was of a half-grown pup and nearly life-size. It had an appealing puppy air as it sat firmly on a plump behind. The black spots were artistically rendered on the white body, and all was covered with a shiny ceramic glaze. She picked it up and it was heavy as a bowling ball. She said, "It's cute, and it would make a great doorstop."

"Do you like it? I'll get it for you." Mitch reached for his credit card. He asked the woman in the booth, "How much is it?"

She replied with a perfectly straight face, "A hundred and fifty dollars."

Lucia hastily put the ceramic dog down. "Oh, Mitch, no! Of course not!"

"Why not, if you like it?"

"The price is outrageous!"

"It's a limited edition," the woman pointed out. "It's signed by the artist on the bottom."

"I don't care if he wrote the Declaration of Independence there," said Lucia, "it's still overpriced."

The credit card slipped back into Mitch's wallet and instead, there was a bill in his hand. He gave the woman the shrewd glance of an experienced trader, holding the bill where she could see it. "Tell you what, will you take a hundred cash for it?"

Lucia protested, "Mitch!"

"Oh, let me buy you something, Lucia. It will give me pleasure."

"You'll have to carry it," she agreed ungraciously.

The bargain was struck and Mitch gamely carried the dalmatian through the rest of the swap meet.

She took it home and put it on one of her hearths. It was too expensive to be a doorstop.

Lucia intended to have an easy week. She would let the housework slide and work on gowns only when she felt like it. Terrilee had other sources for white gowns. There was no hurry.

The only trouble with that plan was that without gowns, she had no excuse to visit Terrilee, and she felt like she owed her an apology. Well, maybe not an apology exactly, but she had been hard on Terrilee about that dinner with Mitch, while Mitch had gotten off without so much as a reproving look.

But did she need an excuse to go call on her best friend? Lucia decided just to go. She wouldn't even take a cheesecake. Terrilee was getting rounder by the day, just the way things were.

When she hauled into the parking lot, it was not yet nine, and the store should have been open, but the windows were dark. A little alarmed, she hurried around to the back, and Terrilee's rooms were lit. She rang the bell.

Terrilee came to the door wearing the caftan that Lucia had designed for her, and her hair was carefully arranged into a huge helmet of curls.

She cried, "Lucia! What did you bring me?"

"Not so much as a carrot stick," Lucia replied. "I only wanted to talk, but it looks like I picked a bad time. Are you about to go out?"

"Sure, sure, but come in. You didn't drive all the way over here to stand on the steps."

Lucia went inside. "I won't stay long. I just wanted to tell you what I decided. Mitch is back in my life and you'd better keep your hands off."

Terrilee laughed. "Get over it, Lucia. I had one dinner with him. Better me than some dame you can't trust."

"Oh, I know I can trust you. It's just that from now on . . ."

"I got my own fish to fry, you know."

"Well, yes, obviously." Lucia took a look at her friend, perhaps her first real look of the evening. Terrilee had a glow about her. The caftan, as it was designed to do, minimized her bulk, and the extravagant curls were so becoming, she looked quite pretty. "Terrilee, are you in love?"

She grinned. "Oh, I wouldn't say that exactly, but I certainly am . . . interested."

"Is he interested, too?"

"Yes. Isn't it funny? We've known each other for years and just never paid any attention, and all of a sudden—"

"Oh, Terrilee, there you go, rushing headlong into something new."

Terrilee managed a reproving look. "I'm having a wonderful time with a man who also happens to be a friend. What's wrong with that?"

"I'm afraid. I'm afraid you're going to get hurt."

Terrilee shrugged. "It wouldn't be the first time, would it?"

"Don't be cynical. It's not like you."

"Me? I'm not cynical. A cynic is somebody who has given up on life."

"That's a pessimist," Lucia said.

"Well, meet Terry optimist! He's nothing to look at, you know. Bald and overweight, just your average C.P.A, but I like him."

"I hope it works for you, Terri, I really hope it does. I've got to go now; I don't want to be cluttering up the place when your beau gets here."

"Stick around. We've got a few more minutes."

"Do I hear a dog howling?"

"Yeah, it's mine. He's been out there in the pen all day and he wants to come in, but I haven't got time for him now."

"He sounds so sad."

"I hate to listen to him, too," Terrilee burst out, "but what can I do? He chews everything and now he's learning to lift his leg. I laughed when he started doing that. I thought it was so cute! He kept walking around, trying to figure out which leg he was supposed to lift; he has so many of them! Then yesterday he figured it out. Lifted up his hind leg good and high and peed all over the merchandise in the store. He has to stay in the pen. I can't afford to have any more stuff ruined."

"I just hate to see him in a pen. He needs company, and it gets cold these nights." Lucia frowned with thought. "I'm going to take him back to Debbie."

Terrilee all but clapped her hands in delight. "Oh, Lucia, would you do that for me? I'd be so grateful! I've been intending to ask her myself, but it was hard to figure out what to say after I'd said I wanted a watchdog so bad!"

"I'll take him right now. Where's the leash?"

Spot was frantic with delight to see Lucia, to see anybody, and he threw himself against her. She was glad she was wearing her office trousers. The stout fabric was protection against his careless claws.

Mindful of what Debbie had said about Spot's tendency to carsickness, she put him in the bed of the wagon, where he couldn't hurt

335

anything, and closed the tailgate window on the end of his leash so he had to stay there.

As she drove out of the parking lot, another car drove in, and there was something about the headlights that made her certain there was a C.P.A. at the wheel. She felt glad for Terrilee, who sure was overdue for some good luck. Maybe this was her time.

Spot bounced around in the back of the station wagon for the whole trip to Los Angeles, looking out the windows and panting with the sheer joy of traveling, but he never was sick. Maybe he had outgrown it.

When she got home she explained to Tommy that Terrilee was not going to be able to keep the dog, and he immediately called Debbie.

When he put down the phone he reported, "She's got a good idea. Her brother Darryl's back in his dorm now, so he can take Spot. It's a guy's dorm, and guys aren't as fussy as girls about things like the carpets."

"Oh, poor Darryl," said Lucia. "What are you going to do with the dog tonight?"

"No problem. We're going to take him over to Westwood right now."

"Now?" Lucia repeated. "It's after nine o'clock."

"It'll be at least ten before we get there. She says that's about the time he usually gets home. Come on, Spot."

"Your car this time?" Lucia questioned.

"Hers is in the shop. I'll be back later."

It was not late when Tommy returned, but Lucia was already in bed. She could tell from the sounds that he had returned without Spot, and that made her sleep easier.

Chapter Eighteen

Lucia was a little surprised when Nancy Larchmont called her. Nancy said, "Hey, look, I don't know exactly how this happened, but day after tomorrow is Thanksgiving."

"Last Thursday in November," Lucia agreed cheerfully. "Happens every year."

"We've been planning for months to spend it at our condo in Palm Springs, and I don't know why I didn't think to ask before, but why don't you join us there? You and your boys. Maybe you could drive down with Mitch."

"Georgie's gone back to San Jose." Lucia was a little confused. "Mitch is spending Thanksgiving with you?"

"He always does. His kids are with Ione, of course, so he'd otherwise be alone. And I know he'd like to have you there, so if you don't have anything planned . . ."

"Ah-ha, I think I've got the picture. You've been talking to Mitch."

"Actually, I have. I called to remind him of our standing date, and what I found out was that there isn't any use talking to him about going anyplace if you aren't going to be there, too."

Lucia admitted, "With all that's been going on around here, I did forget about Thanksgiving. We sort of had our feasts when Georgie was here. Yes, Nancy. Tommy and I would love to spend Thanksgiving with you."

"Oh, thank you, thank you, thank you! I couldn't have put up with Mitch if he thought I was forcing him to spend a whole day without you."

Lucia laughed. "He probably would have survived it."

Nancy laughed, too. "I might not have. We're going to have some of our Palm Springs friends. The Simons are our golf partners and the Hovelands were our neighbors when we lived in Jeddah. They're the ones who talked us into Palm Springs in the first place."

"Will your kids be there?"

"My son can't come, his wife is too near her delivery date to travel, but Jean will be there. And again, I'm sorry I didn't think of this earlier!"

"I'm glad you did think of it. What can I bring? I make a killer sweet-potato casserole."

"Oh, you don't have to do that."

"I'd like to."

"Do it, then. And come early if you'd like. The guys are going to play some golf and we'll have a chance to chat."

Later Lucia checked the whole thing out with Mitch and he apologized. "I should have thought about Thanksgiving earlier, but it slipped my mind. When I was thinking about this week, there was only one thing in my mind, and that was we're leaving for Acapulco on Friday."

"It's been on my mind, too. But I love the idea of going away for Thanksgiving. I'm all cooked out from Georgie's visit. Shall we drive down together? If we do, I think we should take the station wagon. There's no place in your Porsche for Tommy to sit."

"Your wagon? It's a desert out there, Lucia. We'll take the truck."

"That great big truck just to take three people to Palm Springs?"

"Tell you the truth, it rides better than the Porsche. I take it anywhere I want to be comfortable. Don't ever tell Jim I said that, though."

"Okay, truck it is. At least there will be plenty of room for the casserole."

She had just arrived home from work that evening and was putting down her things when the doorbell rang. To her astonishment, it was Debbie on her front porch.

Lucia said, "Oh, hello, Debbie. I'm sorry, but Tommy isn't home now. He has a late lab on Tuesdays."

"That's all right, Lucia," replied the girl. "I want to talk to you."

"Come in." Lucia held the door open, her feelings sinking like a stone in water, for when a girl of Debbie's age wants to talk to a woman of Lucia's, it's either a term project or they are facing some very serious trouble indeed.

Real trouble demands coffee, so Lucia led the way to the kitchen and hauled out the battered coffeepot. "Sit down, Debbie. I'll fix some coffee. Or would you rather have a cola?"

"A cola will be okay." Debbie seated herself. She wore a large, loose overblouse and a pair of designer jeans so fashionably cut as to make her look slightly deformed. Lucia tried to keep her eyes off that overblouse while she measured out the coffee. All those puckers and gathers . . . What might they be concealing?

Toying with the handle of her great pouch of a purse, Debbie admitted, "Well, really, I feel silly."

341

Lucia put ice into a glass for the cola. "Why don't you tell me about it?"

"I locked myself out of my car."

Lucia started to laugh. "Oh, Debbie, you had me scared! Where is the car? Do you need me to drive you someplace?"

"No, not exactly." More toying with the purse. "I . . . well . . . Dad has a duplicate key, and I thought maybe you'd get it for me."

Lucia said, "Huh?"

Debbie leaned forward earnestly. "It would be easy for you. All you'd have to do is slip it off his key ring. You could do it while he's asleep."

Lucia didn't know which shocked her more, the idea that Debbie thought she would do such a thing as to steal a key from the man in her bed, or the realization that this child, this virginal, still-teenage Debbie, knew exactly what her father's relationship was with Lucia.

She managed to say, "Why don't you just ask your father for the key?"

"Oh, you know Daddy. He's forever lecturing us about how important it is to take care of our keys. He'll scold me for a week if I have to tell him."

"Maybe you deserve it." Lucia thought a minute. "Have you considered paying a locksmith to open the car for you?"

"Oh, I couldn't do that! It would be so embarrassing!"

Lucia sat down and folded her arms sarcastically, "Less embarrassing than asking your father's lady friend steal it for you? Don't give me that shocked expression! I've just used some old-fashioned words to describe this very modern situation, that's all I did."

"Well, I . . ." Debbie pushed her cola glass a few inches to the left. "Well, I didn't expect you to say that!"

Lucia explained, "What I really am is an old-fashioned mother type, and old-fashioned mothers have a built-in sensor system. Right now my fib sensor is pointing straight at Debbie Colton. Why don't you tell me what really happened?"

"Well, jeez," said Debbie. "Well, jeez, your coffee is boiling over."

Lucia had rescued the coffee and poured herself a cup and settled again in her chair before Debbie decided she had stalled enough.

"It's all so dumb!" she began.

"I'm listening anyway."

"I went to this party. You knew Darryl went back to his dorm, didn't you?"

"You went to a party at Darryl's dorm?"

"No, listen, will you? This was Saturday night. Darryl wanted to go back to his dorm and I said I'd drive him and we got his things together and I went down into the garage to start loading them into the truck and it was gone! Dad had taken it and gone off somewhere!"

"Fancy that," murmured Lucia.

"We couldn't get all of Darryl's stuff into my car so we started loading things into Sandra's car—"

"Sandra?"

"She's one of the Alphas. My sorority, you know. She'd driven over to talk to me about the quiz we were studying for, and some of the other Alphas were with her. So she and the other two girls rode over to Westwood with Darryl and me, only they were in her car and I was in mine. . . ."

Lucia grunted to assure Debbie that she was listening.

"When we got there we didn't feel like unloading all that stuff, so we got the guys from the dorm to help us and we all got to talking, you know. They said the Betas were having a party. Well, the Betas have a pretty bad reputation on the SC campus and the Betas at UCLA are supposed to be even worse, and some of their parties are supposed to be really gross, and the guys were sort of daring us to go."

"So did you and the other Alphas go to the party?"

"No, the rest of them chickened out, but I went. It wasn't anything, really! They were just drinking beer and singing and there was some horsing around and you know, maybe some of the cigarettes weren't Winstons, but, you know, it was just a party. Only—"

"Only what, Debbie?"

"Only I guess they put something in my beer. Vodka, probably, because I didn't taste it. It made me sick and I was so sleepy! I wanted to go home, but I knew I shouldn't drive my car. Daddy says you should never do that."

"That was a wise decision."

"The trouble was Sandra had gone back to SC, so I couldn't go with her, and Darryl isn't allowed to drive yet because he isn't healed up, so I couldn't go ask him, so I asked one of the Betas to drive me home. So he did, and I was so sleepy, when we got to the Alpha house all I could think about was getting to bed and I just told him good night and went inside and I was in my nightgown before I remembered that he was driving my car."

"What did you do?"

"I didn't think much of it. After all, he had to get back to Westwood some way. I thought he would bring my car back the next day, but he didn't. So I called the Beta house and all they do is give me the business. They say there isn't anybody there named Orson. That's what he said his name was, Orson. So I got Sandra to drive me over there and they wouldn't let me in or answer the doorbell and they were all leaning out the windows on the second floor, laughing like crazy. My car is sitting right there on Landfair and it's locked, but if I could just get the key, I could go get the car and Daddy wouldn't bawl me out for letting Orson drive it. Come on, Lucia, won't you help me? That's not asking too much, is it?

Lucia took a thoughtful sip of her coffee. "I don't suppose you need anybody to tell you that you just had a learning experience," she said. "However, you handled it pretty well. You were right not to drive when you didn't feel you could. Not everything you did was wise, but that was. Now, if that boy Orson has your keys, he must have the whole ring, doesn't he? What's on it?"

"Oh, door keys and such. The key to my room at the Alpha house, the key to Daddy's place, the key to Mother's . . ."

"I think it's clear we need to get the whole ring back." Lucia found the telephone in the breakfast room. It tended to wander around on its long cord as if it had legs of its own. "Beta what?"

"Oh, I don't think it will do any good to call them," Debbie protested, but she supplied the rest of the Greek letters and Lucia got the number from information.

When she had the Beta house on the line, she asked sweetly for the president. She got some smart answers, which she ignored, and at length a voice identified himself as Tag Malone, president of the chapter.

"This is Mrs. Colton," Lucia told him without a qualm. "My daughter, Debbie, attended a party at your house on Saturday."

"Lady, I don't know your daughter," the kid snarled.

Lucia continued, unperturbed. "She left a ring of keys, and I would like to come and get them now."

"What am I? The lost and found?"

"You misunderstand me, Mr. Malone. I didn't say anything about lost; the keys were left. I will be in Westwood in half an hour, and I expect you to hand me those keys."

"I don't have your keys!"

"Perhaps not, but you know where they are, and if you don't, you can find out." Her voice roughened. "If I don't get them, my next visit will be to the dean of men, and I will tell him exactly what sort of party you had on Saturday. I'm going to tell him that you gave hard liquor to a girl who is only seventeen years old."

"Lady . . ."

"While I realize the campus climate is permissive these days, giving liquor to a minor is illegal anywhere in this state, including in fraternity houses. I'm going to nail the boy who gave it to her, and I'm going to see to it that your chapter is on probation for so long, your youngest member will be bald and paunchy before you get off."

"C'mon, lady, have a heart! I can't—"

"Half an hour, Mr. Malone."

Debbie looked impressed as Lucia hung up the phone, her dark eyes round as berries. "Do you think it will work?"

"If it doesn't, we shall have the tedious business of trying to intimidate the dean of men next, but I think we are going to get our own way. They're probably already on probation. They could get stripped of their charter. Let's get in the car."

Lucia picked up her purse and they went out to the station wagon. Still warm from her trip home from work, it started easily.

For a while they rode in silence, but after they had merged into the traffic on the 10, Lucia spoke up. "There's one thing. About your father and me. We are planning to be married."

It wasn't exactly what she had intended to say; somehow it had just come out. Why was it, when she talked to the children, she always brought it up that she and Mitch were going to marry, when they had only talked about it, when she had not yet made a decision? Did she feel that she needed to prove to the kids that their feelings were serious and real?

She went on determinedly. "We aren't ashamed of being in love, but we do try to observe the proprieties, and we do expect a decent amount of reticence from the people around us, including the family. Some things are just none of your business."

In the seat beside her, Debbie stirred resentfully. "Oh, I know all about it. I'm the kid and you're the adult, so you do what you do and we do what we're told. The rules are different for us."

"That's true," Lucia said firmly. "The rules are different for young people because what you do is more important."

Debbie looked at her with sarcastic surprise. "Yeah? How do you figure that?"

"Whatever you do now, to your life, to your body, to your emotions, you have to live with for the rest of your life, and for you, the rest of your life is a long time. At this point your potential is intact, including your potential for children."

"I'm never going to have children," said Debbie with a defiant glower.

She was trying to bait her, Lucia realized,

so she answered only, "That will save you a lot of trouble."

As they drove up the steep street called Landfair, Debbie pointed out the Beta house and her car, parked nearby. Lucia found a parking place and wrestled her station wagon into it. To get a big car into a small space on a hill is always an achievement, and it cheered her when the wagon slid into place with a minimum of fuss.

The Beta house stood high above a long flight of steps. They climbed to the front door and rang the bell.

Immediately the door opened and they were confronted by a very tall, very thin boy with a very grumpy expression. He handed Lucia a ring of keys and said, "There! Does that satisfy you?"

Lucia passed the keys to Debbie, who said, "Yes, these are mine."

Lucia said, "Thank you very much," and, turning, took Debbie firmly by the upper arm and walked her down the steps.

Debbie had her mouth open to say something cutting, and she kept trying to turn around and deliver her line, but Lucia kept her moving until they reached the sidewalk. She let go then, but obviously Debbie felt it would be uncool to stand at the bottom of the steps and scream up at the lanky boy in the doorway above. She contented herself with a sarcastic shrug as they walked down the hill to Debbie's car.

"I'll wait here while you try it and see if it starts," Lucia offered. "It may be out of gas. Do you have money to buy some?"

"I have a credit card." Debbie slipped into the driver's seat and put the key into the ignition. The car started at once, and when it did, she turned to look up at Lucia with a smile so sweet and warm and genuine that Lucia smiled to see it, even while she marveled at the child's resemblance to Mitch.

"Oh, Lucia, thank you for getting it back for me, and you won't tell Daddy, will you?"

"There's no need, is there?"

"Thanks, Lucia. Boy, I'm getting so I hate frats! The guys all act like they owned the world, and so do the girls."

"Oh, not everybody in every frat. They're not all alike, are they?"

"You know, when I moved out of Daddy's, I thought I wouldn't get bossed around anymore, but at least he never told me what I had to rub on my face!"

"The other girls at the sorority tell you that?"

"They've got this whole thing about night cremes and facials. It's gross. If you're going to be an Alpha, you've got to do this, wear that.

They go around checking up on your makeup!"

Lucia grinned wickedly. "So what would happen if you just did your lipstick the way you like it anyway?"

Debbie grinned. "I guess I'd be the maverick Alpha."

"That sounds very serious."

"Oh, it is, but maybe I'll just do it anyway. See ya!" Debbie slammed the door and peeled out of her parking place so fast that Lucia had to step back quickly or have her toes run over.

She didn't mind. She was still smiling as she watched the little white car rush down the hill toward the gas stations in the Village. She wanted to be a friend to Debbie, and not just because they were going to be family. She genuinely liked the kid, even if she did, most of the time, act like a kid.

Chapter Nineteen

It was late on Wednesday evening when the doorbell rang, so late that Lucia had finished sewing and was tidying her workroom. She thought it an unnecessary time for visitors, but Tommy was still studying and may have arranged something. She ignored what was going on downstairs until she heard distinctly, absolutely, a bark.

Lucia went downstairs to the breakfast room and knew at once that the boy she saw there was Darryl, because he was so like Debbie. Bigger, taller, his hair a bit darker, he was the male version of Debbie. And there was one more thing; he had Spot with him.

She said, "Hello, Darryl, I'm Lucia," and Spot threw himself at her ankles as usual.

"I'm Darryl," the kid said unnecessarily.

Lucia bent down to push the dog away.

"Why does he love me so? I've never fed him!"

"He loves everybody," Tommy explained. He took the leash that Darryl was holding and snapped it onto the dog's collar. Then he trapped the loop under a chair leg, limiting Spot's radius of action.

Lucia ventured, "I take it the dog got thrown out of your dorm, too."

"Worse than that," said Darryl. "They threw us both out. I've got nowhere to go unless I sleep in my car, so I came over here."

"Oh, my!" Lucia exclaimed. "Did you explain that you aren't supposed to drive your car so soon after your surgery?"

"They were pretty mad." Darryl smiled, his lips pulled tight against his teeth. "I can go over to Debbie's dorm and have them give me a bed for the night, but I can't take Spot. They won't let him in over there, either. I'm going to Oxnard for four days starting tomorrow, and I can take him with me, but I don't know what I'll do with him when I get back. The guys will probably have cooled off by then and I can go back to the dorm, but I can't take Spot with me. You got any ideas what we can do with him?"

"You mustn't do any more driving," Lucia decreed. "You can sleep here tonight. You can have Georgie's room."

"What about Spot?" Tommy asked. He was

petting the pup, which lay at his feet, delighted with the attention. It was a cute little animal, puppy clumsy, the small, spotted face forever expressing eagerness to pleased without the least idea how to go about it.

Lucia's heart wanted to give him love and a good home, but her mouth said, "I don't know. Perhaps we could shut him up in the storeroom for the night?"

Tommy went on petting. "I figured this was going to happen, so I took a book out of the library about dogs. It says a dog will do anything you want if you can make him understand what it is that you want."

"Maybe I don't speak dog so well," Darryl admitted. "I can't make him do anything."

"The first rule," Tommy lectured, "if you're going to housebreak them, you've got to get him outside a lot. He's probably going in the house because he can't wait any longer. So I'm taking Spot for a walk." He bent to pick up the leash. "I'll keep him in my room tonight and I promise, Mom, there won't be any mess."

Lucia warned, "And should there be, it will be cleaned up before I notice it, won't it, now? Darryl, how are you going to get to your mother's tomorrow?"

"Debbie's going to drive."

"Well, you had better phone and tell her

where you are, so she can pick you up."

Darryl rubbed his hands together gleefully. "Okay if I use your phone? I can hardly wait to tell her we're taking Spot with us to Oxnard tomorrow—in her car!"

Tommy was hauling a book from his bookbag. "There's a section in here about teaching him to ride quietly in the car."

"Yeah? Let me see that." Darryl took the book and turned to the table of contents.

Lucia said, "Don't get started on that. You have to phone Debbie, and Tommy's going for a walk."

"Yeah. Just a minute." Darryl was flipping methodically through the pages.

Oh, well. Lucia went back upstairs to check the room her guest would use, and to lay out some towels.

When she had done that, she went to bed. It seemed to her that both boys were staying up late, but maybe they needed to, to get everything done.

Debbie appeared the next morning in time for breakfast. After everybody had eaten, Tommy turned the dog leash over to her, with instructions to walk Spot regularly and often. When the two boys and their dog rushed off to Debbie's car, Darryl had the library book in the satchel with his texts.

Lucia and Mitch and Tommy had a pleasant

drive to Palm Springs, not a great distance on a fast road. The air was clear and the weather sunny and warm, exactly the sort of day that makes P.S. a place where people go to get away from L.A.

Nancy and Jim had a spacious condo overlooking a golf course. They both rushed out to greet the visitors and proudly showed them around. Lucia dutifully admired the shiny, modern condo with its southwestern decor.

A roasting turkey was filling the house with the aroma of Thanksgiving and the kitchen was crowded with food in preparation. The Larchmont daughter, Jean, was slicing vegetables at the counter. She looked cute in abbreviated shorts and a "P.S. I love you" T-shirt. Lucia found a place to put down her casserole, then introduced Tommy.

Nancy smiled at him. "Oh, I've heard a lot about you! Your mother says you're a chemistry major at SC."

"You know how mothers talk," said Tommy.

Jean put down her knife and moved close to him, smiling. "Tommeee," she said, her voice caressing the syllables. "Is that short for Thomas?"

"I'm only Thomas on exams," he said, grinning.

She fingered the tip of his shirt collar. "I think I'm going to call you Thomas. Come on,

I want to show you the fish pond. There's koi in it."

They left, chattering. Lucia and Nancy went into the living room. As usual, Jim was trying to give everybody a drink. Lucia managed to talk him into providing a tall glass of iced tea, and he went to the kitchen to prepare it.

"This is a lovely house," Lucia said again. "The whole complex is really pretty, and seems very well laid out."

"Oh, it's got everything," said Nancy. "We can play golf every day, and there's a rec center with meeting rooms and Ping-Pong and all that stuff."

Jim returned with the iced tea for Lucia and beers for everybody else. He elaborated. "It's nice here, but the big reason we like Palm Springs is because we have friends here. Some of them are friends from way back, like the Simons; we were visiting them when we found this place."

"You do look pretty comfortable here," Mitch said agreeably.

"I see it as a bolt-hole," Jim went on. "This is where we'll be when we retire. You haven't got a retirement place, Mitch. Why don't you look around here and see if you see anything you like?"

"I'm a while from retirement," Mitch said defensively.

"So you going to wait until you're sixty-five to buy something? Real estate prices are going up every year."

Mitch squinted at him. "You really want to retire and play golf? That's about all there is to do here. What are you going to do when you're too old to swing a club anymore?"

"You gotta be pretty old when you can't golf. Anyways, when that happens, you can still look at the greens and the pond and all that pretty landscaping. It's better'n staring at houses in the city."

"We going to play a couple rounds today?"

"Soon as Hoveland gets here."

Mitch observed, "Lucia doesn't play golf."

Nancy said to her, "If you lived here, you'd practically have to learn. We have a great pro. He'd teach you in no time."

Lucia felt no enthusiasm. "Isn't it sort of like skiing, you have to start learning it when you're a child?"

"It's sort of like everything else," Mitch insisted. "You can learn no matter how old you are."

Jim had drifted out of the room and he drifted back, his beer still in his hand. "Nancy, there're some ants in the bathroom. Have we got any spray?"

"Oh, don't spray in there," she said. "It'll make a smell. I'll just wipe them up with a sponge."

She went off to get her sponge. Lucia chatted with the two men and after a while Nancy appeared on her knees in the hallway.

"I'm trying to figure out where the ants are coming from," she explained. "There're a lot of them."

Lucia went to help her, and together they followed the tiny stream of insects until they found the place where they were marching in under a door.

"They're moving," Nancy pointed out. "They're looking for a new nest. Look, you can see the eggs they're carrying. Sometimes if you let the whole swarm get inside, you can wipe them all out at once and then they aren't ever going to come back. Ants are something of a problem around here."

"Shall we try it?" Lucia asked. "Let them all park themselves in your bathroom?"

"No, maybe we'd better not. It takes a long time and the rest of the guests will be here soon."

"Okay, let's get sponging, then. Where can I find a sponge?"

"Here, take this one; I'll get another." Nancy went into the kitchen and immediately cried out, "Oh, darn, the ants are in here, too! Where are they coming from?"

They went to work with sponges, and forced the insects back in the kitchen. Nancy said,

"Soon as we get them out of here, let's see if we can find the hole where they're coming in, and we'll pour Clorox down it."

From the bedroom came the sound of heavy feet, stamping. They looked in to find Jim dancing on a swarm of ants that covered the floor, the window shutters, the patio floor outside the room.

"We've got to get the ones outside, or they'll just keep coming in forever!" he said. "Get the hose!"

Nancy wiped frantically. "Somebody's got to keep working on the ones inside. Where's Jean?"

"She and Tommy went to the fish pond to see the koi," Lucia reported.

"Koi? The pond that has koi in it is all the way over in the recreation area. That wretched girl! She was supposed to be fixing the relish plate. Oh, my God, the food!"

They rushed back to the kitchen and began snatching up edibles from the counters. Ants were creeping up the cabinets, fanning across the counters. Nancy shrieked with dismay when she discovered that they had already infested the splendid chocolate cake she had prepared. Lucia shoved things into the refrigerator.

Nancy brushed fruitlessly at the cake. "It's ruined!" she sobbed.

"Well, it looked beautiful while it lasted. The refrigerator's full," Lucia reported. "Let's take the stuff that won't spoil, like the salad and the bread, and lock them up in somebody's car. We'll put them in the truck."

Mitch was detailed to rush things out to the truck while Nancy put her cake, along with the unwelcome visitors, down the garbage disposal.

They scrubbed the kitchen and Jim did the bathroom, but even as they worked, the ants were increasing in the rest of the house. Mitch hosed the patio again and again, but at last he came in, looking wet and discouraged.

"We can't fight this," he reported. "And just spraying with a can isn't going to do it, either. You better send for an exterminator."

"The condo association has a service," said Nancy. "I'll call them. We've got to do something. The rest of the guests are going to be here any minute." She went resolutely to the phone.

She returned to report, "They're going to send somebody, but, Lucia, what are we going to do? He says we have to cover all food! It has to be in the refrigerator, or out of the house!"

"We just did put all the food into the refrigerator," Lucia pointed out.

"There's a turkey in the oven!"

"Oh. Turkey." Lucia thought a minute. "Maybe it's done."

"It can't be yet."

"When did the guy say he'd be here?"

"Right away."

"When he gets here, we'll take the turkey out. Good thing you've got it in that deep roaster. We'll wrap the roaster in something that will insulate it and keep it hot and we'll put it in the truck. If there's enough insulation, it will cook for an hour or so all by itself. After the exterminator is gone, we can put it back in the oven."

"Let's take it out now."

"Wait and see. Maybe we'll get another twenty minutes before he shows up, and every minute counts."

They got an hour. The guests began to arrive, and sat on that part of the patio Mitch had managed to clear, sipping beer and watching in fascination the march of ants into the house.

When at last a truck appeared and the men in coveralls began unreeling their hoses, Lucia and Nancy pulled the turkey roaster from the oven, clapped a lid on it, and wrapped it in towels and a thick layer of newspapers. It was then tucked in the back of Mitch's truck.

Of course nobody could be in the house or the patio while the spraying went on, so the whole group walked down to the recreation area, carrying their drinks and sacks of chips. There was an agreeable little park with picnic tables next to the rec center building. There was also a koi pond, with Tommy and Jean sitting on the cement rim, deep in conversation.

Tommy came over to the picnic area to talk to Lucia, and she explained about the ants. Jean followed him, and chatted amiably with her parents' friends. Then she took Tommy to the rec room for a game of pool.

Lucia commented, "The kids seem to be getting along very well."

"Don't believe everything you see," Nancy advised. "Jean isn't usually this flirtatious, and when she steps out of character, there's always a reason. She's probably doing it only because she thinks it will annoy Debbie."

Lucia thought that one over. "I wonder if it will."

In due time somebody checked the house and reported that the exterminators were gone. Nancy was none too pleased.

"I don't even want to go back there," she complained. "I like it here. This is the first chance I've had all day to sit down and talk to my friends."

"So let's stay awhile," suggested Lucia. "The way we wrapped that turkey, it's still cooking."

The guests, comfortable on picnic benches or spread on the grass under the trees, agreed with Lucia, but Nancy went back to the house anyway and Lucia accompanied her. There was a big cleanup job to be done, they both knew.

With brooms and sponges they attacked the mess. Jim appeared outside, hosing down the patio again. There were dead ants everywhere—on the floors, on the walls, on the counters; they had died clinging to the shutters, stuck to the drapes. The smell of insecticide was overpowering. It made Lucia queasy, so much so that as she was cleaning the bathroom she was seized with nausea, and vomited into the toilet.

Nancy must have heard her; she was there at once. "Lucia, what's the matter?"

Lucia wiped her mouth with a tissue. "It's the smell, I think. It makes me feel sick."

"I've got a headache like you wouldn't believe," reported Nancy. "You know something? We've got to get out of this house. We're fools to be in here with all that spray."

"But what about your dinner? Your guests?"

"We're going to have a Thanksgiving picnic down at the rec center," Nancy decreed. "And if that turkey isn't done, well, we'll send for pizza."

Jim had come up from the rec center and his help was enlisted to transfer the contents of the refrigerator to the truck. Lucia collected china, silver, and glasses. Then they trekked back to the picnic grounds to get Mitch, and he came with the keys and drove the truck and the food to where the guests were.

It turned into a highly enjoyable picnic. All the guests pitched in to set the table and arrange the food. Nancy cooked potatoes and vegetables on a barbecue grill. The turkey came out of its wrappings cooked to perfection; Jim carved it to applause from the hungry crowd. Those few fussy people who felt the need of a dessert were dispatched to the yogurt stand.

Nancy sighed happily, "This has been fun. I think I'll do it this way next year."

While she relaxed and digested, her guests cleaned up the table and stacked the dishes in the truck. Mitch drove it back to the house, taking Lucia, Tommy, and Jean with him to unload. The smell was gone from the house, but Lucia put the dishes inside and left as soon as she could. The memory of her nausea in the bathroom was still strong.

She sat with Mitch in patio chairs, taking a breather. "It's quite pleasant out here," she said. "And I'm sure it's safe. The insecticide would have dissipated quickly outdoors. The children aren't in the house, are they?"

"No, I think they went back to the rec center. I'm starting to be sorry I got you invited to this shindig; all you've done all day is work."

"I don't mind helping out. And I'm through now. Somebody else gets to wash the dishes."

He leaned toward her across the barrier of two chair arms. "You want to do something? How about a drink of something?"

"Oh, I don't think so now. I don't often drink in the middle of the day. Have something if you want."

He put an arm around her shoulders, pleased. "I try to be sensible in the middle of the day, too. I've always been a little afraid of the grip drink can get on you. It's the curse of the oil fields."

"Why the oil fields particularly?"

"You hardly ever find oil in the middle of a big city, or even of a little town. It's always way off somewhere, and the people have to be sent there and then they stay and do the work. When they're not working, what have they got to do? They get together and drink. They go off alone and drink. They have parties so they can drink. It turns into a problem for a lot of people."

"I can see how it would," Lucia said.

"I like to watch myself, make sure I'm never drinking just because I don't have anything else to do. You want to go play golf or anything?"

"Golf? Oh, my goodness, no. What I'd really like to do is take off my shoes."

"Go ahead. Take off anything you want." He hunched a little closer and hooked a finger in the neckline of her dress. He was so close she could feel his breath in her ear. "I've hardly got to talk to you all day."

"We'll have the whole weekend to talk."

A second finger joined the first, touching the curve of her breast. "I don't know how much talking's going to get done. Think about it, tomorrow night I'm going to have you all to myself." He kissed her, and tried to get his hand lower in her dress.

She broke the kiss reluctantly and pushed the hand away. "Not here, Mitch. The folks are going to start coming back from the picnic grounds any minute."

He mused, "We can't go in the house, it might make you sick again." Then he smiled engagingly. "The truck's right here."

She gave him a rejecting look, then lost it and started laughing. "It's sure a good thing you brought that truck along."

She followed him to the truck and waited while he pulled down the tailgate, lifted the window. Simultaneously, and with mutual shock, they observed that the truck was already occupied.

A splash of color in the dark interior of the

camper shell turned out to be Tommy, sprawled on top of Jean. They were locked together in a passionate kiss.

Lucia turned quickly away, leaning on the side of the truck. She was nauseated again, and this time her stomach was full of turkey and trimmings. She fought to make it all stay down. Mitch also stood aside quietly, and waited for two subdued children to climb out of the truck.

Jean came out second, pulling down her T-shirt. She tossed a furious glance at Mitch and stalked away, taking the path toward the rec center.

Tommy would have followed her, but Lucia said, "Tommy, I need to talk to you."

Mitch suggested, "Maybe he'd better have a cold shower first."

Lucia thought it an uncalled-for comment from a man who probably could have used one himself, but she managed not to say anything to Mitch. She said to Tommy, "Please go on the patio and wait for me. I'll be there in a minute."

Tommy went. Mitch asked, "You want me to talk to him?"

"I'll do it."

"I'm glad you said that. I've never been any good at this."

"I'm not, either, but he's my kid, so I'll do

it. Why don't you go back to the party?"

He grinned. "I think I've been dismissed."

"For now."

Tommy was sprawled in a patio chair, his legs defiantly stretched out in front of him. Lucia sat down in the chair Mitch had so recently vacated. "I'm surprised at you, Tommy."

"Jeez, Ma, what did you expect? She's been all over me ever since we got here. Anyhow, what did you and Mitch want in the back of the truck?"

"We wanted to be alone together, as you and Jean obviously did. The difference is, we're in a committed relationship. You and Jean hardly know each other."

"We didn't do anything."

Lucia raised an eyebrow. "Whose fault is that? How far would you have gone if you hadn't been interrupted?"

"We weren't going to do anything. We couldn't have. I don't have a . . . you know."

"And what if she had? Some women do carry them around, you know. Would you have gone all the way if a condom had been available?"

"Jeez, Ma! Do we have to talk about all this again?"

"Yes, indeed we do. I concede that we have been through it before, but the dangers cannot be emphasized enough. And don't tell me young people don't have AIDS; it can happen to anybody."

"So what's a person going to do? Join a monastery?"

"The danger is not sex, but promiscuous sex. Uninvolved sex. You were enjoying that girl's body because you had a chance to, and for no other reason. And her motives must have been similarly shallow. You don't believe she fell in love with you at first sight, do you?"

"So what do I get this time? Grounded for the rest of my life?"

"That's a rather attractive thought. I'll consider it. For now, I think it's time we all went back to town."

Chapter Twenty

Lucia wore her knit suit to the office the next day. Her bag was packed and Mitch was picking her up at home at seven. She had her desk cleared long before quitting time, and she was out the door on the dot.

As she drove up to the house she was mildly surprised to note that Debbie's car was at the curb, right behind Darryl's, and Tommy's was in the drive. It wasn't quite time for Tommy to leave for work, but the Colton kids were supposed to be in Oxnard.

As she put her car into its accustomed spot beside Tommy's, Darryl and Debbie came walking along the sidewalk with Spot on the leash. The dog walked just a little ahead, so quietly the leash hung slack, in a graceful curve.

When he saw Lucia he broke discipline and rushed toward her, but Debbie brought him up short with the leash and commanded him to sit. Lucia was able to give Spot a friendly pat and escape with her stockings whole.

"That's remarkable!" she said. "How did you kids do it?"

"It's all in the book," Darryl explained. "We've been training him all day yesterday and today."

"Aren't you back from Oxnard a little early?" Lucia asked. "Oh, no, don't tell me! Your mother didn't like Spot, either."

Debbie laughed. "Well, she didn't much, but we came back because we both need to get some studying done and Tommy promised to help us train Spot. Somehow, he always gets better results than either of us can."

"I think he does speak dog," Darryl contributed.

They continued their walk, and Lucia thought how cute they were together. They were so alike, she wanted to dress them in matching outfits, like twins.

When she went into the house, Tommy was just coming down the stairs, freshly dressed in his work clothes. She praised his success with Spot.

Tommy said earnestly, "He really is a good dog, but nobody can tell when he isn't trained. We figure it will be easier to find somebody who'll give him a good home if he knows how to act nice."

"Seems like a sound theory."

"Uh, Mom . . ." Suddenly Tommy was standing on one foot like an uncertain toddler. "Do you think Mitch's mad at me?"

"What? No, I don't think so. Why do you ask?"

"Debbie and I have a date on Sunday."

All Lucia could think of to say was "Oh."

"You see, I got to thinking. If that girl in Palm Springs, that Jean, thought Debbie was going to be mad if she made up to me, then maybe what I ought to be doing is checking up on Debbie."

"Oh, I definitely think you should."

"You do?" He grinned his thanks. "I've got to go to work now."

Then he came close and gave her a rare spontaneous kiss. "Have a good time in Acapulco."

She was almost too taken aback to return the kiss, but she managed to murmur, "Thank you, Tommy."

And she felt a tug as he strutted toward the door, shoulders back. In the brown slacks and white shirt, the necktie, he looked almost like a man.

And of course her heart, silly as always,

protested, "Oh, no! Not yet!" She wanted to call out to him, "Come back and be a little boy still, like I'm used to!"

As Tommy opened the front door, he remarked calmly, "Oh, the fire engine is here."

"What? What is it this time?" Lucia rushed to the door and sure enough, double-parked in front of the house was a big red pumper with a fire fighter in his yellow helmet sitting on top. Several more firemen stood around on the sidewalk, with Debbie charming them all.

She was smiling and chatting, holding the leash, and Spot, intimidated or imbued with a miracle, remained quietly beside her, sitting still as a ceramic dog on his plump puppy bottom.

"Why is there a fire truck here?" Lucia demanded nervously.

Tommy explained. "Debbie phoned them about Spot. The guy she talked to said they wanted a firehouse dog, but everybody had to vote before they could take one on. Looks like the ayes won." Then he bounded down the steps and joined the group on the sidewalk.

Lucia watched as Debbie turned the leash over to one of the fire fighters. There was a lot of handshaking and dog patting and then somebody hoisted Spot up onto the fire engine. The guy on top took the leash and petted the dog expertly. The rest of the men jumped aboard and the big truck rumbled away, the firemen waving as they disappeared from sight.

Tommy was out of time. He jogged to his car and drove away. Debbie and Darryl came into the house.

Debbie looked about to cry. "He was such a cute little dog," she said. "He did everything just like the book said he was going to."

Darryl grinned. "Right. Once I'd taught him to read, he was never any more trouble."

"Oh, shut up, Darryl," his sister sniffled. "Maybe if I went back to that place where we bought him, they'd still have some pups from that same litter and I could get another one—"

"What for?" Darryl interrupted.

"Now that I know how to train them, I could have a dog of my own. I could keep him in my room at the dorm."

"Aw, come on, Deb," laughed her brother. "A dorm is no place for a dog. He needs attention, and college people are too busy to give it to him. Look what happened the last couple of days! Neither one of us has done any studying. All we've been doing is walking the streets yelling 'Sit!' "

"I guess so. But he sure was cute."

"I've got to hit the books. I can't afford to fall behind again."

"So get your stuff together. Oh, look! We forgot to give Spot's dog biscuits to the firemen!"

"We can drop them off on our way past the firehouse," Darryl began, but changed his mind. "No, let's not take any chances. Let's head for Westwood as fast as we can, before they try to give Spot back!"

"I'm driving Darryl back to his dorm," Debbie explained to Lucia. "We're going to leave his car here for a couple of days. That's okay with you, isn't it? When the doctor says he can drive again, he'll come and get it."

"Sounds a little complicated," Lucia remarked.

"We'll work it out." Darryl raced up the stairs to collect the things he had in the room where he had spent the night.

Debbie turned to Lucia with a smile. "Did Tommy tell you we're going out on Sunday?"

"He did mention it."

"I decided I'm going to wear the kind of lipstick I like, and I'm going to pick my own friends, too. If the Alphas don't like it, that's their problem."

"That's very mature of you, Debbie, and I'm glad you and Tommy are seeing each other again. Only—" Lucia broke off.

"Only what?"

"If you truly do like Tommy, you ought to stop kicking him around." Lucia pressed two fingers to her lips. "Oh, my goodness, did I say that? I sound just like a mother."

Debbie grinned at her. "That's okay. Sometimes even mothers have good advice."

"It is good advice," Lucia agreed. "It's so good, I think I'll take it myself."

"You're going to stop kicking Tommy around?"

"Him, too."

Darryl came running down the stairs with his bookbag and the children were off to Westwood.

Upstairs, Lucia closed her overnight bag, after peeping inside one more time to reassure herself that clothes do not wear out just from repeated packings, from endlessly being put into the suitcase to not go to Acapulco. Everything was ready. There was ample food for Tommy in the refrigerator, clean clothes in his drawers for him to wear. She had inventoried the contents of her purse, checked the suitcase. She was ready. It was her turn. Mitch would be arriving any minute, and she would be away, flying away to sun and sea and sand and two whole days of his undivided attention.

She was coming down the stairs with the bag in her hand when the telephone started to ring. She did not hurry, for she had long since learned that it is counterproductive to run for a ringing phone in a big house. It would either continue to ring, or it would not.

This one would. It rang and rang, and because it kept on ringing, she knew it was trouble even before she found the phone and picked up the receiver.

She said, "Hello?"

She was only mildly surprised when the breathless voice on the other end said, "It's Ione. Is this Lucia? Is Mitch there?"

She came close to throwing the phone, as one would a snake accidentally picked up, but somehow Lucia managed to say quietly, "Hello, Ione. I'm very surprised to hear from you. How did you get my number?"

"Debbie gave it to me. Where's Mitch?"

Good old Debbie. Lucia replied evenly, "Mitch isn't here, but I'll be seeing him later. Is there a message?"

"Yes. Tell him he has to do something right away. Jared's in jail."

"In jail!" Lucia gasped. "What happened?"

"He didn't do anything! He forgot to pay a traffic ticket, that's all, so they put out a warrant!"

Lucia let out her breath. "That's a relief. It isn't much, Ione. All you have to do is go in and pay the fine, and they'll let him go. It's not that big a deal. There's no reason for Mitch to drive all the way to Ventura County to take care of it."

"That's what I'm trying to tell you," Ione snapped. "He's not here, he's in Burbank. They picked him up in Burbank."

Lucia sighed. "Burbank. You're sure it's Burbank?"

"Yes, of course I'm sure."

"Burbank Municipal."

"Yes. You will tell Mitch, won't you?"

"Of course I will," Lucia replied, and was shocked to realize that there was a little glimmer, far down inside her, saying she could just neglect to mention this call to Mitch. She could just forget, and tomorrow she would be basking on the beach and Ione would be taking the flack.

But of course she wouldn't. She pried a few more details out of Ione and had scarcely hung up the phone when Mitch was at the door. He was wearing the tweed suit, the one that traveled the best.

He smiled but did not come into the house. He asked urgently, "Are you ready to go? Get your things and let's get in the car."

"Maybe you'd better come in, Mitch," she said sadly. "Ione just called."

"No, she didn't. You didn't get any call. I didn't hear you say that."

"We can't run away from this one, Mitch. Jared's in jail in Burbank."

He came inside. "Not my son Jared? He lives in Oxnard."

"He was on his way to visit some friends in San Diego and the police stopped him as he was going through Burbank. They had an old warrant for him. A traffic ticket he didn't pay, apparently, when he was living here with you."

"Well, the hell with him!" Mitch said angrily. "He should have paid it. That kid hasn't spoken to me for two years. I'm not going to run down there and bail him out. If he can't watch what he's doing when he's driving, let him stew in his own juice."

"Mitch, you can't mean that."

He didn't. His look told her he didn't, but he kept trying to convince himself. "Our trip, Lucia. We might miss our plane and be cheated out of our trip again."

"It's only a traffic ticket. We ought to be able to get over there, pay it, and have him out in no time. About the worst thing that can happen to us is that we might have to eat on the plane."

"That's a pretty bad thing to happen," he said with a tiny flash of humor.

"Mitch, it's Jared! This is your chance to make up your quarrel with him, to show him you really do care about him."

"Why can't he make up with me?" Mitch grumbled.

"You have to get him out even if it doesn't work and he's still mad at you," Lucia insisted. "Hasn't anybody ever told you what those places are like? He could get beat up. Awful things happen to people there, especially to boys who are young and handsome."

Mitch smiled faintly. "How do you know he's handsome?"

"He's your boy, so of course he's handsome. He's also past eighteen and doesn't even have the protection of being a juvenile. We have to get him out, Mitch."

Mitch's sigh was almost a groan. "We've got to do it, but, oh, Lucia, when is it going to be time for us? When do we get to be together? When are we going to tell the world that we're together and stop all this sneaking around?"

"Maybe after we take care of Jared," she said unconvincingly. "Do you have money? They'll take only cash; you can't write a check or anything like that."

He gave her a shrewd look. "How do you know so much about this?"

382

"Georgie pulled the same trick on me once. Kids think if you throw away a traffic ticket, it's gone forever."

"Really? Georgie the perfect? Somehow, that's kind of comforting. It's nice to know we don't have any angels in our bunch."

"We have had a problem from each kid, haven't we?"

"Perfect score. What do you get for doubles?"

"Gray hair."

Mitch left her in the car when he went into the police station. He seemed to think her presence was going to inhibit his dealings with the police. Lucia suggested that inhibiting his language might be a help, but he only chuckled and kissed her and left.

She read the paperback she had brought along for the plane until it got dark, and then she rested her eyes for a while. She was startled awake when Mitch returned to the car and got in. He was alone, and he climbed behind the wheel and sat there, slumped.

Lucia ventured, "What happened?"

He replied hollowly, "I don't have enough money."

"I thought you did have some."

"I do. I like to travel with some cash on me, so I have more than I normally carry around, but it

383

isn't anywhere near enough, and all the banks are closed now. Where can I get some cash?"

"Do you have a card for the night teller machine?"

"I told you," he answered a little impatiently. "I like to travel with cash. I didn't have time to go to the bank today, so I already took my limit out of the machine."

"We could use mine. You'd have to pay me back, but—"

He raised his head with a small smile. "You'd do that for me? What's your limit?"

"Two hundred dollars, I think."

"Still not enough."

"Why is it so much money? It's only a traffic ticket."

"Three traffic tickets," he corrected her. "With a bench warrant on each. Two are for speeding and one is for not stopping at a red light. . . . That was when he totaled my car. He just ran out on all those tickets. He must have figured if he was in another county they couldn't get him. What time is it?"

"About eight."

"Two hours to plane time. I'm tempted to start for the airport. Let Ione come and get him out, or let him spend a weekend in jail. It probably wouldn't hurt him."

"Probably," Lucia agreed. "But could you really lie on the beach and enjoy yourself while the possibility exists that it would hurt him? You couldn't do it, and you'd be rotten company for me."

"Jim Larchmont," Mitch said suddenly. "I'll ask him to lend me some money. He's a good enough friend to do it, and he lives right here in the Valley. Maybe we can still make it." He started the engine of the truck. "I'm not even going to waste time looking for a telephone so I can call him, we'll just go."

The Larchmonts lived on a lovely, quiet street, thick with trees. It was eight-thirty when they got there. They hurried up the walk to the house and Mitch rang the doorbell. A light went on and the door was opened by the Larchmont's daughter, Jean.

She said cheerfully, "Oh, hello, Uncle Mitch. And Mrs. Morgan."

Mitch said, "Hello, Jean. I need to talk to your dad."

"He isn't home. He and Mother went to Palm Springs for the weekend."

Mitch looked at his watch and then at Jean. He was desperate. He said, "Jean, do you have a card for the night teller machine?"

"Sure."

"I need some cash right now. Can you get me some?"

The child's face showed sympathy and quite a bit of confusion. "Well, sure I can, but I have only about thirty-five dollars in the bank."

"Never mind," said Mitch. "Forget I mentioned it."

As they went back down the walk, Lucia suggested, "We could try Terrilee."

"Do you think she'd do it?" Mitch asked.

"I know she would, and she probably has cash lying around. She usually takes the receipts from the boutique home with her."

"That's kind of a dumb thing to do."

"You have just analyzed Terrilee's personality. It's in Tarzana, but you knew that, didn't you?"

Mitch winced. "At least it's in the Valley."

There was fifteen miles of freeway between them and Tarzana, and it was after nine when they knocked on Terrilee's door. The boutique closed at nine and the lights were on in Terrilee's little suite of rooms.

She came to the door wearing her caftan. Her jaw dropped with astonishment to see Mitch and Lucia at her door.

"Lucia! I wasn't expecting you, and, uh . . . hello, Mitch."

"We won't take up much of your time," Lucia apologized. It looked like Terrilee had a late date, and if so, they were really intruding.

She explained the problem, and with her usual generosity Terrilee provided the money they needed.

Too late, of course. Even if they left Jared in jail and went directly to the airport, they could not have caught their ten o'clock plane. While Mitch wrote out a check, Lucia called the airline and canceled their reservations.

They were both very quiet all the way back to Burbank. Lucia opened her mouth once to ask him where they might eat dinner now that they were not going to the airport, but she only closed it again. The way things were going, they probably could not safely even make plans for dinner.

At Burbank they found somebody to take the bail money and then they sat down to wait for Jared to be released. They sat on dreary dark wood benches in a lobby that was almost dark. The only lights they seemed to have were behind the police desk. Uniformed officers would drift in from time to time, talk a while, then saunter out. It seemed a place where nothing ever happened, or ever would.

Mitch asked, "Have you ever been to Alaska?"

"Only in the movies," Lucia replied. "Ice and snow, right?"

"They have seasons like everyplace else," he

corrected her. "It can get downright hot in the summer, and the bugs . . . On the North Slope summer lasts twenty, maybe thirty minutes, and the rest of the time it's ice and snow. It's on the Beaufort Sea and there's a beauty all its own there. Miles of glaciers. White icebergs floating in the dark sea."

"Doesn't sound like the movies, so you've been there, right?" Lucia hazarded.

"I spent a couple of winters there, and you never learn to love it, but it does have a pull on you. You've got to be tough and smart to survive there. You've got to invent ways to make things work. You've got to invent your own amusements and learn to get along with the people you have to spend the winter with. Then the Northern Lights start flickering across the sky and you're seeing a show you're never going to see anyplace else!"

Lucia said, "What's with you and Alaska these days, Mitch? You're making me suspicious."

He countered, "When are you going to marry me, Lucia?"

"More and more suspicious. What are you driving at?"

He shifted on the hard bench and looked down at her. "I've got to spend the winter in Alaska. We're drilling a series of step-out wells

388

there and they're all started and I don't have a supervisor with winter experience. I've got to train a new guy and the only way he's ever going to learn it is to be in the field when it's really winter. You and I could get married and we'd have the whole winter together. There's no radio communication when the Lights are playing, and the winter nights are twenty hours long."

"Oh, Mitch . . ." she stammered. Why did it sound so good? Why did she long to be shut up with Mitch, alone with Mitch, miles beyond the Arctic Circle for a whole winter? Thousands of miles from distractions and demands and Ione and the innumerable details that kept them apart so long as they were here?

It sounded good because of wishful thinking, Lucia told herself. She was thinking of romantic, cozy nights, and beyond a doubt Mitch was thinking of a lot of expensive equipment that could be lost if the right man were not on hand to take care of it in the months of brutal cold that lay ahead. No doubt he was thinking of having a cheery companion and good cook to take with him, to warm his bed on those long nights.

She said slowly, "We can't just throw away our responsibilities and go away. What would

389

the children do?"

"They'd get along. Why shouldn't they? They always do."

"That's easy for you to say. When you leave town, your children still have a parent available to them. Tommy would be all alone. And what about my house? Who would take care of it? What about my gowns?"

The bench was not only hard, it had sharp edges. Mitch stretched his legs and leaned back, folded his arms, trying to get comfortable. Two policemen hurried in, spoke urgently to the desk sergeant, and then apparently forgot what their errand had been. They idled along the counter, chatting aimlessly.

Mitch asked her, "If you had all the money you needed, what would you do with that house?"

She brought her attention back from the policemen. "If I had all the money I needed, I'd pay Tommy's school expenses and—"

"I'm talking about the house now," he interrupted. "Just imagine you could have all the money you needed for it. What would you do?"

"Fix the kitchen," Lucia replied fervently. "I'd put in a dishwasher and a new sink and some good-looking cabinets. Then I'd build a new bathroom, of course, or maybe two of them."

She was starting to have fun. She went on eagerly. "I'd have a new roof put on, and get the chimneys put back the way they were before they fell down in the 1933 earthquake. And I'd have one of those fancy paint jobs where they pick out the gingerbread with a different color from the rest of the house. I'd buy some new furniture and have the outside landscaped."

"Then what would you do?"

Her eyes glowed with enthusiasm. "Then I'd have an enormous party and invite all my friends to see it and I'd serve punch from an antique punch bowl that I just bought with my magic money."

"Then what?"

Lucia's answer surprised her even as she said it. "Why, then I'd sell it."

"You would?"

"Of course. Fixed up, a house like that is worth a lot of money. That's why I've always wanted to fix it, so I could sell it. Then I would have some money and Tommy wouldn't have to work every weekend. His education would be assured and I'd buy a little place, not too little, big enough so I could have a workroom for the gowns. Everything would be modern and clean and the furnace would work and there would be electrical outlets on every wall and somebody else would do the gardening."

Her eyes were still wide, but her expression had turned thoughtful. "Isn't it funny? My dream house looks an awful lot like your condo."

"Lucia, while you've been dreaming, you've missed a whole revolution in California real estate. You don't have to fix that old place up; it's worth heavy money just as it stands."

"But everything in it is old!"

"You've got something special in that house, just because it never has been renovated. People love that stuff; it's a big fad right now. Everybody wants something authentic and original. For all I know, 'authentic and original' includes the plumbing in that place. You can sell it for plenty. Let the buyer make the repairs."

"He might enjoy doing it," Lucia said. "In fact, he surely would enjoy it more than I ever would. That old place was never my own dream, was it? It was left over from my marriage. I kept wanting it because I had wanted it."

"I thought you loved that house."

"I do, but I can easily learn to love another. Just think, I could have sold the place years ago and used the money for Tommy, for both boys, and maybe then I could have started a business, designing. I've had this way open to me all along, haven't I? I wonder why I never noticed it?"

"Maybe the time wasn't right. The market hasn't always been like it is now. And sometimes you can't see things if you're too close to them. You said once that Tommy wanted to go live in a dorm with his friends. Do you think that's what he still wants? It's sure what Debbie prefers."

"Does that hurt your feelings?"

"I guess so, but at this point in my life I don't really want to be living with my kids. You can let Tommy go, can't you?"

"My Tommy? He can't live by himself. He can't even iron."

Mitch unfolded his arms and made meticulous steeples with his fingers. He said, "You take the birds. Mother birds knock themselves out digging worms to feed their babies, but when the mother sees that her chick is fledged, she kicks him out of the nest. She knows he can fly. He doesn't, but he's going to find out on his way down. Our kids are like those chicks. They'll learn to cope for themselves, like adults, if we aren't always here to rescue them."

"It could even happen to Ione," mused Lucia. "She could learn to get along with just one husband, like everybody else has to."

"We'll never know until we try."

"I wouldn't mind giving up my job with the freight company, but I don't want to lose my contacts for selling the things I design. Can I sew in Alaska?"

"As long as you don't try to do it outdoors."

"I could keep my hand in by mailing things to Terrilee, and when we get back maybe I'll start my own business, like she's always trying to get me to do."

"I'll help you," he promised.

"Oh, Mitch, it sounds too good to be true. It probably is. There's a hitch in it somewhere."

He bent his head and kissed her gently and tenderly, provoking a couple of catcalls from the cops around the desk. She didn't mind them. She closed her eyes and lost herself for a few seconds in the beautiful world that was just hers and Mitch's, the world they created when they were together.

Mitch whispered, "There's no hitch in that, is there?"

She pushed herself away from him and slid along the bench until there was a distance between them, for she was suddenly angry. "You're using that, Mitch. You're using the at-

394

traction between us to get what you want."

He shook his head, baffled. "What else can I use when what I want is you?"

She pounded her hands in her lap. "Why does it have to be so convenient? Such a fair exchange? Your money and my cooking. You have to go to Alaska and it will be such a great thing for me to go, too. . . . That's not exactly the love story of the century, is it?"

"I can't figure out what you want, Lucia. What's the matter with it if we can do good things for each other? What's wrong with me liking the things you can do? Do we have to have obstacles and privations before we can love each other?"

She regarded him from under her brows with a look that could have been a glow or a glower. "I suppose that is the real point, Mitch. Do you love me, or is it just that you're tired of waking up alone in the morning?"

"Well, both, but of course I love you."

"You never said it."

"I figured you knew."

She shook back her hair and the light in her eyes was definitely a glow. "There's no such thing as saying it too much, Mitch."

"All right already! I love you!"

She said, "Why?"

"What do you mean, why? Damned if I know why!" His voice rose, but the cops paid no attention. Used to it, probably.

Lucia's smile was lighting up the whole gloomy place. "That's the right answer! I don't want you to love me for the things I can do. I want you to love me because!"

"Well, I do."

"And because I love you."

"Well, if you love me, why won't you marry me?"

"I will."

"And go to Alaska?"

"Even Alaska."

Jared came out of the doorway behind the desk at just that moment, and the folks in Burbank probably thought Mitch was whooping with joy because they had let his son out of jail.

Probably Jared thought the same thing, but that was okay. The kids don't have to know everything.

Chapter Twenty-one

Jared Colton was lightly built and shorter than his brother, perhaps even shorter than Debbie. His hair was light brown and straight, his eyes blue. Not like a Colton at all, Lucia thought, and then he smiled, pulling his lips back tight against his teeth. He said, "Hi, Dad."

Mitch looked worried. "Are you okay?"

"Sure. I could do with a shower and some clean clothes, though."

"Do you have any clothes with you?"

"I had a bag in the car, but I guess it got impounded along with everything else."

Mitch gave him a friendly pat on the back. "We'll go over to my place. You may still have some clothes there. At least you can get the shower."

"Okay."

"I want you to meet Lucia. Lucia, this is

my son, Jared. Lucia Morgan."

Jared took her hand and smiled. "I've heard a lot about you."

"Now, there's a greeting that's . . . fraught," said Lucia, but she smiled.

"Well, Debbie talks a lot about you. She says you've got a son."

"I have two, but Debbie's dating only Tommy. Shall we go to the car?"

They all sat in the front seat of the truck, Lucia in the middle and, she found, closer than she wanted to be to Jared. He did smell, of stale sweat and of cigarettes, although he didn't smoke. He had been jailed for only a few hours, but, she thought, it must have been a difficult experience for a gentle boy like this.

As they headed down Olive toward Pass, Jared said, "I'm kind of surprised that you're driving around in a truck. Where's the new Porsche you bought?"

Mitch said, "Yeah, I've got another Porsche now, but we were on our way to the airport and I don't like to leave it there."

Jared said casually, "I'm driving a new Accord. I've got a pretty good job, even though I haven't taken my C.P.A. exam yet."

"I guess you can save a lot of money, living with your mother and stepfather," Mitch remarked.

"Oh, I pay my own way."

His tone obviously annoyed Mitch, who said, "You do? Then how about paying me back what I just laid out for your traffic tickets? That came to quite a piece of change."

"Sure, I'll pay you back. You haven't contributed anything to me for two years, why should you have to start now?"

"You're twenty-three years old," Mitch pointed out. "What are you expecting, child support? I paid your way through college. You've got a job. You ought to be off my back by now."

Jared's head was thrust belligerently forward, his lower lip protruding. "If you want me off your back, why did you come and bail me out?"

"I'm starting to wonder." It was a short drive and they already were in front of Mitch's garage. He socked the button that opened the doors and drove in, barely clearing the steel gate as it opened.

When he put the truck into its place, Debbie's car was there, occupying the slot next to the Porsche.

Jared got out of the truck. "That's Debbie's car. I didn't know she was here."

"Neither did I," said Mitch.

"Couple of nice cars right there," pursued Jared, lightly patting the sleek fender of the Porsche. "Darryl's car is pretty nice, too."

"You had a good car," Mitch pointed out, "until you turned it in for an Accord."

Jared took a pugnacious stance, his chin forward again. "Well, I guess if you can't be with your kids, at least you can buy them things. That'll keep them off your back, so you can be with your girlfriend."

"That's about enough, Jared." Mitch stood beside his truck, looking large and dangerous. "I want you to be real careful you don't say anything about Lucia. You're going to treat her with the respect she deserves. And you're going to speak to me in a civil tone and not talk about your mother, either."

Jared tossed his defiant head. "You left my sainted stepfather off your list."

"He's your problem, not mine. What happened between me and your mother is over and done with, and I don't want to hear anything from you about it."

"Maybe it's over for you. Did you ever stop to consider what it was going to do to our lives? We're your children and you don't care what happens to us. You weren't there for any of us when we were growing up. You could let two years go by without ever talking to me. Debbie and Darryl can have what they want, but you were glad to get rid of me."

"You're the one who had to go on a two-year sulk," Mitch said.

"Hold it, hold it, hold it!" yelled Lucia. "What's gotten into you two? You sound like you've been waiting two years for the opportunity to square off at each other!"

"I don't want to fight," said Jared.

"The hell you don't," replied his father.

"Now, hold on, just a minute," said Lucia. "Stand still, both of you. I've been sitting in the middle all the way from Burbank, listening to this, and I'm going to tell you what I heard."

She turned to Jared. "I'm hearing you say that you're sorry your folks broke up, and you resent it that you haven't seen your father for the last two years."

"It was his idea to sulk—" Mitch began.

Lucia stopped him. "It's not your turn yet, Mitch. Is that what you're saying, Jared?"

"Well, yeah."

"And, Mitch, you're saying that you have tried to make a conciliatory gesture and it is making you angry that it's not appreciated."

"You're the one that said it was the chance for me and Jared to finish up our quarrel," he pointed out.

"I said only that it was a chance. I didn't say it was a sure thing!"

"I do want to make up with you, Dad," Jared mumbled. "I guess I just needed to get a couple things off my chest first."

"I got a few, too," Mitch admitted, "but what do you say we call it even for now? If we're friends, well, friends can discuss their differences, but . . . well, they don't have to stand down in the garage in the dark to do it."

"Okay, Dad, friends." They shook hands and tried to exchange an awkward hug. It didn't quite come off, for each still found the other prickly, but it was a start.

When they got upstairs, it was Darryl who was curled up on the couch, deep in a book.

He jumped up, surprised. "Hi, Dad. I thought you were—Jared!"

"I thought Debbie was here," Mitch countered.

"She is, she's studying in the kitchen. She needed a table."

Mitch was puzzled. "You guys moving back home or something?"

Debbie came from the kitchen in time to hear the question. "No, Daddy, I just came over here to study because it's always noisy at the Alpha house and I didn't think anybody would be here. Darryl might be staying a couple days, though. The guys at his dorm tore up all his things."

"It was only the bed," Darryl explained. "They were still mad because Spot chewed on their stuff, so they wrecked my bed. I found out about it as soon as I got back to the dorm. There were cotton blobs all over, and Debbie was driving and she hadn't left yet, so we just came over here."

"Those guys are a bunch of hoodlums," Mitch complained. "Are they going to pay for a new bed for you?".

"I gotta get a shower," complained Jared. "Have I still got some clothes and stuff in our room, Darryl?"

Darryl shrugged. "Probably. Use my stuff if you want. I might as well say that, you're going to anyway."

"Call your mother first," Mitch ordered.

"It's pretty late."

"You know she's going to be worrying."

Jared went reluctantly to the phone. Mitch gave Darryl and Debbie a brief recap of the evening's events, and both children went back to their respective tasks.

Mitch pulled Lucia toward the stairs. "Kitchen's occupied, living room, and we've got to make some plans. Come on into my bedroom. When's the wedding going to be?"

She went along willingly, down the stairs to the lower level. "Yes, we have to figure that out. When do you have to leave for Alaska?"

In his room they sat down on his bed. She was pleased to note it was king-size. The bedcover, however, was downright tacky and would

403

have to be replaced. And the window drapes were deplorable. There was going to be plenty for her to do in this house.

Mitch said, "They're having a mild season up there in Alaska, as those things go. We'll be able to get in, oh, probably another three, four weeks."

"Four weeks! We have to leave in four weeks? Mitch, we're talking about getting married, me quitting my job and breaking in my replacement, finding a dorm for Tommy, selling my house and moving. Oh, my God, moving! All in a month? It's impossible."

"So we'll have the wedding before we go and you can sell the house after we get back in the spring. That way, you won't have to move until then."

Jared called from the living room, "Dad, Mom wants to talk to you!"

"Tell her I'm busy," Mitch hollered up the stairs.

Lucia didn't comment. She even swallowed her little glow of satisfaction, to keep it to herself, and went on with the discussion. "The trouble with selling the house later is that Tommy would have it to look after all by himself while we're gone, and he has his schoolwork to do. It's not fair to him."

"We could close up your house. That's what I'm going to do with mine. Tommy can go live in the dorm if that's what he prefers. I'll pay for it."

"You would? Oh, thank you, Mitch. It will be a loan, and I'll repay you when the house sells. Maybe I can get an agent who will market the house while I'm gone."

"I'm sure any agent would be delighted. I can give you a couple of names. If he should sell it right away, we'll just tell him to put an extra long escrow on it."

Lucia's eyes were bright with plans. "Let's have the wedding at my house. We can have a huge party and invite all your friends and all my friends. We'll have a band in the upstairs hall and dance all night in the big hall below."

"Wouldn't it be less trouble to have it at a hotel?"

"Of course not! We'll hold the ceremony in the big hall, where we first met, and lay out the buffet in the formal dining room."

"Well, okay, but only if you promise to have caterers for the buffet and not to refurbish the house before the party."

"I promise. Could we just carpet the stairs?"

"No!"

"Okay. The house will be just like it always is. Elegant and slightly funky."

"Okay, when?"

"Well, let's see. I'll need a new suit to wear, something dressy in moiré, pale blue, or maybe mauve, and we have to send out the invitations and give people a chance to respond. . . . Three weeks? Saturday, three weeks from tomorrow."

"We'll have to leave for Alaska right away, after."

"The perfect honeymoon."

"Let's go tell the kids."

Jared was out of the shower and had found clothes to wear. He asked at once, "Hey, Dad, when can we go to the impound and get my car back?"

"They probably aren't open until tomorrow" was Mitch's opinion. "We got something to say. Is everybody paying attention?"

Debbie darted in from the kitchen, already smiling. "You're going to do it? All right! When's the wedding? Can I be a bridesmaid?"

Lucia couldn't help laughing. "You sure can take the drama out of an announcement! It's three weeks from now, on a Saturday. We're going to have a party, and yes, you can be a bridesmaid if you want."

"Gee, Dad, that's great," Jared said feebly, and Darryl added his congratulations.

"I have to tell my boys," Lucia fretted. "Tommy gets off work in about an hour. Shall we go to my house and wait for him?"

"Suppose he goes someplace afterward?" Mitch questioned. "He does sometimes, doesn't he? Let's go over to that place where he works. At least we can get a hamburger. I'm hungry."

"I'll go with you," said Debbie. "I want to see his face when you tell him."

"Hamburgers?" said Darryl. "I'll go, too. I'm starving."

"Me, too," said Jared.

Lucia made them wait while she phoned Georgie, rousing him from sleep. He was too drowsy to show much enthusiasm, but he politely wished her happiness.

Lucia and Mitch rode to the hamburger stand in the truck. At Mitch's suggestion, the children went together in Debbie's car. They couldn't seem to stop squabbling among themselves, and it was a relief to get away from them for a few minutes.

At the fast-food outlet Tommy filled vast trays for them with everything the stand had to offer, then joined them at the table. It was the corner booth and held all six of them easily. Tommy explained to his coworkers that he would be on a break until quitting time.

Like Debbie, he had already guessed what the occasion was, but the news about Alaska surprised him. "You'll be away for four months?"

Lucia said, "I'm going to find an agent who will market the house for me and take the responsibility of looking after it. If you want to go live in a dorm, Mitch has offered to advance the money. There's a place you want to go, isn't there?"

"Yeah, I know which dorm I want to be in. I can keep an eye on things at the house, check up on the agent, and so forth. Will we get a gardener?"

"We're going to have a gardener and a house cleaner and a plumber," his mother promised.

Tommy grinned. "All right! I've been wanting to get into this one dorm. Some of my friends are there."

"They'll probably be noisy and tear up your bed," Debbie warned.

"In this dorm, I don't think so." Tommy turned to his mother. "I thought you were going to Acapulco tonight."

"We were, but we missed the plane and now we can't go."

"That wasn't the only plane that ever went to Acapulco. Why don't you get another one?"

Mitch said, "Tommy, that's a great idea. How about it, Lucia? It'll be a short weekend, but we'll still have a good time."

"What about my car?" Jared demanded. "You've got to take me to the impound tomorrow."

"Your brother's right here," Tommy pointed out.

"I can't do it," said Darryl. "The docs won't

let me drive yet, but Debbie can."

Debbie said, "I'm going to be too busy. I've got to drive Darryl around."

"I should think you could spare a little time to help me out," Jared said.

She stuck out a stubborn lower lip. "You're not at home now, King Jared, and Mother isn't here to make sure your every word is law. Go get your car yourself. You can probably get there on a bus."

Tommy asked, "Ma, are you really sure you want to get us mixed up with this bunch?"

Lucia started to laugh. "What, me worry? I'm going to be in Alaska. You're the one who is going to have to cope with them."

"Me?" Tommy grinned and raised his voice. "Okay, now hear this, troops! Tomorrow I'm taking Jared to the impound. Debbie is going to take Darryl wherever it is he has to go to get his bed reinstated. But make sure you get finished by afternoon, Darryl. Debbie has a date with a fireman."

Debbie protested, "Oh, Tommy, I do not."

"I heard him ask you."

"Well, of course I didn't accept. I wouldn't go on a date with somebody I don't even know."

Jared was staring suspiciously at Tommy. "Really? You're going to drive me to the impound tomorrow?"

409

"Yeah. Are you spending the night at Mitch's? I'll pick you up there."

"Guess that's how it is," grumped Jared. "You can't depend on your own family. Got to get help from somebody who's practically a stranger."

"It would have to be a stranger," Darryl pointed out. "Nobody who knows you very well wants to be around you."

"Nobody ever tore up my bed when I was in school," said Jared.

Mitch suggested, "Guys, do you think you could keep it down to a dull roar?"

"Sure," said Jared agreeably. "Let him walk all over me."

"Well, it's the only chance I get," Darryl argued. "When Mother's around, everything's your way."

"That's enough!" shouted Mitch.

"Don't pay any attention to them, Daddy," Debbie advised. "They're always like this."

"Fighting with Jared is my thing," Darryl complained. "How come everybody keeps butting in tonight?"

"Maybe you could take up some sport," Lucia suggested. "Football or croquet . . ."

"Basketball!" said Darryl. "I could cream that little shrimp at basketball."

"I think it's hopeless," Mitch admitted.

Everybody was laughing, even Jared a little

bit, and he murmured again, "I don't want to fight."

"I don't know if I want to bother getting another bed," said Darryl around a mouthful of hamburger. "Dad, how about letting me stay at your place for the rest of the quarter? Those guys at the dorm are always doing something. They make a lot of noise and some of the things they get going, you have to drop whatever you're doing and defend yourself. I got behind when I couldn't go to classes for two weeks, and I'm still trying to catch up, so I need to go someplace quiet."

"Kind of a long commute to Westwood," Mitch pointed out.

"Doc says I can drive again after my exam next week."

Mitch thought it over. "I was planning to close the place up while I was gone, but I suppose you kids might as well use it. We got to have some ground rules, though."

"We won't destroy anything," Darryl promised.

"Keep it clean. No wild parties . . ."

"Lock up when we leave . . ."

"And don't forget to pay the utility bills. Pay them on time."

Darryl was grinning. "Thanks, Dad. I'll take good care of it. Tommy'll probably get me if I don't."

Mitch said, "I'm going to call the airport and find out when we can get a plane. That's a phone over there, isn't it?"

"Yeah," said Tommy. "I've got to close this place and clean up."

Lucia whispered to him, "As soon as I get some money, I'm going to pay your car expenses so you can quit this job."

"Quit? Gee, Ma, I'm the weekend night manager!"

"Oh, dear, I wouldn't want to spoil your career," murmured Lucia, and watched with astonishment as her son efficiently cleared the table and deployed his minions to clean up behind the counter.

He was almost finished before Mitch came back from the phone. The Colton children had left, and Tommy was standing by the door to let out the remaining employees.

Mitch took Lucia's arm firmly. "We can make the plane if we hurry. Let's go."

Lucia gave her son a quick squeeze and they rushed to the truck. It was so late, the streets were quiet, and they headed toward the 10.

Lucia leaned back on the upholstery, wishing she dared kick off her shoes. "What an evening! I'm already worn out, and we have a plane trip ahead of us!"

"Well, we don't," Mitch confessed.

"Huh?"

"The next plane for Acapulco leaves tomorrow, and it's booked solid, so I got us a room at the Long Beach Hilton."

"Long Beach?"

"It's got sun and sand and sea and practically everything Acapulco has, and it's right down the road from here. I'll have you in bed in an hour."

Lucia started to laugh. "What a wonderful idea, Mitch! People come from all over the world to spend a weekend on Southern California beaches. But the children think we're in Acapulco. Suppose there's an emergency? They won't be able to reach us."

"If there's an emergency, they're going to have to handle it. Be good practice for them. We've got to let them think we're in Acapulco. If they know we're just around the corner, they'll drop in for breakfast or something."

Lucia said, "Oh, yes, Mitch, I agree."

She leaned back luxuriously on the thick upholstery and surreptitiously kicked off the shoe that was pinching.

"It's true, what they say," she said happily. "The kids don't have to know everything."